Jackson snarl  vhen I kill 'im."

"Matt Price."

Jackson blinked once. "I heard a you . . . Somebody tole me you were dead."

"Somebody got it wrong."

"An' now I'm s'pose ta be a-scaird. Is that the deal?"

"You have a choice to make," Price said. "That's all."

He saw the choice in Jackson's piggy eyes and moved before his adversary reached his pistol. Price beat him to it with his Peacemaker, thumbed back the hammer as it cleared leather, and fired almost without conscious thought.

His slug took Jackson left of center, spinning him half around. Slumping against the bar, Jackson squeezed off a shot that drilled the floor between his feet, struggling to turn and raise his weapon while the life pumped out of him and stained his unwashed clothes. Price waited with his Colt rock-steady for another shot, until the man folded and his six-gun clattered on the boards.

Retrieving it, Price put it on the bar beside his glass of beer, holstered his own, and told the barkeep, "Let me have a whiskey while we're waiting for the law."

BOUNTY GUN

Lyle Brandt

BERKLEY BOOKS, NEW YORK

THE BERKLEY PUBLISHING GROUP
Published by the Penguin Group
Penguin Group (USA) Inc.
375 Hudson Street, New York, New York 10014, USA
Penguin Group (Canada), 90 Eglinton Avenue East, Suite 700, Toronto, Ontario M4P 2Y3, Canada
(a division of Pearson Penguin Canada Inc.)
Penguin Books Ltd., 80 Strand, London WC2R 0RL, England
Penguin Group Ireland, 25 St. Stephen's Green, Dublin 2, Ireland (a division of Penguin Books Ltd.)
Penguin Group (Australia), 250 Camberwell Road, Camberwell, Victoria 3124, Australia
(a division of Pearson Australia Group Pty. Ltd.)
Penguin Books India Pvt. Ltd., 11 Community Centre, Panchsheel Park, New Delhi—110 017, India
Penguin Group (NZ), Cnr. Airborne and Rosedale Roads, Albany, Auckland 1310, New Zealand
(a division of Pearson New Zealand Ltd.)
Penguin Books (South Africa) (Pty.) Ltd., 24 Sturdee Avenue, Rosebank, Johannesburg 2196,
South Africa

Penguin Books Ltd., Registered Offices: 80 Strand, London WC2R 0RL, England

This is a work of fiction. Names, characters, places, and incidents either are the product of the author's imagination or are used fictitiously, and any resemblance to actual persons, living or dead, business establishments, events, or locales is entirely coincidental.

BOUNTY GUN

A Berkley Book / published by arrangement with the author

PRINTING HISTORY
Berkley edition / March 2006

ISBN: 0-425-20886-9

BERKLEY®
Berkley Books are published by The Berkley Publishing Group,
a division of Penguin Group (USA) Inc.,
375 Hudson Street, New York, New York 10014.
BERKLEY is a registered trademark of Penguin Group (USA) Inc.
The "B" design is a trademark belonging to Penguin Group (USA) Inc.

PRINTED IN THE UNITED STATES OF AMERICA

10 9 8 7 6 5 4 3 2 1

For Marg

PROLOGUE

Four riders in the dark.

They passed unnoticed from the mountains into gently rolling foothills, shadows moving in a world of shadow, being quiet for the most part. Silence wasn't absolutely necessary, but they did their best. No talking when they didn't absolutely need to, and what difference did it make? They'd used up all the words they knew beforehand, arguing and planning for this night.

Four men of grim determination and resolve, although they weren't in absolute agreement on their goal. They could resolve that problem later maybe, hoping that it wouldn't come to blood.

And if it did . . . so what?

Their leader had conceived the mission, talked the others into joining him against their better judgment, stacking the rewards until only a fool would say it wasn't worth a try. The trouble was that now, at night, their worries and misgivings didn't seem so foolish anymore. As they rode through darkness, four against the world, it seemed like

anything could happen and they might not make it home
alive.

Still, if they pulled it off, it would be something that
was talked about forever and a day. The big score of all
time. Big scores meant bigger risks and being hunted like
an animal, maybe for years on end, but once they had the
payoff in their hands, three of the four were reasonably
certain they could find a comfortable place to hide.

The fourth, their leader, didn't give a damn.

He wasn't in it for the money, strictly speaking, though
he damn sure wouldn't turn it down. Money and happiness might be two different things, the way most preachers told the story, but in his experience they went together
mighty well. Like bread and jam, for instance. Gravy and
potatoes.

Sex and danger.

Passing from the foothills into flatlands, they were
doubly cautious. Anyone could spot them now, and anyone they met would be an enemy. The leader had been
careful, plotting out their route, tracing a path across his
homemade map that would avoid the grazing herds. The
great spread's southern quarter wasn't being used this
month, which shaved the odds of them encountering pa-
trols. Still, it was possible. And if it happened, they would
have to strike before the other side had time to think.

They had been through it time and time again, planning
exactly what to do if anything went wrong. Shoot fast and
straight, then ride like fury for the house, to get it done before the family and hired help could collect their sleepy
wits. There'd be no turning back, no matter what.

Their leader had demanded a blood oath that none of
them would quit before the job was done. It was a do-or-
die agreement, with a hint of romance to it and the promise of a great reward. When they were done and paid in
full, they could decide if it was best to scatter or continue
on together for a while.

They'd have the luxury of choices then.

Tonight, they only had the urgency of greed and fear.

The land was flat and open where they rode, the soil beneath their horses' hooves as rich as he who owned it. Crops would've done well there, but the Big Man liked his cattle. Nothing wrong with that, the riders thought, as long as sales were brisk and kept the coffers full.

As long as he could pay up on demand.

The leader had them sold on that. There'd be no haggling over price, no hesitation, no attempt to hem and haw. The Big Man would deliver, if they forced him to it, but he'd likely also try to kill them first.

They were prepared for that.

Their leader welcomed it.

Their mission wasn't *just* about the money. The job meant settling old scores, finding a semblance of the peace that had so long eluded him.

He hoped the others understood. If not, to hell with them. The money would suffice.

A quarter hour later, they could see the big house, barn, and scattered outbuildings. The place was dark and quiet, not so much as chimney smoke to hint at human habitation. They were in there, though. The family.

There was the Big Man and his lady wife. The son, a shadow of his sire but still a force to reckon with. And finally the daughter, Daddy's golden child.

Their ticket to a life of ease.

"You remember what we talked about," the leader said, not really asking them. "The way we planned it out."

The others nodded silently, doubly reluctant now to speak when they could see the dark house waiting for them.

"Keep all your wits about you," he ordered, getting more nods back. "Somebody tries to stop us, you know what to do."

They might've smiled at that another time, but it was deadly serious tonight. Their leader shared a silent look with each of them in turn, then spurred his pinto toward the sleeping house.

•   •   •

The Big Man woke up all at once, no easing into it. He lay rock-steady for a moment, wondering what had roused him from a muddled, swiftly fading dream. He listened to the house, willing the walls and floors to speak if there was anything amiss, but they kept silent.

No—not quite.

Somewhere beyond the Big Man's bedchamber, a floorboard creaked. Barely a whisper, but his ears were sharp. He knew the house and all its varied sounds, by day or night.

The Big Man recognized that creaky floorboard, thankful now that he'd been slow repairing it. It lay just outside Marcy's bedroom door, meaning that she was up and on the move when she should rightfully be sleeping.

What was that about?

The Big Man reckoned he should go and find out for himself.

Dark doings were the sort he liked to find out for himself, see with his own two eyes. And if correction was required, what better instrument than his two hands?

The Big Man left his woman sleeping, rose without disturbing her. He had no need of her just now. His slippers were forgotten as he padded barefoot to the door. It stood ajar, the way he liked it when he slept. To let him know if anyone was on the move.

There were no secrets underneath the Big Man's roof, except his own.

He wasn't worried as he left the master bedroom, pausing on the threshold. Just ahead of him, a railing overlooked the ground-floor family room below, its massive stone fireplace and chimney to his left, stairs to the right. Beyond the staircase, catercornered from the Big Man's bedroom door, was Jubal's room, unoccupied tonight. Beyond it, last door on the upper level, firmly shut, was Marcy's.

There was no one on the landing, no one on the stairs. The Big Man paused, breathed in the sudden silence of his home, and slowly rolled his shoulders.

Check it out.

He hadn't imagined the sound. It was real. He trusted his ears. And if Marcy had been prowling, he was bound to find out why.

A small adventure. Something extraordinary in a life that sometimes verged on a predictable routine.

He moved along the landing, quiet for a man his size, with naked feet and nothing underneath his nightshirt. There was just a hint of chill to make his senses more alert. His big hands flexed, as if preparing for a test of strength.

Passing the stairs, he paused again, surveyed the spacious room below. A small army could hide there, in the shadows, but his eyes found nothing out of place.

Get on with it.

He was approaching Jubal's door when Marcy's opened. Frozen in his tracks, the Big Man watched two figures exit. He knew one of them immediately, and was squinting into recognition of the other when they saw him standing there.

With recognition came the flare of rage inside him, overwhelming his surprise. He knew within a heartbeat what was happening, and felt the anger coursing through his veins like vintage whiskey, setting him on fire.

"Goddamn you!" Almost whispering at first, he lumbered forward, arms outstretched, his hands the only weapons he would need. The Big Man found his voice when he was halfway to his target. "God*damn* you! I warned you, didn't I?"

The intruder clutched Marcy's arm, spun her back and away from the Big Man, shoving so hard that she stumbled and fell. It was his first mistake. If he expected mercy, he had come to the wrong place.

"You bastard!" raged the Big Man. "I'll—"

He saw the gun but couldn't stop himself. The rage had a momentum of its own, and if he tried to run, where could he hide? Better to charge and take his chances with the prowler than to let himself be humbled underneath his own damned roof.

The first shot was like thunder, with a lightning bolt that burned into his torso, underneath his rib cage on the left. The Big Man staggered, but he kept on coming, hands outstretched to clutch the gunman's throat.

One chance was all he needed.

Just a twist, and he could put things right.

"Somebody get this bastard offa me!" the leader hissed through clenched teeth, fighting just to breathe. He'd dropped his Smith & Wesson when the Big Man tackled him—his first shot wasted, damn it—and felt fingers like a iron talons clamped around his neck.

Jesus!

He could've sworn his first shot hit the Big Man fair and square, but if it had, the bastard should be writhing on the floor instead of wringing his neck like a farm wife with a chicken.

Desperately, the leader brought his knee up, fast and hard into the Big Man's groin. It didn't seem to faze him. Nothing did. The sumbitch had to be a lunatic, with strength like that, immune to pain.

When scratching at the Big Man's wrists and knuckles did no good, he drove a fist into the washboard abdomen, putting his weight behind the short, sharp blows. The Big Man didn't seem to notice, but the leader's hand was bloody when he raised it, scrabbling at his adversary's face.

Where did the blood come from? His bullet must've hit the Big Man after all, but if it had—

"Somebody . . . get . . . this . . . bastard . . ."

He was fading, saw a swarm of black motes dancing in his field of vision, almost covering the Big Man's florid face, the bristling mustache, teeth like aged piano keys. Dear God, the bastard was about to kill him. It was all for nothing, everything he'd planned and—

Someone struck the Big Man hard across the head, tearing his scalp and spraying blood into the leader's face. The fingers didn't loosen on his throat, but now the Big Man turned to show his other enemy a snarl. A brown hand drove a pistol butt into his nose and mashed it flat.

The Big Man roared and staggered, letting go with one hand while the other held its crushing grip. The leader kicked out with his sharp-toed boots, hitting the Big Man's knees and shins, making him roar again. Another pistol slashed across the Big Man's face and broke his grip at last, driving him back against the rail.

"Watch out!" somebody said, a voice the leader should've recognized, except his ears were ringing now and he could barely hear at all. One of his people stepped in close and fired into the Big Man's chest, scorching his linen nightshirt with the muzzle-flash.

The Big Man felt that one, sagging against the rail, blood pumping from a wound that must have struck his heart or something close to it. The leader wasn't taking any chances. Dropping to one knee, he wrapped both arms around the Big Man's legs and lifted, groaning at the weight. He used the railing as a fulcrum, lifting in a rush of heat and pain that made him feel he might've ruptured something, letting go as the Big Man tipped over backward and was gone.

The leader found his pistol, then the cringing girl. He grabbed her wrist and dragged her after him, telling the others, "Let's get out of here. We're running goddamned late."

Reaching the stairs, he glanced in the direction of the mother's room, but didn't see her in the doorway. It was just as well. He didn't want to shoot a woman if he could avoid it, and they needed someone to negotiate the payoff anyway. He wasn't sure a hireling would have the authority or interest to complete the deal, but family was different.

Blood cares.

Blood pays.

Now, all they had to do was clear the Big Man's land and they were—

"Stop!"

A skinny, balding man was rushing toward the bottom of the staircase. He was dressed in shirtsleeves and a pair of baggy trousers, black. His feet were bare, and the expression on his face was struck somewhere between outrage and panic. More imposing than his stature was the double-barreled shotgun in his hands.

"Who's this prick?" someone asked the leader.

Answers weren't important now. Only reactions mattered. Crouching as he fired, the leader saw his target stagger, falling, and the scattergun went with him. When the old man jerked its double triggers, it was aimed somewhere above and to his right of the staircase. Its blast was echoed by a piercing scream.

The leader spun and saw the mother clinging to the rail with one hand, while the other pressed against her face, blood streaming through her pale fingers. Her lips parted to loose another wailing cry.

"Mama?" The girl recoiled from him, straining in his grasp. *"Mama!"*

The leader jerked her arm, half-dragging her downstairs behind him. "Hurry up, dammit!" he snapped. "We got no time to waste!"

They hit the porch running, heard voices from the general direction of the bunkhouse, but no shooters had emerged to challenge them as yet. The girl didn't resist as they manhandled her aboard the extra horse and got her settled.

"Two men dead already," someone groused. "I didn't count on that."

"So what?" another answered. "They can only hang us once."

"An' it's the once that worries me," the first replied.

"Shut up and ride," the leader told them all, "before these bastards find the nerve to take us here and now."

•   •   •

The bedroom had a strange, flat look about it that the lady of the manor didn't recognize. She understood that two eyes were required for depth perception, but it took some getting used to. She had trouble gauging distances, exacerbated by the dull pain in her head and the foul-tasting laudanum she'd swallowed to relieve it.

The doctor hovered at her bedside, nervous, plainly wishing he was somewhere else. "There's nothing I can do to save the eye," he said. "I'm sorry, ma'am."

"My husband?" Was her voice really a breathless whisper, or was it the ringing in her ears that muffled sound?

"He's gone," the doctor said. "Again, I'm sorry."

"Jubal?"

Leaning past the doctor now, the foreman frowned at her, rolling his hat in bony hands. "Ma'am, he's been sent for. Should be here tomorrow evening, at the latest."

"My daughter?"

Words were difficult to form, for some reason. They slithered off her tongue and down her throat before she could give voice to them. Each syllable required an effort she did not recall from normal speech.

"They took 'er, ma'am," the foreman said. The grimace on his face told her it cost him something, saying that. "Me an' a few boys follered 'em a ways, but then we lost 'em in the foothills. We'll be goin' back an' try again at first light, ma'am, I promise you."

In idle moments past, she had sometimes amused herself by wondering what it must feel like, losing everything at one fell swoop. It was impossible, of course. Such things were never meant to happen—yet they sometimes did. Within a span of moments she had lost her eye, her husband, and her daughter. As the laudanum began to do its work, her pain gave way to emptiness, a sense of being left completely, utterly alone.

Not yet.

Her son was still alive and well, coming to join her in this hour of trial, but he was not the man she needed. Jubal could be fierce, but he was seldom focused. For the job

she had in mind, an altogether different kind of man
would be required.

"Listen," she said, and waited while the others bent
over her bed of pain, their blurry faces drawing close. "I
want to offer a reward."

I

It was half-past noon when Matt Price entered Santa Rosa from the east, leaving scrub desert thankfully behind him for the moment. Four days on the trail from Yuma, and he knew the Salton Sea was somewhere up ahead of him, but Price was damned if he could smell it on the dry wind blowing in his face. His roan was thirsty, and Price would've said the same, had anybody asked.

The town was of a decent size for rural southern California. Most of the shops seemed freshly painted, which was testimony to a certain level of prosperity. It would be cattle country, Price supposed, if there was grass enough to graze on farther north and west. If not, he didn't have a clue what they were up to, and he didn't care.

The man Price wanted, if he hadn't come too late, would gravitate to whores and whiskey. He'd have money left, unless his last score had been smaller than the Tularosa bankers claimed. It happened that way sometimes, when one thief tried blaming some of his work on another, but again, Price didn't care. The only sum of interest to him at the moment was the five-hundred-dollar price on Dermott Jackson's head.

Dead or alive, the poster folded in his pocket said.

Price reckoned he'd let Jackson make that call.

He had been tracking Jackson for the best part of a month, had missed him twice by no more than a couple days in dried-up little desert towns that offered nothing to an outlaw on the run. Price hoped that Santa Rosa would be different, that his quarry would relax and stay a while, thinking that he was safe because he'd never pulled a job in California.

It would be his last mistake.

Jackson had left two dead in Tularosa, one of them a deputy, the other an eleven-year-old boy who'd gotten scared and run the wrong way when the shooting started. Price supposed the kid had been an accident, but rope was waiting for the shooter any way he sliced it. That meant Jackson would most likely fight, in lieu of going back to face a jury.

Just as well, Price thought. The prospect of a long ride back with Jackson hadn't thrilled him anyway.

Let's end it here.

Whoever wore the badge in Santa Rosa would be authorized to pay up on the warrant, once he got the confirmation from New Mexico. Price didn't mind if he was forced to wait a day or two. He'd use the time to rest and choose his next quarry.

That was the good thing about bounty hunting.

There was never any dearth of fugitives.

Price stopped at the first water trough he saw, outside a freight office, and waited for his mount to drink its fill. Horses had better sense than people, and he knew the roan would drink enough to satisfy itself, but not go overboard. While he was waiting, Price scanned storefronts, looking for a marshal's office, but he got distracted by a funeral procession coming down the middle of the street.

The hearse was drawn by two black horses, nearly

twins, except that one had a white blaze between its eyes. The undertaker and his boy sat close together on the driver's seat, dressed just alike in frock coats, string ties, and tall hats. The hearse was one of those with open sides, to show two polished caskets wedged inside, each with a floral wreath on top.

A stylish buggy trailed behind the hearse, keeping its distance so the mare that pulled it wasn't eating too much dust. The driver was a grim-faced man of twenty-something years, wearing a pistol with his mourning clothes. The passenger who sat behind him was a woman who concealed her face behind a long black veil.

Price watched the small procession pass, noting that several shopkeepers came to their windows, staring through the glass. A couple actually stepped outside and bowed their heads, presumably to show respect.

Dead folk of substance then.

If Dermott Jackson chose to fight, he wouldn't get this kind of send-off.

And neither would Price, he supposed, if Jackson had a faster gun.

The roan snorted to let Price know that it was finished drinking. With a light tug on the reins, he put the horse in motion, walking east along the town's main street. He saw the marshal's office now and passed it by, more interested in the two saloons that faced each other from opposite sides of the street's western end. He felt eyes tracking him along the way, the greeting every stranger got in frontier towns, but Price paid no attention to them.

He was focused on payday.

The dive on Price's side of Main Street was the Sundance, while its competition called itself the Lucky Strike. As gin mills went, they seemed fairly respectable. Fresh paint, clean windows, and no naked strumpets dangling from the upstairs balconies. Price tied his animal outside the Sundance, stamping off a layer of pale dust from the trail before he pushed through batwing doors into the shade.

The midday drinking crowd was sparse, which made it easy. He had memorized his quarry's face and didn't have to haul the poster out right now. None of the eight men he could see was Dermott Jackson, so he turned and left before the bartender had time to wipe another glass.

Price crossed the street, feeling as if he had a target painted on his back. That was ridiculous, of course. Jackson had never seen him, likely never heard of him, and Price had never tangled with the law in California. It was just a feeling that came over him sometimes, most often in a new place, when he hadn't fully scouted out the ground. A small reminder that the worst thing that could happen to him hadn't happened yet.

Another set of swinging doors flapped shut behind him, fanning hot air at his back. The Lucky Strike was doing slightly better business than its neighbor, with perhaps a dozen drinkers at the bar and half as many more at scattered tables. Price ticked off their faces without seeming to, and made a point of showing no reaction when he spotted Jackson at the far end of the bar.

It would've been too obvious to turn and leave immediately, might've spooked his man if Jackson wasn't already too drunk to notice. Price found a slot at the bar, paid for a beer, and drank it slowly, savoring the taste. He watched Jackson's reflection in the mirror without seeming to, noting the Colt worn in a backward holster, butt foremost.

When he was finished with his beer, Price turned and left. His man was busy drinking at the moment, and it wouldn't hurt to let him down a few more shots. If Jackson left the Lucky Strike, he wouldn't travel far.

Price found the barbershop and livery stable.

First things first.

"Full treatment?" asked the barber after Price had settled in his chair.

"How much?"

"A dollar even."

"Might as well."

The hot towel stung his face and made Price feel a trifle claustrophobic, blinding him to movement in the street, but he tried to relax. Nobody knew him here. He had no history in Santa Rosa, and it seemed impossible that anybody could be waiting for him. All the same, Price kept the Colt Peacemaker in his lap, thumb on the hammer, index finger resting on the smooth curve of the trigger guard.

"You're new," the barber offered while he stropped his razor.

"To Santa Rosa anyway," Price answered.

"What I meant, yessir." The barber waited for elaboration, finally compelled to add, "It's hot weather for traveling."

"That's true."

"I guess you've ridden quite a spell to find us."

Price let silence hang between them for a moment, then replied, "I didn't know a quiz came with the shave and haircut."

"No, sir, you're exactly right. I got the gift of gab, is all."

"Give it to someone else."

The barber forced a chuckle. "That's a good one, yessir. I'll have to remember that."

Price heard the barber mixing lather in a cup, humming a tuneless melody to keep himself from asking any further questions. Took his time about it too, but that was fine. Price kept his eyes shut as the towel lifted away and foam was slathered on his face.

The barber had a steady hand, no jerkiness or trembling with the razor. Price was happy that he concentrated on his work, instead of gabbing while the cool blade glided over skin. It was a closer shave than Price could often manage by himself, with cold water or none at all, and left him feeling fresh, a sharp dash of witch hazel for the chaser.

"Halfway home," the barber said, trading the razor for

a comb and pair of shears. He pumped a lever on the back-side of the chair, changing its angle, and began to work on Price's hair.

Price had a thought and said, "I passed the undertaker's wagon, coming in."

The barber sighed, releasing pent-up pressure. "Yessir, I expect you did," he answered. "That's all folks have talked about the past two days."

"A funeral?"

"The murders, that would be. Big news for Santa Rosa, but the wrong kind, if you follow me."

Price didn't want to ask, but what if there was money in it somehow, and he let it slip away from simple lack of interest? "What happened?" he inquired.

"Oh, it was turrible," the barber said. "A gang went on the Schaefer spread, out north a town, and raised all kinds a hell. They killed Mr. Uriah Schaefer and a hired man, Old Isaiah. Tried to kill the Widow Schaefer too, but missed it by a smidge an' only put her eye out. Quite a looker, that one used to be, if I do say so."

"Sounds to me," Price said, "like someone in the family made enemies."

"They weren't no *friends,*" the barber granted. "That's for damn sure. And that weren't the worse of it."

"There's more?" Despite the tale of woe, Price had a job of work to keep from smiling at the barber's melodramatic delivery style.

"Worst bit of all," the older man replied, still snipping Price's hair. "Afore they left, the scum made off with Miss Marcella."

"Who would that be?" Price inquired.

"Marcella Schaefer. Apple of her daddy's eye, she was, and better looking than her ma. I mean, afore them bastids shot her eye out."

"So, they kidnapped her?"

"Yessir, right outa bed, the story goes, with nary time to grab a stitch of decent clothes."

"What did your marshal do?" asked Price.

"Oh, *him*." The barber didn't try to hide his scorn. "He's hell on drunks come Satiday, when they run outa money for their poison, but he ain't what anybody calls a real lawman. No jerry . . . jersey . . ."

"Jurisdiction?"

"Right you are, sir. None a that outside the city limits, so he says, and not much inclination to be shot at neither. If the bastards come in town and give theirselves up to him, I suppose he's got the nerve to lock a cell."

"Did anyone go after them?"

"Oh, hell, yes. Jubal Schaefer—he's the Big Man's son and heir, Marcella's brother—took some hands to run 'em down, but they got lost or somethin'. Come back empty-handed anyhow."

"And this all happened when again?"

"On Sunday night," the barber said.

Three days ago, while he was on the trail from Yuma.

"Was that Mrs. Schaefer in the buggy, following the hearse?" Price asked.

"The very same."

"She must be tough, out riding this soon after she was shot."

"The lady is a strong'un, yessir. You called that exactly right."

The barber turned away, set down his shears, and held a mirror up in front of Price's face. "How's that look to you, sir?"

Like someone who's been through the mill and out the other side, Price thought. "It's fine," he answered.

"Someone special oughta be impressed."

Price frowned into the looking glass and said, "I'll let you know."

Leaving the barber's shop, Price thought about a steak and beans, but then decided it could wait. An empty stomach was the best hope for survival if he happened to be gut-shot, and the hunger made him feel a little meaner than he might have otherwise.

It couldn't hurt.

Price felt no animosity himself toward Dermott Jackson. Granted, bank robbers had killed the woman that he loved some months ago, but that had been a different place and time. He'd settled with them privately and didn't bear the rage some others might've carried to their graves, although the hurt of it was never far away. He dreamed of Mary still, sometimes, and thought about—

Stop it!

Distraction was a fatal error in his business, and he didn't mean to give Jackson an edge by walking into the saloon with one eye focused on a past he couldn't change. The fugitive would have his full attention, until Price had seen him caged or put him down.

The Lucky Strike had picked up ten or fifteen customers while he was in the barbershop, but Dermott Jackson was still drinking by himself. Same place, the far end of the bar, with ample space around him as if other drinkers knew they shouldn't press too close.

Price took advantage of the bad man's comfort zone and stepped up to the bar. He ordered beer again, received it with no sign of recognition from the bartender, and paid in coin. After a sip to wet his throat, Price took the wanted poster from his pocket, carefully unfolded it, and smoothed it with his palms against the shiny surface of the bar.

Price knew his man without confirming it, but he'd developed something of a ritual in recent weeks, since he had turned his hand to bounty-hunting. After Mexico, that is, where he'd avenged himself on Mary's killers, then allowed himself to be diverted for a time by dreams of revolution and redemption.

The revolt was going on without him, Price supposed, but it had failed to show him whatever the hell he had been looking for since Mary's death. Salvation was too strong a word for it, something beyond his grasp or hope.

On morbid nights, when whiskey did the talking, Price wondered if he was simply looking for a faster hand to pull the trigger for him. Anyway, he hadn't found it yet.

Price watched his quarry in the back-bar mirror while he smoothed the poster's wrinkles. Jackson wasn't watching him, or didn't seem to be. Unruly hair the color of a rusty saw blade hung down to the fugitive's eyebrows once he had taken off his dirty, almost shapeless hat. There was a chance his narrow eyes might've examined Price, and Jackson might even remember him from his first visit to the Lucky Strike. If so, he gave no sign.

A cagey bastard, or a careless one.

Which was it?

Dermott Jackson was the fifth man Price had tracked for money since returning to the States from Mexico. He'd given each of them a chance, but only one of them had looked into his eyes and seen enough of what was waiting for him there to go along without a fight. The other three were dead, and if somebody missed them, Price had yet to find out who it was.

When he had smoothed the poster to his satisfaction and enjoyed another sip of beer, Price spoke to Jackson's image in the mirror. "I know you," he said.

The shooter first pretended not to hear Price, or to know the comment was addressed to him. Jackson consumed his final dram of whiskey with a steady hand and set the empty glass back on the bar.

Price used two fingertips, skimming the flattened poster down the bar. With no friction to speak of, it slid all the way to Jackson's whiskey glass and stopped there, with the drawing of his round face scowling up at him.

"That *is* you, I believe," Price said.

Jackson seemed to address the poster as he answered, "So, what if it is?"

They hadn't raised their voices yet, but customers were making room around Jackson and Price, withdrawing from the line of fire but lingering within earshot. The bartender was suddenly engaged in polishing his spotless woodwork.

"So," Price said, "the paper says you're worth five hundred dollars. There's a judge and rope waiting for you in Tularosa."

Jackson turned to face Price for the first time since they'd started talking. "What if I don't feel like going back?" he asked.

"'Dead or alive,' the paper says. It's all the same to me."

"You have a high opinion of yourself."

Price answered with a smile, watching his quarry's eyes and hands.

"You wanna take this to the street?" asked Jackson.

"I don't think so."

"Suit yourself. Barkeep, I'll take another whiskey now."

"After," Price told him. "If you've still a mind to drink."

"I like to know a man's name when I kill 'im. D'you mind?"

"Matt Price."

Jackson blinked once. "I heard a you, way back. Somebody tole me you were dead."

"Somebody got it wrong."

"An' now I'm s'pose ta be a-scaird. Is that the deal?"

"You have a choice to make," Price said. "That's all."

He saw the choice in Jackson's piggy eyes and moved before his adversary reached the pistol in its backward holster. Price beat him to it with his Peacemaker, thumbed back the hammer as it cleared leather, and fired almost without a conscious thought.

His slug took Jackson left of center, striking with sufficient force to spin him half around. Slumping against the bar, Jackson squeezed off a shot that drilled the floor between his feet, struggling to turn and raise his weapon while the life pumped out of him and stained his unwashed clothes. Price waited, with his Colt rock-steady for another shot, until the dead man folded and his six-gun clattered on the boards.

Retrieving it, Price set it down beside his glass of beer, holstered his own, and told the barkeep, "Let me have a whiskey while we're waiting for the law."

The marshal lived down to his reputation, from the barber's brief description. He was heavyset, muscle turning to fat without resistance from the man who wore it, and defeat was written on his face. Although well groomed, he had an air of general neglect about him, covered by too much cut-rate cologne. The lawman eyeballed Price and read his poster twice from top to bottom, standing with a fat hand resting on his gun.

"I didn't know this man was wanted," he declared at last.

"Good news for me," Price said. "I might've missed the bounty otherwise."

"You might've checked with me before you turned this place into a shooting gallery," the marshal said. "That's what you might've done."

"I saw the opportunity, Marshal. It didn't call for any help. Nobody's hurt except the one who called the play."

The marshal scuffed at Jackson's bullet hole with one wide boot. "Who's paying for the damage to the Lucky Strike?" he asked.

"My guess would be, the hole pays for itself in extra customers before the night's over. You want to turn his pockets out and keep the difference, it's fine with me."

The lawman had a look that wanted to demand respect but didn't dare. Instead, he twitched his ruddy nose above a thick mustache and said, "You'll have to wait until I get the confirmation back from Tularosa."

"Fine. Let's do the paperwork."

"All right then. Come with me."

Price trailed the marshal through a crowd of muttering observers who had flocked into the Lucky Strike after word of the shooting spread. Some of them were already drinking, driving up the tavern's profit, and he guessed most of the rest would join them when the undertaker finally got Jackson's corpse out of their way.

Later afternoon was scarcely cooler in the street than it had been when Price rode into town. He let the marshal go ahead without him, while he fetched the roan and followed in his own good time. There was no hurry. Dermott Jackson wasn't going anywhere but in the ground, and Price would have his money by tomorrow or the next day, latest, even if the lawman tried to slow it down.

The marshal's office stood between a dry goods store and sundries shop that had a headless dummy in the window, dressed up in a woman's fancy gown. It had been hanging there a while, based on the marked-down ticket, and Price wondered who would ever buy it now that Santa Rosa's richest female had put on her widow's weeds.

Inside, the office had a desk, one chair, and two small cells in back. A message board hung on the west wall, thick with overlapping posters. Price looked through them while the marshal took some papers from his desk and found an inkwell. Price had to smile at sight of Dermott Jackson's wanted sheet, half-covered by a flyer advertising two Mexican rapists. The dead man peered around limp paper with one baleful eye.

Price worked the poster loose and dropped it on the marshal's desk without comment. The lawman took an awkward swipe at his mustache and said, "I don't know how I missed that."

"Well, you've got a lot of faces here," Price said, still poking through the rest. "Hard to remember all of them, I guess."

"I'll need the usual particulars," said his disgruntled host.

Price took the marshal's pen, dipped it, and scratched his name across the standard form's top line. The date came next. He got to the address line, paused, and asked, "Is there a decent hotel hereabouts?"

"The Rockford, half block down, across the street," the marshal answered. "They're a mite particular about their patrons, though."

Price smiled. "Let's hope I pass inspection. Otherwise, I'll have to stay with you until the payment clears."

That made the marshal doubly ill at ease. "They give you any problem, I can have a word," he said. "I know the owners."

"Glad to hear it." Price wrote down the hotel's name and followed it with Jackson's on the line allotted. In the blank reserved for CIRCUMSTANCES he wrote "Resisting" and left it at that. "I guess you know the witnesses?"

"Most of 'em, yeah. That ought to be enough."

"I hope so, Marshal. And before you put a slowdown on the paper, bear in mind I'll be in town until I'm paid."

"Not likely to forget it, am I?"

"I hope not."

Price left the office, stepping into meager shade outside. A woman dressed and veiled in black stood waiting for him on the dusty sidewalk, with a grim-faced man at her elbow. It was the first surprise of any consequence since Price had ridden into town.

"I understand you've killed a man," she said.

Price watched her male companion as he answered. "Not a friend of yours, I hope."

"Hardly." She almost laughed at that.

Almost.

"Well, ma'am, in that case—"

"You're a bounty hunter." Not quite asking him.

"That's right."

"A good one?"

"I'm alive," Price said.

"And would you like to earn ten thousand dollars?" she inquired.

2

The lady wouldn't talk about it in the street, wouldn't accompany Price to the hotel or Santa Rosa's only restaurant. She countered with an invitation to her ranch.

"Ma'am, I've been on the road a while," Price said. "I'm tired and hungry. So's my horse. I don't mind talking money with you, but I've put on enough miles today."

"Two miles, due north. That isn't too far surely, Mr. . . ."

"Price. Matt Price."

"I'm Joan Schaefer. This," she said, half-turning, with a gloved hand raised, "is my son Jubal."

Jubal didn't nod, stick out his hand, or offer any other sign of life beyond his glare. Price had a feeling that whatever happened in the next few minutes, they would never be the best of friends.

"I'm pleased to meet you both," Price said, stretching the truth a bit. "But as I said—"

"Of course," the lady interrupted him. "You're waiting for the money."

"Ma'am?"

"You shot this person for a bounty, yes? May I inquire how much it was?"

"Five hundred dollars."

"Jubal, please."

Price watched the son reach in a pocket of his black trousers and palm a wad of greenbacks. Breaking eye contact just long enough to make the count, Jubal peeled off three hundred-dollar bills and four fifties, extending them to Price.

"Ma'am, I already filed my claim for the reward."

"And when it comes, you'll have a bonus, Mr. Price. Consider this my payment for your time. Come hear my proposition, please. The money's yours, whether you take the job or turn it down."

"Where is this ranch of yours?" Price asked.

"Two miles due north of town. I have a carriage waiting. You can ride with us or follow, as you please."

Price thought about it for another moment, coming up with no one in that part of California who would want him bad enough to front five hundred dollars for a shot, when they could snipe him on the street for free. This didn't smell like bait.

Price put the money in his pocket. "After four days on the trail," he said, "my animal needs seeing to, and so do I. Assuming you don't want to wait, I'll take directions to your place and follow in an hour, give or take."

"An independent man," she said. Was there a bare hint of a smile behind the veil? "All right then. One mile north, along the county road, you'll see our gate. The Circle S. Follow the trail another mile, and we'll be waiting for you. Bring an appetite and open mind."

"I'll be there, ma'am."

Price stood and watched them walk away, the tall son glancing back at him one time with an expression on his face that looked like anger mixed with curiosity. Price guessed that Jubal Schaefer was accustomed to the locals doing what he wanted, when he wanted it. It rankled, hearing "no" or even "maybe," but he guessed the man would learn to live with it.

Or not.

Price led his roan down to the livery and paid the boy in charge to brush and feed the horse, then have it ready for him in an hour. That done, he walked back to the barbershop along a street the waning afternoon had cast in shadow.

"Back again so soon!" the barber said, trying to smile. "Nothing amiss, I hope?"

"You advertise hot baths."

"Yessir. Indeed I do! If you'd be kind enough to follow me . . ."

Price soaped and soaked for half an hour while he thought about Joan Schaefer's offer. First, he ran the bait-and-trap scenario again, but couldn't make it work, no matter how he tried. Price hadn't been within two hundred miles of Santa Rosa previously. Anyone who knew him there must be an immigrant from somewhere else, and it defied logic that his name had traveled fast and far enough outside the Lucky Strike to set some old hate simmering, much less allow transplanted enemies to lay a snare for him. And if it *had,* if someone in the area *was* gunning for him, would they use the richest woman in the county, lately widowed, as the lure?

Impossible.

That left the lady and her son, who were complete strangers to Price before she stopped him on the street. He knew the bare bones of her story, or one version of it, from the barber. With five hundred dollars in his pocket and a day or two to kill in Santa Rosa, Price could well afford to hear the lady's side. He guessed there would be vengeance at the end of it, ten thousand dollars' worth, but what was wrong with that?

Price knew the sweet taste of revenge. He'd killed for free and fought for pay in range wars once or twice. Now he was tracking wanted men for money, and of five he'd hunted down so far, only one gutless weasel made it to the calaboose alive. Price wasn't an assassin in the common sense, meaning he wouldn't backshoot strangers for a fee, but he supposed most casual observers would consider it a fine distinction.

Kidnappers and murderers were fair game, any way he broke it down. And ten grand was enough to get him off the circuit for a good long while. Price could retire on that perhaps, if he could find a place where no one recognized his name and young guns didn't come sniffing around to earn a reputation for themselves.

Why not?

He'd already been paid, and very handsomely, to hear the widow's story. They had supper waiting for him at the ranch, a little conversation, and he could reject the offer if it went too hard against the grain.

Or so the lady said.

Price had known people, rich and poor, who changed their minds when things began to go against them. Promises went out the window sometimes, and sore feelings took control. The lady or young Jubal might feel cheated if Price turned them down and tried to leave with their five hundred dollars in his pocket. Mood swings of that nature could be lethal if he was outnumbered, caught on unfamiliar ground.

Price didn't brood about the risk. Joan Schaefer had already paid him for his time. The least he owed her was a ride into the country and the open mind she'd asked for. If her offer didn't suit him, he would pass and take whatever followed as it came.

When he was dry and dressed, Price cut the barber's gossip short and walked back to the livery. His mount was waiting, seemingly content. They took the dry road out of town as afternoon stretched into dusk, still ample light remaining for a brisk two-mile ride. It meant returning in the dark, but Price had no objection on that score.

The ghosts that haunted him were careless as to whether they appeared by night or day.

The northbound road was clear and relatively straight,

well used from all appearances. When he was twenty minutes out, Price found the gate Joan Schaefer had described. It was constructed out of rough-hewn logs, double a tall man's height and wide enough to let a large freight wagon pass with room on either side. It was surmounted by the Schaefer brand, a barrel hoop surrounding barbed wire bent to form an S. Price guessed the gate was meant to be symbolic, like some classic monument, since there was no fence trailing off to either side. A trail led through the gate and off through open grazing land, toward distant trees and buildings in the east.

Price had a choice of passing through the gate or circling around it, but he didn't feel like playing games. Straight passage didn't mean he was committed to the lady's offer. He was free to come and go as he desired, and God help anyone who told him otherwise.

A lookout must've seen him coming from a distance. As Price rode into the yard, he found Joan Schaefer and a hired man waiting for him on the front porch of a long two-story house, flanked by live oaks, a barn, and other outbuildings. She had shed the veil, and Price was startled by the large black patch that hid her left eye and a portion of her face.

"You found us, Mr. Price," she said.

"No problem, ma'am."

"In that case, welcome to my home."

The hired man took his reins as Price dismounted, but the roan stood fast until Price spoke to it, clearing the stranger for a short walk to the barn.

"Your animal's well trained, I see."

"The only kind to have," Price said.

"We have something in common then." His hostess tried a smile for size.

"Could be," Price answered, thinking to himself, *Not much, except for loss*.

"Please, follow me."

The steps and porch were solid underneath his feet, no sagging to the boards. Price thought the house was built to last, not just for show. It wasn't new, but it had weathered well and it was well maintained. Price didn't bother guessing what it must've cost to build.

Inside, the rustic charm gave way to luxury without apology. The hardwood floors were polished to a lustrous shine, and there were life-sized portraits on the walls. Price didn't recognize their subjects, mostly military men who posed in uniform, but he was able to identify the hunting trophies that competed with the paintings for wall space. Whoever did the Schaefer family's shooting had collected a menagerie including cougar, bear, moose, prong-horned antelope, bobcat, and peccary. There was a snakeskin over one doorway, stripped from a rattler close to six feet long. A giant severed foot of some kind had been hollowed out to make a stand for walking sticks.

Joan Schaefer caught Price looking at the foot and told him, "That's a hippopotamus. One leg at least."

"All right."

"They live in Africa," she said.

Price nodded, wondering how big the creature must have been to walk on feet like that.

"My husband bought it at an auction in New Orleans," she went on, as if he'd asked. "Uriah never went as far as Africa."

"Few of us do," Price said, for want of any other answer.

"No. I thought we'd sit in the library, if you don't mind."

"Fine with me."

She led him through a few more well-appointed rooms, all stocked with heavy wood-and-leather furniture, until a doorway opened on the left and she passed through it. Price followed her into a room whose walls were lined from floor to ceiling with bookshelves, all of them filled with volumes fat and thin. Price guessed an avid reader could've spent a few years in that room without feeling the need to step outside. Chairs occupied the center of the room, and one of them was occupied by Jubal Schaefer, lounging with a glass of some dark liquor in his hand.

"You know my son," the hostess said.

It wasn't strictly true, although Price recognized him. Jubal didn't rise or speak, leaving the silence from their first encounter solidly intact.

"We'll dine after we talk, I think," Joan Schaefer said. "Would you like anything to drink, meanwhile?"

"No, thank you."

"I believe I'll have a sherry. Jubal?"

While she sat, directing Price to one of four identical deep chairs, the son got up to pour his mother's sherry, choosing one of half-a-dozen bottles on a nearby sideboard. Price waited until his hostess had been served and sipped her wine, no hurry on his part.

"Are you acquainted with my situation, Mr. Price?" she asked at last.

"Talk gets around," he answered.

"So it does, especially in Santa Rosa."

Price was getting used to the eye patch. The portion of Joan Schaefer's face that he could see was handsome, stopping short of beautiful. There was a strength beneath the stylish surface too, or else she wouldn't have been interviewing gunmen so soon after she was nearly killed herself.

"Unfortunately," she continued, "much of what you'll hear in town is either incomplete or fabricated from thin air. You won't mind if I set the record straight?"

"It's your story," he said.

"Quite so. You see before you half of what I used to call my family. My husband was murdered on Sunday, in this very house. He fell near the stairs that we passed, coming in."

Price thought someone had done a decent job of cleaning up. His hostess told the story straight, without revealing much of what she felt inside.

"You have my sympathy," he said.

"Keep it." Jubal Schaefer's first two words were muffled by his whiskey glass.

"Jubal," his mother said, "if you cannot be civil, then I must insist you leave us."

"Yes'm. Sorry." Speaking to his mother, not to Price.

"No doubt you will forgive my son his grief," the lady said to Price.

"It's understandable," he answered, thinking to himself that Jubal sounded more pissed off than sad.

"In any case, as dearly as I loved Uriah, losing him to violence was not the worst of our unfolding tragedy. The murderers also kidnapped my youngest child, Marcella."

"How old is the girl?" Price asked. He'd barely stopped himself from saying *was*.

"She's just turned seventeen."

Price didn't have to tell the lady that was bad. The recognition of his silent thought was visible in her good eye.

"A party tried to overtake them, but the search was unsuccessful." Here, she looked at Jubal, something like reproach. The object of her scrutiny refused to meet his mother's gaze. "Needless to say, we're worried sick."

And rightly so, Price thought. He asked them both together, "Is that all of it?"

"No, Mr. Price. The killers left a message when they fled our home. They have demanded ransom for Marcella's safe return."

"How much?"

"One million dollars."

Price considered the amount, trying to picture it in cash. He'd have to shoot two thousand Dermott Jacksons for a million dollars—twenty of them just to make the ten thousand he'd already been offered.

He was looking for the catch.

"A sum like that—"

"Is not a problem," said Joan Schaefer, interrupting him. "Marcella means the world to me, of course—to us. I'll gladly pay."

The look on Jubal's face told Price *he* wasn't glad about it. "If you mean to pay, ma'am, I'm not clear on what you need from me."

"It's quite a lot of money, you'll agree."

"Yes, ma'am."

"The ransom message specifies delivery at San Felípe. That's a small town on the Gulf of California, roughly two days south."

Old Mexico. Or rather, Baja California. It was all the same to Price, and he had no desire to cross the line again so soon. Still, he had never worked in Baja, wasn't known there. And ten thousand dollars carried solid weight.

"I'm not clear on exactly what you want," he said.

"If you accept our proposition, you would help deliver payment for my daughter. Keep the money safe from thieves until the kidnappers are paid and satisfied."

"Go by myself, you mean?"

A snort from Jubal, washed down with another shot of alcohol.

"Alone? Good heavens, no! Jubal will join you, with another pair of men who've served us well."

Price frowned. "If you've got three men going, ma'am, you likely don't need me."

"That's what *I* said," Jubal reminded her.

Ignoring him this time, Joan Schaefer told Price, "While I trust them with Marcella's life, they're not professionals. I need a man who knows exactly what he's doing in that kind of situation."

"A killing situation."

"Yes."

"You want more than delivery and pickup," Price suggested.

"Yes, I do."

"Let's hear the rest of it."

"Once the exchange is made, when you have seen my daughter safely back in Jubal's hands, I want the devils punished."

"That's the law's job, ma'am."

"Which law would that be, Mr. Price? American authorities can't touch them while they hide in Mexico. As for the *federales,* who can trust them to do anything?"

She had a point. The Mexican police he'd met in recent weeks were a mixed bag, at best. The worst of them were nothing more than bandits dressed in uniforms, endowed with the authority to loot and maim at will. As for the rest, they worked within a system built on bribery—*mordida*—and if they were personally honest, few of them would buck the brass to seek reform. Most treated their own people badly and had no respect at all for gringos who had strayed across the line.

"So, Mr. Price," she prodded him, "what will it be?"

"I'm thinking."

"Are you philosophically opposed to shooting kidnappers and murderers?"

"No, ma'am. But I'd prefer to know how many shooters are involved before I swat a hornet's nest."

"That's easy," Jubal told him. "Four."

"Four that you saw."

"Four, period."

Joan Schaefer said, "I was about to tell you that we know the men responsible."

"I guess you'd better tell me how that works, ma'am."

"Of course. The leader is Reese Johnson. He's from Bakersfield, I think. White trash. He and his brother Abel worked around San Rafael, doing odd jobs for pocket money. Somehow, he developed an obsession with Marcella and began to make her life—*our* lives—unbearable. Uriah chased him off the property time and again, but madmen are persistent, don't you find?"

"Sometimes," Price granted, having known a few. "The marshal couldn't help you?"

"Oh, he locked Reese up for trespassing," the lady said. "Fined him some trivial amount and told us it was all the law allowed. We planned to send Marcella East next month, to boarding school. For safety's sake. Perhaps, if she'd gone sooner . . ."

"Was the brother in on this?" Price asked.

"He was."

"That still leaves two."

"Their cousin, Frank Bodine, participated in the crime. More trash from God knows where. You'd think one member of the family would have some common sense or decency."

"Inbreeding," Jubal quipped.

"And number four?"

"Ed Timmons, I believe he's called." She glanced at Jubal.

"Timmons, right."

"Related to the other three somehow?" Price asked.

"Not to my knowledge," Joan Schaefer replied. "They likely met in some saloon or brothel. Lord, it makes my skin crawl to imagine those four with Marcella."

"You shouldn't dwell on it," Price said, knowing before he spoke that his advice would be impossible to take.

"You're right." Her one eye met his level gaze. "I need to focus on recovering Marcella, then on punishing the men who've spoiled our family. Will you help me, or not?"

"I'll take the job," Price told her. "But you have to understand in advance, there are no guarantees."

"Meaning?"

He reckoned she'd been down this mental road already, but Price wouldn't lie to spare her feelings. "First," he said, "we can't be sure your daughter's still alive."

"Reese won't have killed her yet," the lady said. "You'd have to know him, Mr. Price. He claims to *love* her, and insists that *she* feels love for him."

"Men kill for love. Some women too."

"Trust me—or trust my mother's instinct. If my girl was dead, I'd know it, Mr. Price."

"All right. The second risk is trusting Johnson and his bunch to give her back. It doesn't fit so well, him loving her that way and offering to sell her back."

"The man's insane."

"Which means unstable. There's no telling what he'll do at any given time, or why he'll do it. Once he gets the money, he may just as well decide to keep the girl."

Jubal leaned forward in his chair, clutching an empty glass. "So what? We'll *take* her back."

"The very risk I was referring to," Price said. "A shootout with Miz Schaefer in the middle."

"What do you suggest?" his hostess asked.

"There's nothing to suggest, until we're at the drop. Once it unfolds, we wait and see. No guarantees that anyone will walk away."

"You paint a grim picture."

"It's a grim business," he informed her.

"Do you lack self-confidence?"

"I lack the gift of prophecy," Price answered. "I don't know these men, how fast they are, how steady under fire. I don't know whether Jubal and your other hands will be a help or hindrance in a fight. And *you* don't know for sure if there'll be four or forty men at the exchange. Crazy or sane, these fellows may decide to take out some insurance."

"Should I just give up my daughter then?" she challenged him.

"You should be ready for bad news," Price said.

"I've seen the worst that they can do."

"Not necessarily."

"I want Marcella back. If you won't help—"

"I didn't say that. Count me in."

The first smile of the evening blossomed on Joan Schaefer's face, seeming lopsided underneath the black eye patch. "In that case, we should celebrate."

As if on cue, a stoop-shouldered servant appeared in the doorway, announcing that dinner was served.

The food was plentiful and well prepared, including beef, potatoes, green and yellow vegetables, fresh bread, coffee and apple pie to follow. Joan Schaefer and Price carried

the conversation while it lasted, Jubal interjecting sour
notes disguised as jokes from time to time. They didn't
talk about the trip to Baja or its dangers anymore, the lady
seeming to prefer stories about her land and family when
it was still intact.

She didn't ask Price to describe his own adventures,
which was likely for the best.

They planned to leave next morning early, after breakfast, forcing Price to stay the night. His hostess told him
she would send word to the marshal, making sure his pay
for Dermott Jackson would be waiting for him when—or
if—he made it back to Santa Rosa. At the same time, she
invited Price to sleep beneath her own roof, in a guest
room, but he chose the bunkhouse.

There was no point in pretending he was family.

Price checked the roan and found it situated nicely in
the spacious barn, with feed and water handy. It was pushing ten o'clock when he entered the bunkhouse. Price had
guessed the Circle S would have at least a dozen hands in
residence, but there were only five men in the bunkhouse,
playing cards when he walked in. They ranged in age from
late teens to mid-fifties, by his estimate, all staring at him
curiously.

"You's the shooter," one man said at last.

"Matt Price," he told them.

If it registered, they covered well enough. "You're
goin' south with Jubal," said another, still not asking.

"Some of you are coming too, I understand. Who
would that be?" Price asked.

A forty-something cowboy with a red beard, thinning
hair, and ample stomach raised his hand. "I'll be along.
Tom Landry."

"Pleased to meet you," Price replied. "Who else?"

"That's me," answered a young one, slender, with a
straggling ghost of mustache on his lip. "Name's Early
Brooks."

"Early?"

"He couldn't wait the whole nine months," one of the others said. "Or else his mama wanted shed of him."

"You see why I'm not sorry to be leaving this bunch in the dust," Brooks said.

Price chose an unmade bunk and dropped his gear. "Who's been to San Felípe?" he inquired.

"I spent a night there," Landry answered. "Four, five years ago. It's nothin' special."

"Maybe you could fill me in, whatever you remember, while we're on the road," Price said.

"Don't see why not."

Price nodded. "What time's breakfast hereabouts?"

"Five-thirty, more or less," said Early Brooks.

"In that case, I'll turn in and leave you to your game."

"Hey, mister," Brooks called after him.

"It's Matt."

"You think it'll be bad?"

"Be ready for the worst," Price told him. "That way, if you're disappointed, it'll be a nice surprise."

3

Breakfast was ham and eggs, with fried potatoes on the side and coffee strong enough to wake the dead. The bunkhouse crew ate quickly, keeping conversation to a minimum, which suited Price's mood. He found his roan well rested, glad to see him, seeming anxious for a chance to stretch its legs.

His dreams the night before had been of Mary Hudson, as they often were. Those nights, he rarely saw her dead, which was a blessing, but she always lingered just beyond his reach. Price often woke from such dreams feeling guilty, frustrated, and angry at the world.

Because her death had been his fault.

He couldn't shake that feeling, sometimes thinking he would take it to his grave. And why not? Mary Hudson had saved his life and come *that* close to saving his soul, before her fatal chance encounter with a gang of badmen in New Harmony, Texas. Price had been marshal at the time, his one stint with a badge, but he'd been out of town tracking a fugitive when Mary died.

Too late to help her, but in time to take revenge.

For all the good it did.

To break the morbid train of thought, he concentrated on the job he'd undertaken. Price had no idea whether Marcella Schaefer was alive or not, but if her mother was prepared to pay the ransom—and to pay *him* handsomely for escorting the money to its destination—Price had no objection to the plan.

As for the other part of his assignment, taking out the kidnappers, he'd have to wait and see what happened at the drop. Price had explained the pitfalls to Joan Schaefer and her son as clearly as he could. The lady didn't want to hear it, ruling out disaster with a mother's wishful thinking, and the son had yet to drop his surly mask for any kind of glimpse inside.

Price guessed that there was something he had not been told about the kidnapping and murder. Joan Schaefer made it sound a relatively simple case—obsession and rejection spilling over into blood—but Price wasn't convinced she'd told him everything.

Why should she?

Every family harbored secrets, Price's being no exception, and he wouldn't normally have cared. He had accepted the commission to retrieve a hostage and bring justice of a sort to her abductors, who were also murderers. It was a variation of the same thing Price did every time he stalked a fugitive for bounty.

What was different this time?

Something, but he couldn't make it out.

Not yet.

There'd be time on the trail to look for answers. Jubal wouldn't spill, but Price could work on Brooks and Landry, maybe pry some information out of them if he was slick enough and didn't push too hard.

By 6:15, three quarters of the ransom party was prepared and waiting in the barnyard. Jubal Schaefer was the last to appear, picking his teeth where breakfast traces lingered stubbornly. One of the hands who hadn't introduced himself to Price last night brought Jubal's horse around, saddled and ready for the trail. He also led a fifth horse, this one bearing satchels of supplies and a large suitcase planted squarely on its back, secured with rope.

"I take it that's the payoff?" Price asked Brooks.

"Must be. A million dollars needs some room."

"Good morning, gentlemen." Joan Schaefer's voice drew Price's gaze from the packhorse back to the house. "I hope you all slept well."

Landry and Brooks answered politely, out of habit. Price decided there was no point lying, so he kept his mouth shut.

Standing on the porch, dressed all in black from her eye patch to the ankle-length hem of her dress, Joan Schaefer reminded Price of temperance crusaders he had seen in Wichita and Kansas City. They were always solemn in demeanor, burdened with the gravity of their crusade, but raw fanaticism glimmered in their eyes.

In this case, Price supposed it must be grief.

"Before you go," the lady said, "I want to thank you all for helping to retrieve my daughter from captivity. Although you will be risking life and limb, I know your courage will prevail. The evil we've already suffered will not be compounded. God won't let it!"

The roan snickered and shifted restlessly. Price shared the animal's impatience now. The pitch sounded rehearsed, as if it had been written down and memorized. It had a hollow ring somehow.

"My prayers go with you, gentlemen," his new employer said. "Return safely, with our Marcella, and you shall be handsomely rewarded for your bravery. God speed you on your way."

Landry and Brooks both thanked the lady, as if she was doing them a favor by allowing them to risk their necks in Mexico. Or maybe, Price decided, they were simply looking forward to the handsome but unspecified rewards. He had assumed the two were acting as employees of the Circle S, but maybe they were mercenaries too. That left only

Jubal riding strictly for his sister's honor, and presumably to guide them on their way.

He led them westward first, back to the fenceless gate and through it, turning south from there. Their road took them through Santa Rosa without stopping, people on the sidewalks watching them ride past. A few men doffed their hats, as if the party was another funeral procession.

Price had considered raising an objection to the ride through town, and then thought better of it. If the townspeople knew there was ransom money on the move, they wouldn't need a quick glimpse of a suitcase on a horse's back to start them talking. On the other hand, if they were ignorant of Jubal's mission, they could not spread tales.

The truth was bound to leak, sooner or later. That was human nature and a fact of life. Given a choice, though, Price would make it later.

Money drew scavengers and thieves the same way dung drew flies. Big money made the odds of reaching San Felípe without incident remote.

So be it.

Price had signed to do a job, and he would see it through, no matter who stood in his way.

"So, Matt, you ever done a thing like this before?"

Brooks had been quiet all the way through town, but now that Santa Rosa was behind him, dwindling in the morning heat haze, he had found his tongue again.

"Not this," Price said. "It's new."

"But you're a bounty man, somebody told me. No offense."

"None taken," Price replied. "Somebody's right."

"If you don't mind my askin', how's a man get into that?"

"I didn't plan it," Price explained. "Some months ago I was in Gallup—"

"That's New Mexico?" Brooks interrupted.

"Right. So, one night as I'm coming out of a cantina

there, I heard a ruckus in the alley. Some hardcase was roughing up a woman and I called him on it. Next thing I knew, he was slapping leather and I put him down."

"Who was he?"

"Ever hear of Big-Nose George McDuffy?"

"Nope."

"I hadn't either," Price said, "but he had two hundred dollars on his head for holding up a stage outside Roswell. The sheriff recognized him from a poster."

"And you got the money."

"Right."

"And just kept doing it?"

"So far."

"Big-Nose George." Brooks smiled and shook his head. "I thought *I* had a stupid name."

"There's nothing wrong with Early," Price assured him. "Beats Late anyway."

"I heard that one before."

"Sorry."

"It's no big deal." Brooks shifted in his saddle, glancing furtively at Schaefer's back and lowering his voice as he asked Price, "You reckon we'll find Miss Marcella?"

"If the boys in San Felípe want that money, they'd best have her standing by."

"They might not, though."

"That's true."

"Hard to believe Reese done a thing like that," Brooks said.

"You know him?" Price hoped his surprise wasn't too obvious.

"Sorta. It ain't like we's great friends or anything. More of a 'Howdy, howya doin'?' kind of knowing, if you follow me."

"Acquaintances," Price said.

"Like that. He come around some, after Miss Marcella. Old Man Schaefer run him off the place a couple times, and Jubal had a fight with him in town."

"About his sister?"

"I suppose."

"Who won?"

Brooks shrugged. "I wasn't there."

Something in his demeanor made Price wonder whether Brooks was showing loyalty to his boss or truly didn't know the fight's outcome. In either case, Price didn't want to press.

"Tell me somethin' else about the bounty trade," said Brooks.

"Like what?"

"Can anybody do it?"

"Anybody who can pull it off," Price said.

"You don't need any special trainin', though?"

"None I'm aware of."

"'Cuz I'm gettin' tired of cattle."

"It can happen," Price allowed.

"You reckon I could do it?"

"That, I couldn't say. You may find out on this trip, though."

"I think so too." Brooks dropped a hand to pat the double-action Schofield on his hip. "We just might see."

Most young ones liked the thought of fighting, Price reflected. After they'd been in a real fight—not the happy, drunken push-and-shove kind, but a killing battle—they began to split along the fault lines of their personalities. Some loved it still and craved more of the same, while others were put off in the extreme and shied away from any threat of confrontation in the future. Most fell somewhere in between, learning from the experience but going on with life as best they could.

Assuming they survived.

Price didn't know Brooks well enough to judge him, and wouldn't until he had seen how Brooks reacted in a situation where his life was on the line. Their errand was the kind wherein bloodshed was probable, if not dead certain. When it happened, Early Brooks would have to prove himself or pay the price.

Tom Landry rode a bit behind them, with the packhorse

tethered to his saddle horn. He didn't seem to be eavesdropping, but Price didn't know *him* either, so he kept the conversation vague and friendly. He said nothing of his doubts about Joan Schaefer's story, asked no questions about family and such. After another mile or so, however, he had worked his way around to the logistics of the crime.

"I'm thinking," he told Brooks, "about what's waiting for us at the other end."

"What's that?" Brooks asked.

"My point exactly," Price replied. "I don't suppose you've seen this ransom note I heard about."

"Not me." Brooks shook his head.

"Apparently, there's no details on who'll be meeting us or when, no mention of how many they'll be bringing to the table."

"Oh." The cowboy looked concerned now, frowning thoughtfully. "I reckoned it would just be Reese and them."

"The other three, you mean?"

"Tha's right."

"Were you there when they took the girl?"

"I slept through most of it," Brooks answered ruefully. "The first shots sorta brung me half-awake, like; then I heard Isaiah's twelve-gauge plain as day. It took a minute in the dark to grab my Schofield, get my boots on. By the time I come outside, they's riding hell-for-leather outa pistol range."

"But you saw four?"

"Five," Brooks corrected him.

"How's that?"

"They brung a horse for Miss Marcella."

"So they wouldn't have to double up, I guess."

"I s'pose." Brooks had moved on, thinking ahead. "You reckon they'll have more boys waiting for us?" From his tone, Price guessed the prospect didn't much appeal to him.

"I wouldn't rule it out," Price said, "but if they're tight we may get lucky. Could just be the four."

"I'll keep my fingers crossed."

"Not while you're shooting," Price reminded him.

"Well, no."

"Are you acquainted with the other three we're after?" Price inquired.

"I know Abel about the same as Reese," Brooks said. "They spend mosta their time together, bein' kin and all."

"Have you seen either of them fight?"

Brooks studied Jubal Schaefer's back before he answered, making sure the boss was far enough ahead to miss his answer. "Jubal had a go at Reese one time and got the worst of it. They's drinkin' at the Sundance, Reese and Abel with their cousin Frank, when in comes Jubal spoilin' for a dustup."

"And?"

"He got it. Reese weren't gonna fight at first, it looked like, but then Jubal said somethin' about his sister— meaning Miss Marcella—and next thing I know, he's on the floor."

"Was that the end of it?" Price asked.

"Nosir. Jubal was heeled and mad as hell. He went to draw, but Landry and a couple more hands talked him out of it."

Bad blood, Price thought. *The killing kind.*

"Beyond what you describe," he said, "you never saw Reese or the others fight? No thoughts about their skill with guns?"

"I never seen 'em shoot," Brooks said. "But they killed Mr. Schaefer and Isaiah pretty good."

"I guess they did."

Ahead of Jubal Schaefer, fifty yards or so, Price saw a rider break from cover in a copse of trees and canter toward the road. He waited for them, morning sunlight glinting on the star pinned to his vest. "Jubal!" he called out in a deep, strong voice. "We need to have a word."

•   •   •

"That's Corey Tharp," Brooks said. "Chief deputy for this part of the county."

Price waited for other lawmen to emerge from hiding, but the new arrival seemed to be alone. Kneeing his roan a few yards off to Schaefer's right, Price stopped and waited for their leader to address the deputy.

"What do you want, Corey?"

"That's easy, Jubal. You lot turn around and head back to the Circle S."

"Why should we?" Schaefer challenged.

"It's the right thing to do," Tharp answered. "It's the *smart* thing."

"Maybe, if your sister's safe at home. Mine isn't."

"You'd be making a mistake."

"How's that?"

Tharp answered, "You have no authority in Baja."

"So what? This is a business deal, not politics."

"I can't protect you once you cross the line."

"Protect me?" Schaefer barked a grating laugh. "Where were you when they killed my father, Corey? When they kidnapped Marcy?"

"You won't help her this way."

"Did you have another plan in mind?"

"You know the sheriff's been in touch with Washington."

"Negotiating, right." Schaefer was scornful. "Let me know how that works out, when I get back."

"What if you *don't* come back?"

"Then you can tell your friends in Washington I died trying."

"We have too many dead already, Jubal."

"That depends on where you're standing. Seems to me we're still four bodies short."

"I'm looking at them," Tharp replied. His eyes found Price. "Three men I used to know and one new face."

"We're wasting time, Corey."

"What's your name, friend?" the deputy asked Price.

"You talk to *me*, goddamn it!" Schaefer snapped.

"We're bound for Mexico on business that is none of yours. We've broken no laws here, and where we're going is outside your jurisdiction. If you try and stop us, be prepared to lose your badge—at least."

"That has the ring of threat about it, Jubal. Are you threatening the law?"

"I haven't and I won't," Schaefer replied. "Three witnesses against your none."

"You need to hear me, boy," Tharp said. "If you ride into Mexico with that much money, chances are that none of you will ever see your sister, much less bring her safely back to this side of the line."

"So be it, Corey. Now you've done your job. Let us do ours."

The lawman turned to Price once more. "I'd like to know your name, mister. In case your next of kin come askin' after you."

"I've got no next of kin," Price answered, though it wasn't strictly true.

"Then satisfy my curiosity, why don't you. Just a name."

"Matt Price."

"I heard of you," Tharp said. "You killed the Deegan brothers at Prescott."

Price thought about that night, five years ago, as he replied, "I might've missed one. It was dark."

"Somebody told me you were dead."

"Somebody got it wrong."

"Or maybe not." The deputy turned back to Schaefer. "I can't stop you being foolish, that's the truth. You need to think about it, though, before this goes too far."

"It's gone," Schaefer replied.

"Awright, then. Nothing I can do within the law to hinder you."

"Or help me either."

"That's the truth," Tharp said. "There'll be no help for you down south."

"I brought my own."

The lawman cast another glance at Price, stern-faced in the shade of his hat brim; then he slowly reined his horse off to the roadside.

"Hope you boys enjoy your ride," he said as they filed past him. "Adiós."

Price felt Tharp watching them, but he refused to turn and meet the lawman's eyes. Instead, he watched the road ahead and Jubal Schaefer, who had spurred his piebald mare into the lead once more.

When they were out of earshot, Early Brooks remarked, "I coulda done without the send-off."

"Did he spook you?" Price inquired.

"Hell, no!"

"He has to say he tried."

"You mean, in case something goes wrong."

"Correct."

"Because we got the son and heir along." Brooks tipped a nod at his employer.

"That would be my guess." Price knew the deputy wouldn't have tried to stop *him* riding south. Most likely, he'd have urged Price to be moving on the same day he hit town.

"You think he's right? About us getting killed down there, I mean."

Price ducked the question, saying, "I don't think he sees the future."

"But it *could* happen."

"When you wear a gun and look for trouble, yeah. It could."

"We're doin' right, though."

"Makes no difference to a bullet."

Brooks was silent for a quarter mile or so, then said, "I'm ready for it anyway. Just so's you know."

"Ready's the way to be."

"What was it Corey said about them brothers?"

"That's old news."

"I musta missed it. Can you fill me in?"

Price wasn't much for storytelling, but he saw Brooks

slipping, reaching for an anchor. Was it better to encourage him or let him go, if he was working on a change of heart? *None of my business,* he decided, and began his tale.

"It wasn't Prescott," he began, "but close enough. Skull Valley, in Yavapai County."

"Arizona?"

"Right. They had a range war going, back in '85. I didn't ask them how it started. It was just a job. Squatters and cattlemen. The usual."

"Which side were you?" asked Brooks.

"I always seem to pick the underdog. Can't say I recommend it, but it seems to be a trend."

"So, what about the Deacon brothers?"

"Deegan," Price corrected him. "Four of them signed on with the cattlemen. They had a reputation working for them."

"Fast?"

"They did all right."

"You took 'm, though?"

"We had a couple run-ins," Price allowed. "I guess they took it more to heart than I did."

"So, they called you out?"

"Not quite. I'm in the barbershop, having a shave one night, when they start firing from the street. Winged me and dropped the barber, but it went against them after that."

Brooks blinked. "You killed 'm all?"

"Deke, John, and Walter. It was dark out, like I told the deputy. Hank got away."

"He musta wanted you."

"I saw him later, in Tucson."

"What happened?"

"He's still there."

"Jesus."

"Something to think about," Price said. "You always want to make the first shot count."

• • •

"So, you've been to San Felípe?" Price asked Landry two miles later.

"Just the once, but I don't reckon it's changed much."

"Tell me about it."

"What's to tell?"

"We're going there to pay a million dollars for a girl who may be dead already. We don't know how many shooters will be waiting for us at the drop. I'd like to know something about the place before we ride into their sights, and you're the only one of us who's seen the place before. It's time to share."

"Awright, no need to get excited." Landry thought about it for a moment, chewing his whiskers absentmindedly. "There ain't much I can tell ya. It's a little pissant town, no more'n a hunnert yards from end to end. Mostly adobe buildings, with an old church at one end."

"Which end?" Price asked.

Landry considered it. "The south. It faces you as you ride in."

"What else?"

"They got a fountain in the square. Ya see that in a lota Mex towns. It was dry when I was there, weeds growin' out of it. I spent mosta my time in the cantina there."

"Sleep over, did you?"

"Yeah."

"You rent a bed?"

"Tha's right. They got a couple places, more like boardin' houses than hotels. Just small. The whole thing's small, except some a the whores. Ya like meat on 'm, San Felípe might surprise ya."

"I'll keep that in mind. They have a lawman?"

"Didn't see 'im if they did. There weren't no call for any law when I passed through. Most country towns just let the *federales* handle any problems. Everything's *mañana*."

Price knew that could change, and quickly, if the residents of San Felípe knew a million U.S. dollars were en route to their community. What would they do to get their hands on so much wealth? What would the *federales* do?

Hell, what would *anybody* do?

A man could live forever on that kind of money, and still pass a fortune to his children when he died. Price thought about it, knowing he could drop his three companions if he wanted to, and ride off with the greenbacks to someplace where no one knew his name. If he possessed a million dollars, folks would call him anything he liked and put a big fat "Sir" in front of it. The Deegan brothers would've done exactly that, and never lost a minute's sleep.

Daydreams.

Price wouldn't kill these three and take Joan Schaefer's cash because he wasn't the assassin some people imagined him to be. There would be killing on this journey, he was almost certain, but he wouldn't start by murdering his comrades, even if their leader was a cocky horse's ass.

Price was concerned about the townspeople of San Felípe both as enemies and obstacles. If they found out about the money, it was possible they'd arm themselves and try to take it, maybe even kill Reese Johnson and his friends to cut down on the competition. On the other hand, if they were ignorant of what was happening around them, any play Price made against the kidnappers could turn into a bloodbath with bystanders in the line of fire. Price knew he'd have to watch that, even as he watched his back.

The thing about a million dollars—any fabulous amount, for that matter—was that it seemed almost impossible to keep its movements quiet. Guards on bullion shipments and the like were sworn to secrecy, but something always leaked. It was a law of nature. Water flows downhill, the day begins at sunrise, and some people *always* talk.

Which meant they could have trouble long before they got to San Felípe.

"How far is it?" he asked Landry.

"To the town? We oughta be in there tomorrow, close to sundown. Only one night sleepin' rough."

One night, and two days on the trail. Price knew the residents of San Felípe weren't the only risk they faced. Marcella Schaefer's kidnappers might lay a trap along the way and try to take the cash by force, especially if she was dead and they had nothing left to sell. He also had to think about the danger from third parties, any shooters who had picked up whispers of a fortune on the move and ripe for picking.

Anything could happen on the way to meet his quarry. Anything at all.

They crossed the border into Baja California without incident, an hour past midday. No river lay between the nations here, as in Texas, and if there'd ever been a sign to mark the crossing, it had long since been torn down and dragged away.

Schaefer announced the transit with a wry, "Here's Mexico. Smell anything?" When no one answered him, he laughed at his own joke, then lapsed back into moody silence.

Another two miles farther south, Price asked Brooks, "Is your boss always like this?"

"I've never known him to be sociable," Brooks said. "O' course, he's just lost half his family."

Price hoped that wouldn't make him reckless. He could cover Schaefer to a point, but wet-nursing a rich boy hadn't been part of his job description. His employer had assumed that Schaefer could retrieve his sister and return her to the Circle S, assuming she was found alive.

Price had been hired to do the dirty work.

As usual.

No problem there, unless the men he hunted took him by surprise somehow, or had him so outnumbered that he couldn't catch a break. In that case, he supposed Joan Schaefer would hire someone else to do the job. It wouldn't be his problem anymore.

But if he pulled it off and lived to tell the tale, ten thousand dollars ought to keep him for a while. Price didn't need a million to retire and take it easy.

All he needed was an edge.

The sun was low when Schaefer spied a stream off to the left side of the trail and said, "We may as well camp here."

One day behind them, more or less.

Now Price could work on living through the night.

4

They trailed the creek a while before deciding on the perfect campsite, set back fifty yards or so from the main road. From there, Price thought, they'd be aware of strangers passing by, but might not be observed themselves if they could stand to let the fire die.

"Go all night without it?" Landry asked him as he unloaded the packhorse. "Wha's the point a that?"

"I'm saying," Price replied, "that if we put the fire out after supper, when we're turning in, we make it harder for someone to spot us in the dark."

"I didn't see nobody trailin' us today," the bearded man replied.

"You wouldn't necessarily."

"My eyes're sharp as anybody's."

"Be that as it may."

"He's right about the fire," said Schaefer as he spread his saddle blanket on the ground. "I don't want any more attention drawn to what we're carrying."

"Awright, then," Landry grumbled. "But it gits damn cold out here at night."

"I'd rather catch a chill," Brooks said, "than wake up with my throat cut and the money gone."

"Which brings us to the watch rotation," Price remarked.

"Say what?" Landry was standing with the heavy suitcase in his left hand, dragging down his shoulder on that side.

"We need to stand guard on the camp and cash tonight," Price told him. "Break it up in shifts, nobody loses more than two, three hours sleep."

"I guess that's fair," said Landry, still not liking it.

"Who cooks?" Price asked.

"That's me," Brooks told him. "All we got tonight is beans an' taters."

"Right. I'll fetch some wood."

Price got his roan well situated, then went out to prowl the scrubland that surrounded them for deadwood. First, he marked a pile close in, convenient for their breakfast fire, and left it there after recording its position in his memory. Price wanted time away from his companions while he scoured the terrain for logs and kindling, mostly choosing dried mesquite, watching for snakes and scorpions along the way.

Their first day had been uneventful to that point, but a full night still lay before them, and Price cherished no illusions that tomorrow would be just another day. Even if they were lucky and advance word of the ransom payoff hadn't leaked to thieving trash on both sides of the border, they would be in San Felípe by this time tomorrow, waiting for the kidnappers to make contact.

And what would happen then?

Price was a firm believer in preparing strategy ahead of time, but there was no way to anticipate the moves an unknown enemy would make on unfamiliar ground. His only strategy at this point was to wait and see what happened next, hoping that any action wouldn't take him too much by surprise.

Landry was right about the trail, as far as Price could tell. He'd checked the skyline at their back sporadically all day, searching for riders in the distance or their telltale plumes of dust, and there'd been none. The test wasn't infallible, of course. If trackers knew where they were going, there'd be no need to stick close behind them. Enemies could hang back out of sight, or ride ahead and lay in ambush. Let the money come to them. It might be pure dumb luck that they had come this far without a hitch.

Or maybe no one knew about the money. Maybe they were safe until they got to San Felípe.

Maybe.

But he didn't think so.

Back in camp, Price helped Brooks start the fire, then scouted the perimeter once more. He walked back to the road and stared in both directions, checking out as much distance as sundown would allow. Still nothing that resembled trackers gaining ground.

So far, so good.

Brooks gave them what he'd promised—beans and fried potatoes with a hardtack biscuit on the side, washed down with coffee. Price had eaten worse, though he wasn't about to recommend Brooks as a full-time chef. He wondered if there would be some variety at breakfast, but he wasn't counting on it.

Landry cleaned his plate before he asked, "What do we do about the *federales* if we meet 'm?"

"That depends on them," Schaefer replied.

"Four gringos, they might have some questions," Brooks suggested.

"Questions I can handle, but we don't give up the money."

"S'pose they try'n take it?" Landry asked.

"In that case," Schaefer said, "we treat them just like any other thieves."

Price didn't join in the exchange. He understood the

risk of being waylaid by the Mexican authorities. Some of them were no more than bandits dressed in military uniforms, and Price had fired on *federales* more than once— some fairly recently. He hoped they could avoid that kind of trouble, but he would defend the ransom from all takers until it was time to make the deal.

"Well, then," said Landry, smiling, "did I ever tell ya'll 'bout this trail drive where the foreman got a snakebite on his ass?"

"Believe I missed that one," said Brooks.

"So tell us," Schaefer prodded.

Landry launched into a rambling tale about a foreman on a cattle drive who left camp to relieve himself one night and crouched too near a sidewinder. The gist of it was that none of his cowboys would agree to suck out the venom, but one worked up courage enough to examine the wound—and discovered cactus needles sticking in the man's backside.

Price laughed with the others, neglecting to tell them that he'd heard variations of the story in Texas last spring, and in Denver the year before that. If Landry had an urge to entertain them for a while, Price didn't mind.

It gave him time to think about tomorrow, and whatever happened after that.

"A spider bit my old man once," said Brooks, "when he went to the privy."

"Does this one have a funny ending?" Schaefer asked him.

"Naw. He nearly died."

"We'll let that go then."

"You got any funny stories, Matt?" asked Brooks.

"None come to mind right now."

"I got another one," said Landry.

"Fire away then."

Price tuned out the story, focused on his private thoughts. If they survived the ransom payment and whatever followed it, his work still wasn't done. His payoff and the money he was owed on Dermott Jackson would be

waiting for him back in Santa Rosa. Price had to retrace
his route, presumably returning all or most of the one million dollars, before he could claim his prize.

He wondered if he would be riding back alone.

Or if he'd make it back at all.

"Who wants first watch?" asked Schaefer when they'd
cleaned their plates and drowned the fire with sand.

"I'll take it, Boss," said Brooks. "The coffee's got me
wide awake."

"All right then. I'll go second. Landry, you're up third,
and Price can take the last bit."

Price offered no objection to his placement on the
watch. He had adjusted to the thought of losing sleep, and
now it made no difference whether he was first or last in
the rotation. Price checked on the roan once more to put
his mind at ease, then rolled into his blanket with his saddle serving as a pillow. Underneath the blanket, he kept
one hand on his Colt, ready to cock and fire the weapon at
a moment's notice even as he drifted off to sleep.

It was a talent Price had cultivated over time, sleeping
in nearly any situation where the opportunity was offered.
In the life he'd led since adolescence, the incessant traveling and episodes of mortal danger interspersed with pe-
riods of tedium, he'd learned to sleep whenever possible,
because he might not have the chance tomorrow. Sleep, in
Price's estimation, was a method of recharging vital energy to face the next demand, his next crisis.

But he could do without the dreams.

Most nights, if he remembered anything at all, it was a
vague parade of faces from the past. Price recognized
most of them, though he guessed a few were composites
or represented someone he couldn't recall—or maybe
someone he had yet to meet. He put no stock in seers and
fortune-tellers, but a Gypsy in New Orleans had surprised
and spooked him once, saying he should beware of a left-
handed man. Price thought no more about it until two

weeks later, when a shooter with a hook in place of his right hand had tried to take Price in a Texarkana whorehouse.

Still, it could've been coincidence.

Or not.

Most of his bland face-dreams involved passing encounters with the people who had mattered, more or less, at some phase in his life. A time or two, Price had to stretch his memory—a hostler who had fed and groomed his horse in Laramie; the writer who had interviewed him once in Amarillo for a penny dreadful—but most were more significant. Friends, dead or living. Women Price had bedded. Men he'd killed.

The latter group had grown considerably, though he didn't bother keeping score. Young guns with something yet to prove were fond of notching rifle stocks and pistol grips to mark their kills, but Price had never seen the point. One shooter he'd known briefly had collected souvenirs from each engagement—trinkets, for the most part; sometimes locks of hair—but Price thought that was symptomatic of some sickness. He had taken nothing from the showdown where he'd left the grim collector facedown in a dusty Arizona street.

Why kill a man at all, Price sometimes wondered, if the slayer meant to drag his victim's memory around like shackles, clanking every time he took a step?

Which didn't mean Price had escaped the memory of those he'd killed, or those he'd failed to keep alive. Far from it. He rarely thought of them in waking hours, Mary Hudson being the exception to that rule and every other, but they visited his dreams. Approximately once per year, Price glimpsed his first, a young man named Gilley who tried to rob Price in a cattle car, crossing from Kansas to Missouri. He was larger, stronger, but dull-witted and a trifle slow. Ironically, the only thing Price had worth stealing was the knife he planted under Gilley's ribs, to keep himself from being strangled.

Faces.

They appeared in no coherent order, playing fast and loose with the chronology of Price's life. A man he'd killed last month in Mexico might show up squiring a saloon girl Price had met in Oklahoma six or seven years ago. They wouldn't know each other in real life, if they were thrown together on the street, but that was part of what made dreams so unpredictable.

The other part was seeing dead men walk and talk, while folk Price guessed (or hoped) were still alive appeared to him as silent wraiths. Sometimes Price saw his son, the boy he barely knew, watching or waving to him from the far side of a street Price couldn't cross. Each time he tried, a wagon or stampede of livestock forced him back, and when the dust settled, his boy was gone.

It didn't take a medical degree to figure out that one. His son was nearly ten years old when Price first learned of his existence from a woman he'd once loved. She had a new life by that time, and while it needed some assistance from a killer, Price had seen no percentage in turning the boy's young world upside down. Some revelations were best left for deathbeds—or better yet, taken to graves.

This night, sleeping beneath the stars in Baja California, Price was visited by Gray Wolf, an Apache warrior who had shared some of his recent time in Mexico. They'd taken turns saving each other's lives, until Gray Wolf ran out of time and luck. Price had avenged him, but he'd long since learned that corpses couldn't fill a void.

They simply added weight to Price's soul.

Most days, he didn't feel it. Those he'd slain had nearly all been trying to kill Price or someone else. He didn't think the world would miss them much, even if scattered friends or relatives tried settling the score. Most of his dead were strangers, met in passing on some killing ground they'd chosen. Some of them had died without Price bothering to learn their names.

He recognized their faces, though, when they returned. There was no fear associated with his ghosts. They didn't threaten Price or offer baleful glimpses of his future, like the shades in fairy tales. Mostly, they stared at him. A rare few laughed. Now and again, one asked him, *Why?*

To which he always answered, *You know why.*

And if that didn't satisfy them, they could go to Hell.

Price only woke up feeling guilty when he dreamed about his boy or Mary Hudson. One, he'd never really known; the other died because Price broke a silent promise to himself that he would always keep her safe.

No judge or preacher living could absolve Price from the sentence he had passed upon himself.

Faces were forming in the mist, still undefined, when Price was shaken from his sleep. Before his eyes snapped open, Price had cocked his Peacemaker and jammed the muzzle under Early Brooks's chin.

"Don't shoot!" the young man hissed.

"What is it, Early?"

"Fire," Brooks said. "I see a fire."

Price rose, holstered his piece, and left his blanket rumpled on the ground. Schaefer and Landry slept, bundled up on either side of the suitcase that held the ransom money. Landry snored softly, interspersed irregularly with a louder, piglike grunting sound. It was repulsive, but it didn't keep his boss from sleeping like a stone.

"Show me," Price said.

"This way."

Brooks led him past the cold remains of their campfire, traveling a dozen paces farther north. The night seemed more profound there, Landry's snuffling noises quieter, divorced from any human origin. Brooks pointed, but he didn't have to.

"There."

"I see it," Price replied.

It was a fire, all right. The flicker of its yellow light was unmistakable. A lantern's light would've been steady,

and a candle's probably too small to see at such distance.
Price guessed the campers were three quarters of a mile
behind them.

Close enough to see his own fire earlier, and smart
enough to watch it doused before they lit their own.

"You think they're trailing us?" asked Brooks.

Price shrugged. "I wouldn't know."

Why risk a fire at all, he asked himself, if their unknown companions on the trail were stalking Schaefer's
party with malign intent? A dark camp would've kept
them safe from observation. Better yet, they could've
moved in after nightfall, creeping close and taking their
positions for a sudden blaze of gunfire that would cut their
targets down without a fight.

"It could be anybody," Brooks suggested.

"Right."

"They mightn't even know we're here."

Price glanced at Brooks and saw him wince by
starlight. It was farfetched, and he knew it. Even if the
other campers had kept riding well past sundown—more
particularly then—they would've seen the campfire
glowing like a beacon on the flats ahead of them.

They know we're here, Price thought.

But did they care?

There were a hundred reasons for a solitary rider or a
group of travelers to journey south this time of year. They
could be Mexicans, returning from a sojourn in the States.
Or livestock buyers, seeking cattle, sheep, or horses. Im-
migrants in search of cheaper land than California offered
lately, hoping that a meager cache of dollars would allow
them to live comfortably in the land of pesos. Maybe out-
laws on the run, or bounty hunters tracking fugitives.

Maybe.

The campers might be any of those things, or something else entirely—but Price didn't think so. Something
in his gut told him the campfire was a warning sign of
trouble following their path to San Felípe.

"Would they light a fire like that if they were after us?" Brooks asked.

It was the voice of common sense, but Price had known enough cutthroats to understand that ruthlessness and keen intelligence weren't always complementary. Most criminals, in fact, were short on wits except where raw survival was concerned.

Which made Price ask again, *Why light a fire?*

Because they're cold or hungry, maybe both. Because they planned to overtake his party in the daylight, maybe try some ruse they deemed so clever that no adequate defense was possible.

Price couldn't read a stranger's mind, much less judge the intelligence of someone he had never even seen. And as he stood there in the dark, he knew that there was only one way to be sure about their fellow travelers.

He'd have to go and see them. Judge the strangers for himself.

"It could be nothing, right?" Brooks prodded him.

"It could be something."

"Sure, I guess. But—"

"I make the distance right around three quarters of a mile," Price said, interrupting him, still speaking softly in the night. "Call it a mile, to be on the safe side. Walking along the road and being quiet, it should take me fifteen, twenty minutes."

"To do what?" asked Brooks.

"Get over there."

"What do you mean?" The concept seemed to baffle his companion.

"We don't know who's camped around that fire," Price said, "but we need to find out. If it's a family headed south, some preacher looking for a soul to save, more power to them. But if someone's dogging us, we need to cut it short before they choose the ground and make their move."

"Jesus."

"If he's a comfort to you, have a word with him," Price

said. "But keep your eyes and ears open the whole time that I'm gone."

"The others—"

"Are asleep. There's no point waking them right now until we know what's happening."

"But if you go—"

"You'll know if anything goes wrong," Price promised him.

"*How* will I know?"

"You'll hear it, Early."

"Oh."

"All right?"

"Jubal is gonna be real mad if you get shot and he ain't there."

"He'll have to catch the show some other time."

"No, hey, I didn't mean—"

"We're wasting time. I could be halfway there while we're debating it."

"I still think I should—"

"No," Price said.

"It won't be you he takes it out on, if you're dead."

"My lucky day then. Just stand here and listen, like I told you. Understand?"

A footstep crunched on sand behind them just as Jubal Schaefer said, "Maybe you wouldn't mind explaining it to me."

Price turned to find the boss watching them, holding his gun belt coiled like a dead snake in his left hand. His hair was tousled, sticking out on one side where he'd lain against his saddle, but the sour expression on his face eliminated any urge to laugh at him.

"Out there," Price said, cocking his head toward darkness.

"What? I don't—" Schaefer stepped closer, narrowing his eyes. "Is that a fire?"

"It is."

Brooks blurted out, "He thinks somebody follered us!"

Price frowned, correcting him. "I said it's possible."

"What makes you think so?" Schaefer challenged.

"Everyone in Santa Rosa knows your sister was kidnapped. By now, the word's most likely spread beyond the county, maybe out of state. We're headed south now, with a million dollars in a suitcase. Think about it."

"No one knows about the money," Schaefer said.

"*We* know," Price answered. "And I'll bet my paycheck that the others on your spread all know it too. The only word that travels faster than bad news is money talk."

"You could've spilled it," Schaefer answered.

"How? I spent the night in your bunkhouse, and you've been with me since sunrise."

"Okay, then. Let's say you're right. They don't know where we're going to make the payoff."

"They're *behind* us. They don't have to know."

A grunting snore reminded them that they were one man short. Shooting a glare at Landry in his bedroll, Schaefer snapped at Brooks, "Go wake him up, for God's sake. It's like sleeping in a damned pigsty."

"Yessir."

When they were momentarily alone, Schaefer rounded on Price. "You're slick," he said. "I give you that. But don't think I'm some witless rube."

"Is there a point to this?" Price asked him.

"Bet your ass there is. I didn't want to take you on for this. It was my mother's choice. She calls the shots for now, but only back in Santa Rosa. Do we understand each other?"

"Clarify it for me," Price suggested.

"Right. I don't trust strangers, and I don't trust bounty hunters. You impressed my mother, taking down some saddle tramp nobody ever heard of. That's her call, but I don't have to like it. Is that clear enough?"

"And yet," Price answered, "here I am."

"On suffrage," Schaefer said.

"That's sufferance."

"What?"

"Suffrage is voting, Jubal."

"Yeah? Well, maybe you should bear in mind that I can vote you off this team whenever I feel like it."

Price felt a familiar anger stirring in his belly, knowing from experience that he could tamp it down before it interfered with his reflexes. "What would Mother say?" he asked.

"Damn you! If I—"

"Here's Tommy, Mr. Schaefer," Brooks announced, cutting the boss's tirade short. Beside him, Landry was a rumpled vision—barefoot, with his shirt half open, fingers of his left hand rummaging through bristly whiskers while a six-gun dangled from his right hand.

"Wha's the trouble?" Landry asked.

"Somebody's follered us," Brooks said.

Price let it go, addressed himself to Schaefer. "I was on my way to visit them when you distracted us," he said. "So, Boss, what should we do?"

It was apparent from the look on Schaefer's face that he loved giving orders but was queasy when it came to making a command decision. He'd be fine on daily chores, bossing the help around the spread, Price guessed, but having grown up in the shadow of his parents, he'd be short on field experience where hard decisions were concerned.

"We need to find out who they are, all right." A flash of inspiration seemed to hit him. "And I'm going with you."

"Are you sure that's wise?" Price asked.

Schaefer was buckling on his gun belt as he spoke. "Why not?"

"You've got a million dollars sitting over by the fire."

"And two men left to watch it. So?"

"I need a private word," Price said.

It caught Schaefer off guard. He hesitated, on the verge

of telling Price where he could go, then turned to Landry. "Tom, get dressed, for God's sake. Early, help him."

"What?" Brooks blinked surprise.

"Give us some room, all right?"

"Yessir."

The two cowboys retreated, leaving Price and Schaefer to themselves. Schaefer seemed ill at ease, fumbling with his belt buckle. "All right," he demanded. "What's the private word?"

"I'm wondering if you really want to leave the money with those two."

"Why not? You saying they'd make off with it?"

"Nothing like that," Price answered. "But you need to think about the repercussions if they make a critical mistake and something happens to the ransom while you're gone."

"Like what? They start a fire and toss the money in by accident?"

"No accident," Price said. "Wrong fire."

"Talk plain, dammit!"

Price pointed back across the flats, through darkness. "What if *that* fire is a lure to get some of us over there and leave the money short of cover?"

"Then we don't go," Schaefer told him. "Simple."

"Not so simple. Either way, we need to check it out. Maybe just sneak around and eavesdrop, find out it's a bunch of pilgrims seeking Jesus in the wilderness, but we still need to know."

"And have the money covered too."

"That's right."

"You want to go out by yourself, I guess."

Price nodded. "Leaving you to watch the kitty, so you've got no doubt that it's done right."

"And have you out there, doing who knows what with God knows who? I don't think so."

"Your call. I guess you've faced enough guns that you'll have no problem coping if there's trouble."

Schaefer glared suspicion. "Eavesdropping, you said. Spying."

"Unless you pick up something that would indicate a threat. I'll just stay here and watch the money for you, with the boys."

"No good."

"You're running out of options, Boss."

"Here's one," Schaefer replied. "*You* go, and take Brooks with you."

"He means well, but he's green as grass."

"How's he supposed to get experience, sitting in camp?"

"Wrong place, wrong time."

"Use Landry then."

"They'll hear him farting in the brush and reckon it's a peccary. Start shooting in the hope of breakfast bacon."

"Brooks or Landry, take your pick. I won't send you alone. That's final."

"Brooks, if he can watch his step and keep his mouth shut."

"Tell him what he needs to know. Watch over him."

"I'm not a tutor."

"Think of it as saving Early's ass." Putting the weight on Price, that way, if anything went wrong.

Landry and Brooks were coming back, the former shod and buttoned to the throat, his younger comrade looking out of sorts. It didn't seem to cheer Brooks up when Price said, "Get your rifle, son. We're going for a walk."

5

"Why me?" Brooks asked as they were trudging out of camp, back toward the road.

"You wanted to find out if you could do it," Price reminded him.

"Well, sure. I mean, why didn't Jubal wanna come?"

"He did. I talked him out of it."

"What for?"

"I need a cooler head," Price answered. "Someone who'll do as he's told and not fly off the handle. I'm hoping that's you."

"I'll do just like you say," Brooks replied with a measure of pride in his voice.

"Then we should be all right."

They reached the road, pale in the wan light of a quarter moon. Price didn't mind the darkness while it covered them, but it could also work the other way. For all he knew, a team of gunmen from the other camp might be advancing on Schaefer and Landry even now. They wouldn't have to use the road, though Price preferred it as familiar ground with no surprises.

"Is it safe to talk out here?" Brooks whispered.

"For a while. Not when we're closer."

"Right. You'll let me know?"

"Count on it."

"'Cuz I'd rather not do somethin' that'll get us killed."

"That isn't high on my list either," Price assured him.

"So, you done this kinda thing before?"

"Night hunting? Once or twice."

He'd done it more than that, in varied circumstances, but Price didn't think Brooks wanted details. Brooks was trying to inflate his nerve, convince himself that he could face another armed man in the dark and kill him if he had to, without fumbling when it counted, maybe getting killed himself.

"You never know," Price said, anticipating the next question.

"What?"

"How you'll react, the first time."

"Oh. No tricks, huh?"

"Plenty of them," Price admitted. "But it's best to find your own and make them work for you."

"I hope to get the chance."

"All right, try this. No fancy shooting. Don't try winging anyone, shooting the gun out of his hand, or any other hoopla from a Wild West Show. Aim for the center of the body when you can and put your target down."

"What else?"

"Do what you need to, to survive."

"But keep it fair, you mean."

"The fair fights are the ones you walk away from," Price replied.

Brooks chewed on that one for a while, the silence spinning out between them, broken only by the rough sound of their boots on gritty soil. When they were halfway there, a mournful, wailing cry erupted from the darkness, causing Brooks to jump.

"Coyote," Price informed him.

"Right. I knew that."

"Is that Henry primed?"

"It's loaded," Brooks answered.

"Right now, you need a cartridge in the chamber, with the hammer down. Go easy when you lower it. Don't strike the firing pin."

"It could go off that way."

"Do you intend to drop it, son?"

"Nosir."

"No problem then."

Price listened to the *click-clack* of the Henry's lever-action, waiting while Brooks eased the rifle's hammer down.

"Okay," Brooks said.

"Now keep your finger off the trigger till you mean it, and you'll be all right."

"You reckon these 'uns really trailed us for the money?"

"Only one way to find out," Price said.

"What's that?"

"Ask them."

"You're kidding, right?"

"Maybe. If we get close enough without a ruckus, maybe we can work out their intentions."

"And suppose they *did* come for the money?"

"Then we have a choice to make," Price said. "Deal with them now, or later, when they pick the time and place."

"Now's better, I suppose."

"Let's wait and see."

"Okay?"

A sidewinder slithered across the road in front of them. Price watched it go, wishing the hunter well. When it had vanished into darkness, they moved on.

"Try not to fret," Price said. "We have advantages."

"Like what?" Brooks sounded dubious.

"Surprise, unless we mess it up. They aren't expecting company. Also, the firelight works against them."

"How?"

"You ever try to look outside the bunkhouse after dark, when you've got lamps burning inside?"

"Oh, right."

"Also, we'll flank them."

"Say again?"

"When we get close enough," Price said, "we'll find a place for you to watch from; then I'll move around and pick my own."

"Cross fire," Brooks said.

"In case we need one. If we don't, I'll circle back and pick you up on the way out."

"You mean we just might leave 'm?"

"If it's plain they mean no harm to us, that's all we *should* do."

"Right. O' course."

"But otherwise, follow my lead. Don't start in blasting on your own."

"I won't."

"And don't plug me."

"Nosir."

"In that case, we should do all right."

"I hope so."

"Hope can't hurt," Price told him. "But you need a clear eye and a steady hand."

They'd reached a point directly opposite the campfire, separated from its small light by a quarter mile of scrubland, give or take. Once they were off the road, Price knew that every step was critical, and any unintended sound could raise alarms within the strangers' camp.

"All right," he told Brooks, "this is where we button up our lips. Step easy now, and watch the ground in front of you the best you can. No kicking stones or falling into gullies. Any noise we make might carry to the camp and set them off."

"I hear you."

"If you absolutely *have* to tell me something, like a snake crawled up your trouser leg, be sure to tap me on the shoulder first and whisper like you've got no voice at all."

"Okay."

"And once we've covered half the distance, don't say anything for *any* reason. I don't care if you've got *ten* snakes in your pants."

"Okay," Brooks said again.

"Stay right behind me, with your rifle pointed somewhere else."

"No finger on the trigger," Brooks confirmed.

"All right, let's go."

It wasn't far to walk, but darkness doubles distance in the mind, and Price was apprehensive as he left the road. Taking his own advice, he watched the ground in front of him by moonlight, simultaneously searching well ahead for any sign of lookouts posted there.

The campers might've left someone on guard, as his group had, even if they had no designs upon the Schaefer ransom money. It was only common sense to take precautions in a hostile land, and Baja California was as hostile as they came toward careless travelers. Evil intent wasn't required to bring down trouble on a pilgrim's head. Danger lay waiting in this country like a trapdoor spider, primed to spring at the approach of prey.

Price heard Brooks following, but some amount of sound was unavoidable. They couldn't float across the desert, and each step they took was bound to make some noise. He tried to minimize those warning signs, however, hoping that the wayfarers they'd come to see weren't ready for them.

Hope can't hurt.

But would it help?

Price thought ahead to what would happen if he deemed the campers dangerous. If there was killing to be done. The easy way would be to lie back in the darkness and unload on them with rifles, drop as many as they could before the targets rallied to defend themselves. It would be relatively safe, and yet it went against the grain for Price.

Do what you need to, to survive.

No problem there. He was a master of survival, not afraid of fighting dirty in a pinch. But there was still a difference between survival and assassination, sniping strangers at their fireside in the middle of the night.

Be sure, he thought. *That's first. Then do what must be done.*

The look of them would tell him something, and he'd learn more if he had a chance to hear them talking. Any indication of an interest in the ransom money was enough to dictate action, but the setting and opponents would decide what action was appropriate.

Numbers, for one thing. Facing one or two men was a world away from bracing six or seven. If he found himself critically outnumbered, Price would have to reevaluate his definition of fair play.

And there was Brooks, of course.

The young hand's nerves were working on him, understandably, but Price had yet to learn if Brooks would stand or fold in action. Brooks wouldn't know that himself until it happened, and by that time it would be too late for substitutions in the game. If Brooks froze on the firing line, then Price would be alone against however many guns he found in camp. The burden shifted back to him.

And there was no way to be certain he could carry it.

No matter.

Having shouldered the responsibility and come this far, he couldn't turn around and change his mind. Schaefer and Landry counted on him, just as Brooks did, to confront this riddle in the night, assess it—and, if necessary, make it go away.

They'd covered roughly one third of the distance to the fire when Price stopped for a moment, taking in the desert night sounds, studying the new terrain. He glanced off toward the dark campsite he'd left behind and was relieved to find no trace of his companions visible. If anyone had left the strangers' camp to hike in that direction, they would have to use dead reckoning, without a guiding beacon in the night.

Price turned to study Brooks a moment, by moonlight. The young man wasn't quaking, but his eyes were nervous, darting here and there. Price waited for the restless eyes to find his, held them there, and raised a warning finger to his lips.

Brooks nodded understanding, one time, up and down.

Price started toward the fire again, gripping his rifle loosely in both hands. He'd cocked it prior to leaving camp and thumbed the hammer down, as he'd instructed Brooks to do. Between the Winchester and Colt, he could fire eighteen shots without reloading.

But if that wasn't enough . . .

Price heard a rustling in the dry scrub to his left, some varmint by the sound of it, and pivoted in that direction anyway, just to be ready if his ears were playing tricks on him. The noise continued for a moment, then subsided with no sign of what had caused it, leaving Price to go about his business unopposed.

Five minutes later they were at the halfway point, as near as Price could calculate. The campfire had grown larger as they closed the distance, and Price froze again as he saw shadows move across it, briefly interrupting his view of the flames.

How close?

The shadow passed again, and he could make out legs. Someone within the camp was moving, but they weren't obstructing Price's path.

What did the movement mean?

It could be anything, or nothing. Someone reaching for a coffeepot or slipping off to do his business in the brush, for all Price knew. Conversely, it could mean the strangers were preparing for a march across the desert, to face Jubal Schaefer and demand the ransom.

For a moment, Price considered that this might be part of the kidnappers' plan. It could make sense to fix a destination, then lie waiting somewhere else along the route of travel, to achieve surprise. How would he know upon arrival at the camp?

One indication, he supposed, would be a girl in her teens surrounded by at least four gunmen. That would make his task more delicate, depending on the girl herself, whether she was restrained or free to move about the camp. He wouldn't recognize Marcella Schaefer, but Brooks should. And if they found her in the camp, it wouldn't do to shoot her with the rest.

Another possibility Price bore in mind was that the girl already might be dead. In that case, Price couldn't be sure the men around the fire were her abductors, unless they did something to betray themselves.

And if they did, his job was simplified. He had a chance to leave them here and take the ransom home to Santa Rosa, pocket his reward, and leave the Schaefers to their grief.

Simple. Except it never really was.

Even straightforward killing offered twists, sometimes, to complicate the job. And unexpected twists could get a shooter killed.

A hundred paces from the campfire, Price stopped short and pulled Brooks close enough to whisper in his ear, lips almost touching skin. "Go slow from here," he said. "Follow my lead and stop when I do."

Brooks nodded understanding.

Price moved on, watching for lookouts, until he could count the shadow-shapes around the fire. Five men were visible, no females anywhere within the ring of firelight, and no place for one to hide.

All right, Price thought. *We do it the hard way.*

He drew Brooks forward, ten slow steps, then made it clear with silent gestures that he wanted Brooks to wait exactly where he was. Another hand sign told Brooks that Price would be circling to his left, or north, around the camp to find another vantage point.

Brooks nodded once again and gripped his Henry repeater in hands that seemed steady to Price. Leaving him there, Price set off through the darkness, looking for a place where he could spy and eavesdrop on the camp, without catching a bullet if his backup jumped the gun.

Price stayed well clear of firelight as he made his creeping circuit of the camp. When he had finished two thirds of the journey back to where Brooks stood, he smelled horses. Price stopped before he spooked them with his presence, kneeling next to a saguaro cactus taller then himself.

Five horses. Five men hunched around the fire with coffee cups. Unless they'd sent companions toward the Schaefer camp on horseback, all the pilgrims were accounted for. They all wore pistols, two of them with matching pairs. Rifles and shotguns were within their reach.

But who were they? What did they want?

Price waited on the edge of darkness, listening, his Winchester braced flat across his upraised knee.

"I still don't follow why we're waitin'," said a red-haired fat man, three days from his latest shave.

"We been all over that," another answered. Black oily hair hung nearly shoulder-length from underneath his hat. He was the tallest of the five, but stooped in posture, elbows planted on his knees.

"I *know* we been all over it," Red Beard replied, "but I don't *follow* it. Why ain't we doin' it right now?"

"Because they'll be expectin' it tonight," the other said. A couple of the silent coffee drinkers nodded in agreement, while the fifth remained impassive.

"So the hell what?" asked Red Beard. "They'll be expectin' it tomorra, just the same. An' by tomorra night they'll be in San Felípe."

"They hope to be," the seeming leader of the band declared.

"More trouble takin' it in town than out here in the middle a nowheres," the fat man groused.

"This is the part we been all over, Cletus. If you can't remember simple shit like this, how are you gonna spend the money?"

"Spendin's easy," Cletus answered. "Gettin' it's the goddamn risky part."

"So clean yer ears this time and *listen,* will ya? Come first light, we're ridin' fast as can be to a place I know about, three miles along. Good cover there, on both sides a the road. We hunker down and wait, then drop 'em cold before they knows what hit 'em."

"We could hit 'em *now,*" said Cletus, stubborn in defeat.

"Could maybe. But we ain't, and that's an end to it."

The fat man plainly longed to argue, but he glanced around the circle, judging firelit faces, and apparently decided it would be a bad idea.

Price had no doubt that Schaefer's party was the band these riders planned to ambush in the morning, but he lingered in the darkness for a moment longer, seeking confirmation of the fact before he showed himself. It took a while, the conversation drowned in snuffling sounds as coffee was consumed, before another of the gunmen spoke.

"You reckon they's really got a million dollars?" asked a long-faced man with a mustache and sideburns the color of dirt.

"I wouldn't guarantee no *million,*" said their leader, "though I guess it ain't impossible. Schaefers are rich shits, ever'body knows. Whatever cash they're packin', it'll be a damn sight more'n we seen up to now."

"Too bad the girl ain't with 'em," said another. He had

freckles and a scar bisecting his left nostril. "That way, we could have the money an' a poke besides."

"You get that kinda money," Cletus told him, "there'll be no shortage a pokes, I guarantee."

They shared a laugh at that and poured more coffee all around, draining the pot. Price had his confirmation now, but he was torn between courses of action. He could double back and tell Brooks what he'd heard, in case the young man's nerves had plugged his ears, and they could make their move together. Or Price could proceed alone, trusting in Early Brooks to back his play without some major hitch that got them both killed on the spot.

It was a gamble either way. He had better control of Brooks if they were fighting side by side. That way, if Brooks proved worse than useless, Price could always knock him out and face the shooters on his own, without a wild card in the game. If he went solo with a backup from the kid, Price guessed there was a sixty-forty chance that Brooks would do all right, not piss himself or shoot Price by mistake.

"They musta seen our fire by now," the scar-nosed shooter said.

"Jes' like I planned it, Bob," the leader told him, with an echo sounding from his upraised coffee cup. "Right now, they're wonderin' if somebody's comin' to cut their throats or gun 'em in their sleep. Tomorra they'll be half dead in the saddle from a night like that."

"Not watchin' close along the way," said Dirty Sideburns.

"Tha's exac'ly right," the leader said, turning to Red Beard once again. "*Now* do you follow, Cletus? Do I gotta draw a pitcher for ya in the dirt?"

"I hear ya, dammit. I jest want the money now."

"You need ta learn some patience, boy. That cash'll spend the same tomorra as it would tonight."

"We oughta talk some more about the shares," said Cletus, stubborn even in defeat.

"The shares'll be what we agreed. We split six ways,

an' I get two shares 'cuz I put the job together an' I brung you all along. That was the deal agreed to. Who's the sumbitch wants ta change it now? Jus' raise a hand an' lemme see the bastid's face."

"That would be me," Price said as he stepped out of darkness into firelight.

Five startled faces snapped around to stare at Price. Five shooters started reaching for their pistols.

"Not the best idea you ever had," Price cautioned them. He added, for the leader's benefit, "Real bad for you."

His Winchester was pointed toward the campfire, meaning his first shot would pierce the leader, in and out, before it reached the coals. Whatever happened after that would be decided by a mix of skill and luck, tempered by the surprise of Brooks's Henry, if he didn't freeze.

"Who are you, mister?" asked the leader.

"One of them you planned to bushwhack in the morning," Price replied. "Rest easy, Cletus, if you want to keep on breathing."

"Yeah, awright." The fat man settled back onto the stone that served him as a perch.

"You got some sand, I give ya that," the leader said. His smile was flat, reptilian. "You shore outsmarted us, comin' around tonight."

"You think so?" Price inquired. "It mightn't be too smart, five against one. If I was by myself."

That set their eyes to darting every which way, bright with firelight, sizing up the night beyond their range of vision.

"You got friends," the leader said, "let's see 'em. Lemme put more coffee on an' sort this out."

"It's sorted. I just have a couple questions for you, while we're in a talking mood."

"Questions?" The long-haired gunman lost his smile. "What kinda questions?"

Price's eyes were constantly in motion, covering the

circle, shifting to avoid a pattern they could count on. "First," he said, "I'd like to know if you came up with this idea yourselves, or if somebody put you up to it."

"I do the thinkin' here," Long Hair retorted.

"How did you know about the ransom?"

"Ever'body in the county knows about it, mister. I jest got the nerve ta grab my share."

"Meaning the whole thing," Price replied.

"Not fer myself. These boys all got shares comin'."

"You don't care about the girl, I take it. What'll happen to her if the ransom's not delivered."

"Wha's the girl to you?" asked Long Hair.

"Nothing. I'm just making sure the money doesn't go astray before it gets to San Felípe."

"That'll keep ya busy, boy. About the Schaefer gal, I gotta tell ya hones'ly, a snotty rich bitch don't mean shit ta me. If she was here right now, I couldn't git the time a day, much less a li'l ole piece a comfort."

"Never mind," Price said. "We'll comfort you—"

"Who's *we*?" asked Cletus, interrupting. "Sittin' here, I don't see nobody but you."

"An' like you said," Long Hair reminded him, "it's five ta one."

"All right, Early," Price called into the darkness. "You can shoot the fat one now."

"Now wait a goddamn min—"

A crimson geyser spouted from his chest as gunfire echoed through the camp. Cletus pitched over backward, dying with a stunned expression on his florid face, fat legs and dusty boots churning the air.

Price shot the leader as he rose and knocked him back into the fire. Long Hair was already past feeling it as flames began devouring his clothes, seeking the flesh within. Heart-shot, he twitched from muscle memory rather than any conscious effort to fight back.

Price pumped the rifle's lever-action, ducking to his right as Brooks fired from the darkness, missing this time, kicking up a spout of dust between the scar-nosed shooter

and his dirty-sideburned friend. It sent them lurching off
in opposite directions, sprawling as they grabbed for hard-
ware, leaving Price to face a stocky man who hadn't spoken since Price reached the camp. Still silent, the fifth
man was hauling a short-barreled six-gun from its holster,
cocking it before it cleared leather.

Price fired on instinct, without aiming, and he nearly
made it three for three. His shot was six inches off center,
though, and spun his adversary with a hard punch to the
right shoulder, dropping the man to one knee with the
shock of it.

Still fighting for his life, the wounded man clung to
his weapon with a numb hand, reaching to retrieve it with
his left. He had to know it was a hopeless play, but still
he tried. Price gave him points for that and shot him in
the forehead, dropping him beside the smoking body of
his leader.

Scar Nose had his twin Colts drawn and blazing toward
the shadows where he guessed the hidden sniper ought to
be. His partner, Dirty Sideburns, fired at Price too late to
score a hit, as Price dropped to his stomach in the dirt. The
Winchester was cocked and at his shoulder when the bullet whispered overhead.

He fired again, no textbook shot, but good enough. His
slug bored home beneath the target's breastbone, lifting
him completely off his feet before he fell hard on his
backside, woofing air out of his lungs. The fall would
probably have stunned him, but the bullet got there first,
mangling around inside him, shearing through whatever
made him almost human. Dead before he toppled over
backward, he still managed to get off another shot into the
sky by pure reflex.

Price rolled out to his left as slugs from twin Colts
started knocking divots in the soil around him. He was
busy with the lever-action, thinking through his next shot
in a blur and hoping he'd have time to make it, when a
shot took Scar Nose from behind and made him stagger
forward, grimacing in pain.

They finished him together, Price drilling a hole above the shooter's heart while Brooks shot him again between the shoulder blades. The double punch kept Scar Nose upright for a moment after he was plainly dead; then he collapsed into a slack heap by the fire.

"We're clear," Price told the darkness as he scrambled upright. "Come on in."

Brooks joined him in the firelight, covering the nearest corpses with his Henry as if he expected them to rise and fight anew.

"They're done," Price said. "All five."

"Jesus, he's cookin'."

Price leaned in to grab one of the leader's boots and drag him from the fire. That done, he kicked dirt over shirt and pants until most of the hungry flames were doused. It left a scorched-meat smell that wouldn't go away.

"I made out mosta what they said," Brooks offered. "Bastards."

"The good news is, we got them all," Price said. "That's if Old Smoky wasn't lying through his teeth."

"You think somebody back in Santa Rosa set it up?"

"I doubt it," Price replied. "The way they talked about the money, none of it was going anywhere outside their circle."

"They'll never see it now." Brooks was a little green around the gills, his voice a little younger than his body, standing there among the dead.

"You did all right," Price told him.

"Yeah?"

"I wasn't sure about the first shot, but you came through fine."

"That was the tough one," Brooks admitted. "After that, it weren't so hard. No time to think about it really."

"That's the way of it."

"What now?"

"Now," Price replied, "we live with it, explain it to your boss, and try to get some sleep."

6

They broke camp at sunrise, all anxious to be on their way and find out what the new day would bring. None of them had slept well, though Price managed it better than most. Riding out, he could look back and see vultures circling the spot where five corpses were offered like meat on a platter.

The day shift, he thought, coming in where coyotes had fed through the night.

They'd ridden back to camp after the shooting, leading five spare horses that the dead men wouldn't need. It was agreed to leave the saddles, while they took the horses on to San Felípe. Jubal Schaefer saw a profit in it, and Price didn't argue, since the two alternatives were shooting them or leaving them to forage in the desert on their own.

Schaefer and Landry had been nervous when they heard the horses coming. Price had called ahead to warn them, and he got the feeling that it had been none too soon, the way his left-behind companions held their rifles cocked, with fingers on the triggers. They'd relaxed a bit at sight of Price and Brooks, then had to hear the story twice before they were convinced the threat had passed.

At least for now.

Schaefer had been for going back to search the bodies, until Price told him that Brooks could lead the way. Schaefer had dropped it then, deciding it would be a waste of time and energy, but Price saw through the change of attitude. Whatever happened during the remainder of their journey, Schaefer wouldn't leave Price with the money if he had another choice.

It seemed to gall Schaefer that anyone in Santa Rosa would discuss his family's private business, much less scheme to rob them on the sly. To Price's ear, the money sounded more important than the threat a holdup would've posed to Schaefer's missing sister, but he granted that his own dislike of Jubal might be coloring his judgment.

Either way, they knew the word was out. And that meant they would have to be prepared for more trouble along the way, before they reached their destination.

Early Brooks seemed different in the morning, less inclined to laugh at trifles, more reserved. He didn't replicate the first day's running chatter as they paced off arid miles. Instead, he focused on the horses he was leading and the road ahead of them, with frequent glances back along their trail. Watching for dust or riders, Price supposed.

Price couldn't judge exactly what was going on in Brooks's head, but he recalled the first few men he'd killed and how he'd felt about it afterward. Mechanically, the act got easier with repetition, practice making perfect, but each man who took another's life reacted to the deed in ways that were uniquely personal. Some gloried in it, others never felt a thing. Most registered some kind of feeling, but it faded over time. A few were paralyzed by guilt or grief and never got beyond it, shrinking back into a turtle's shell of isolation from the world.

Price didn't see that kind of grim withdrawal when he

watched Brooks on the sly, but he was no mind reader. If the youngster was concerned about their chances on the trail, he had good cause to be. If he was fretting over how to cope with having shot two men last night, Price reckoned it was only natural. His real concern was what would happen the next time Brooks confronted a life-or-death choice.

And he thought they might find out today.

One bungled ambush didn't mean there'd be another, but a million dollars was the kind of lure that would draw scavengers from both sides of the border, making life in Jubal Schaefer's company a risky proposition for the next full day, at least. That was *before* they met the kidnappers and paid the ransom for the hostage's release.

If she's alive.

His mind kept coming back to that, no matter how Price tried to dodge it. There was no way he could find out in advance whether Marcella Schaefer had been killed the night she was abducted, or if she was waiting for them with her kidnappers in San Felípe. Keeping her alive would be good business if the gang planned any further kidnappings, but with a million dollars they could well afford to disappear, retire into a life of ease. That made supportive word of mouth irrelevant and turned their captive from a thing of value to a liability.

It finally came down to nerve and ruthlessness. How heartless were they really? They'd killed twice already, that he knew of, but those shootings could be sold as self-defense once they committed to the kidnapping. Killing a helpless female took a different kind of man entirely.

Not that there was any shortage of that type in California, Mexico, or any other place where Price had been. Cold-blooded killers weren't the norm, by any means, but they were reasonably plentiful.

Price had been tagged as one himself by some who didn't know him well enough to pass that judgment. They were wrong, but Price could understand the way he looked from where they stood. He had no time to waste selling impressions of himself to strangers.

Most days, he had his hands full just staying alive.

The day warmed rapidly as they rode south, and soon the circling carrion birds were lost to sight. Price closed his mind to what was on the menu, joining Brooks to scan the countryside around them, watching out for riders on the road ahead.

Schaefer was in the lead, as he'd been yesterday, still playing boss to the hilt. Price didn't know yet how he'd cope with leadership when it was more than ceremonial, but instinct told him Schaefer would be well tested before the day was out.

Landry was glum, leading the packhorse and two extras. He'd been quiet since he heard details of last night's shooting. His red beard in the morning sun put Price in mind of the first gunman Brooks had shot, but there was no other resemblance Price could readily identify. All things considered, he supposed a silent ride was best this morning, when alertness was required from all of them.

There would be time enough for small talk after they had done their job in San Felípe, Price supposed. And thinking about it, he wondered which of them would still be talking when the sun came up tomorrow.

Near noon, they found what Price supposed must be the ambush site he'd heard the leader of the nameless gunmen talk about before their plans went fatally awry. A spring rose near the road, feeding a healthy stand of cottonwoods with honest grass around their roots, and Price made out a rough-hewn gully on the other side.

"Good cover," he remarked to Brooks, "on both sides of the road."

"I noticed that. You think there's more of 'em?"

"One way to tell," Price said. His right hand found the hammer thong on his holster, releasing it.

Schaefer mounted and reined up, turning in his saddle to confront them. "What's the trouble?" he demanded.

"This's where them others meant ta jump us," Brooks declared.

"You know that for a fact?"

Brooks shrugged. "Well, now—"

"It fits," Price interjected. "Ample cover for a cross fire, and they could've been here well ahead of us, if they rode hard enough from daybreak."

Schaefer scanned the roadside, left and right, seeming uneasy with his right hand resting on the curved butt of his pistol. Finally, he said, "All right then, shooter. Earn your money."

Price handed the reins of his spare animal to Brooks and nudged his roan into a trot. He swung around behind Schaefer, not fretting about a backshoot, but aware that anything could happen. Price rode toward the cotton-woods and in among them, slightly cooler in the shade there, though the midday heat was inescapable. The stand of trees ran twenty yards along the road and fifteen back, with cover for a dozen men, but Price found no one there.

He rode from shade to sunshine, back across the road, and came onto the gully from its southern side. The roan shied from its crumbling edge, but Price could see enough from where he sat to satisfy himself that they were safe. No snipers in the trees, none in the gulch.

But they were still a full half day from San Felípe, with the rich word of a million dollars on the hoof preceding them. No place was truly safe just now.

"All clear," Price said.

"Okay," Schaefer replied. "We may as well stop here and have a bite, where we've got shade and water."

Brooks and Landry tied the horses in a relatively cool place, left them space to drink and graze, then built a small fire out of deadwood for the midday meal. Price wasn't shocked to see it come up beans and hardtack once again, but he dug in beside the others, never certain when or where he'd find another meal.

"We's more'n halfway there," said Landry, talking with his mouth full. "Should be in town by sundown, if we don't git bushwhacked."

"All of you stay sharp, that's not a problem," Schaefer said. He stared at Price. "You feelin' sharp, shooter?"

"Beans slow me down a little when I eat them every day."

"They speed me up," said Landry, grinning proof that he enjoyed the menu. "Git me all fired up."

"Don't strike a match around him, though," Brooks warned.

"The hell is that suppose ta mean?" Landry demanded.

"Never mind."

"Gimme your ears a minute," Schaefer said. "The *real* game starts once we're in San Felípe now. We don't know how Reese and his shit-heel bunch'll try to reach us. Maybe flag us down or send some Mex out with a note. No way to tell. Thing to remember is that we're packin' a million dollars here."

"Hard ta fergit it, Boss," Brooks said.

"You'd better *not* forget it, any of you." Once again, his eyes stuck longest when they got to Price. "Because we don't turn loose of one red cent until we've seen my sister. Understood?"

Quick nods from Brooks and Landry satisfied Schaefer. He waited, watching Price, until Price asked him, "What if they won't play that way?"

"We've got the money," Schaefer said. "They want it. I imagine they'll play any way I tell them to."

"Imagining's one thing," suggested Price. "It may not go your way regardless."

"Oh? So tell me how *you* think it's gonna play."

Price shrugged. "Who knows? They may want money first, before they show your sister. Then again, they may not *have* her anymore. You've thought of that?"

"I've thought of everything," said Schaefer.

"Good. Then we'll be ready if they try to take the cash by force, without negotiation or a by-your-leave."

"Damn right we will. That's why you're here, shooter."

Part of it anyway, thought Price. "I may get lucky against four," he said, "but you'd be dumb to count on it. On top of which, it's likely we'll be facing more than four guns when we get to town."

"Says who?"

"The talker from last night. We told you what he said, about the word out on the ransom. There's a good chance Johnson and his friends could get lost in the crowd."

"We'll face whoever's waiting, right?" Schaefer replied.

"Something like that needs talking out."

"Details, you mean."

Price nodded. "Some of it we can't work out until we've seen the killing ground. Numbers, ranges, angles. All that kind of thing. We need a basic plan, though. What to do in town before they hit us."

"*If* they hit us," Brooks amended.

"If," said Price, convinced it would be *when.*

"All right," Schaefer replied. "What did you have in mind?"

"We'll need a place to stay," Price said, "in case they don't make contact right away. Someplace to leave the horses too. Landry can show us that."

"No problem," Landry answered, gnashing beans.

"No disrespect to what we're eating now," Price said, "but we'll want food by then, some sleep, maybe a bath."

"Bath, hell," said Landry. "I been thinkin' of a little señorita."

"Think about her on your own time, Tom," Schaefer commanded. "We're not riding all this way to get you laid."

"Awright, Boss. I jest thought—"

Price interrupted him. "We can't walk off and leave the money, so we'll have to go in turns."

"Go sneakylike," Brooks said, "so they don't know we left the loot short-handed."

"Screw the bath," said Schaefer. "We can pay some Mex kid to go fetch a meal."

"And maybe have somebody spike it," Price suggested.

"Jesus." Landry eyed his dwindling share of beans as if suspecting *they* were poisoned.

"Anyway," Price said, "it may be better if they think we're careless with the money."

"Better how? For who?"

"For us," Price answered. "Let me tell you what I have in mind."

The sun was merciless all afternoon, baking the riders and their animals. Schaefer muttered about their sluggish pace but didn't push it, stopping twice when they found water near the road, to let the horses drink. They met no ambush on the way, and if they were pursued, the hunters were too smart to show themselves.

Schaefer had gone for Price's plan, with reservations that owed more to pride than any defect in the scheme. By sundown, Price imagined Schaefer would convince himself it was his own idea, or at the very least behave as if it were.

No problem.

Ego and survival didn't always work in tandem. Price was more concerned about the trouble that lay waiting for them in a town he'd never seen before. Schaefer could have the glory, if he found some. Price wanted to do his job, get paid—and stay alive.

By four o'clock the sun was well off to their right, stretching their long, distorted shadows eastward. If the day was any cooler, Price still couldn't feel it. Treasuring his hat brim's shade, he watched the road ahead with narrowed eyes, trusting in Early Brooks to watch behind them.

"Nothing," Brooks announced after his latest backward glance.

"That's good."

"If anyone was chasin' us, we shoulda seen their dust by now, I guess."

"Depends on when and where they started," Price replied.

The answer didn't cheer Brooks. "Right," he said. "That's right." Another quick glance to the north. "I don't think anyone's back there."

"I hope you're right."

"In San Felípe, now, that's somethin' else."

"It may be," Price agreed.

"You don't go out on many limbs, do ya?"

"I find they have a way of getting sawed off near the trunk."

"That's good." Brooks smiled. "I best remember that one."

"Be my guest."

"You gonna kill Reese and them others?"

"That depends."

"On what?" Brooks asked.

"Mostly on what they have in mind," Price said, "for us and for the money."

"And for Miss Marcella."

"Right. She's why we're here." Price wondered whether Brooks would pick up on his sheer lack of conviction.

"Jubal's mama'll be grateful if we fetch her back."

Will she? Price wondered. And replied, "I reckon so."

"I get the feelin' you don't think it's likely, though."

"I don't have an opinion on the matter yet."

"If it was me kidnappin' her, I'd have ta figure she was trouble while she lives."

"It wouldn't be you, Early."

"No, I reckon not. But Reese might think that way, if he's stopped lovin' her."

"How likely do you think that is?" Price asked.

Brooks studied Schaefer's back and dropped his voice. "The way Jubal an' Old Man Schaefer did him, I guess it could fall out either way."

"Bad news for Miss Marcella then."

"It could be, yessir."

Dusk was velvet blue and gray around them when they sighted San Felípe in the distance, buildings huddled on the flats as if seeking safety in numbers. It was worth a try, Price thought, but trouble wouldn't balk at walls or windows.

Not if there were appetites to satisfy and money to be made.

When they were two miles closer, seeing lighted windows, Landry started giving them a quick tour of the town. "The livery's over that way, east." He pointed. "The hotels, if you wanna call 'em that, face one another more or less smack in the middle. Got a couple a cantinas in there, and a whorehouse, use ta be."

"Forget about the whores, I told you." Schaefer was tired and gruff.

"Yessir. They's forgotted."

"And shut up about them, while you're at it."

This time, Landry made a face at Schaefer's back, but there was no trace of defiance in his voice as he repeated, "Yessir."

No one ran to herald their arrival as they entered San Felípe from the north, but Price knew word would get around. It always did. Four armed, hard-bitten riders could be trouble at the best of times. If they were hauling pounds of cash and it was known to local residents, the trouble factor blossomed exponentially.

"You get a lot of drifters passing through?" Price asked.

Landry considered it. "No more'n usual, I guess. Ya gotta bear in mind I only been here once an' spent two nights. It ain't like I's an expert on the place."

"You're what we've got," Price said.

"In that case," Landry groused, "I hope we ain't shit outa luck."

"You and me both."

"Look sharp," said Schaefer, as if he expected gunmen to appear and brace them in the street. It wasn't totally impossible, of course, but Price was counting on a bit more subtlety from their opponents.

Hoping for it anyway.

They passed along the town's main street until Tom Landry steered them to the left, stopping before one of the few buildings constructed out of lumber. It was narrow and three stories tall. The fading foot-high letters painted blue above its door told Price they'd come to the hotel.

"I stayed in this'n," Landry told them, "but we got a choice across the street. They ain't much differ'nce."

Turning in his saddle, Price beheld another building, similar in all respects to the hotel on their side of the street, but for its one-word sign painted in fading red. "You got that right," he told Landry.

"Same Mex owns both of 'em, from what I recollect." To Schaefer then Landry said, "Which'n ya want, Boss?"

"Blue suits me." He glanced at Price, remembering the plan he had agreed to over lunch. "I'll get the two rooms under Smith and Jones. You all wait here till we can bring the money in."

Schaefer dismounted, gave his reins to Brooks, and went inside. Ten minutes later he was back, shoving the spare change from their rent into his pocket, telling them, "We're on the second floor. Bring in the gear."

Schaefer retrieved his saddlebags, leaving his hired help with the rest. Landry was quick to take the suitcase from the packhorse, grunting from its weight as he retrieved his saddlebags and rifle. Price and Brooks tied up the horses, crowded with their heads together at the hitching rail, then claimed their saddlebags and long guns for the trek inside.

The hotel wasn't much to speak of, but the owners kept it reasonably clean. The stairs were solid but they had a creak to them, which Price appreciated. On the second floor, their two-man rooms were on the small side, sparsely furnished, both with windows facing on the street. Schaefer and Landry paired in Room 2A, guarding the ransom. Price and Brooks had Room 2C, next door. When they had stowed their gear and rifles, Schaefer met them in the narrow corridor outside their rooms.

"Early," he said, "you go with Tom and get the horses settled at the livery. Tom knows the way. You tell whoever runs the place that I may want to sell the extras, but do not—and I repeat, *do not*—discuss a price. You hear me?"

"Yessir."

"Right then. Go."

Brooks called for Landry from the threshold and they went downstairs together, out of sight.

"Come in here for a minute," Schaefer said to Price, then turned and passed into his room. Price followed, stopping just inside the open door.

"You want to close that?" Schaefer asked him.

"No. This way, we know if someone's listening."

"All right then," Schaefer said. "Run through this plan of yours again."

When they paired off that evening, Schaefer called on Price to join him, leaving Brooks and Landry with the case. They didn't seem too thrilled about it, but they didn't argue with the boss, either. Price supposed Schaefer still didn't want him sitting with the ransom, unless Schaefer was on hand to supervise.

Downstairs, on the rough sidewalk, Schaefer said, "I need a bite to eat first. You?" Landry had pointed out a couple of cantinas that served food.

"I'll check the horses, then catch up with you."

"Landry took care of that already."

"Then I won't be long," Price answered.

"Suit yourself. I mean to see if they serve anything but goddamn beans."

He moved off toward the nearest tavern, while Price crossed the street and walked down to the livery. The "man" in charge still wasn't old enough to shave, but he was obviously good with animals. He ran a tidy, quiet stable with a tiny blacksmith shop out front. Price tipped him extra for his soft touch with the roan and left the horse seeming contented in its stall.

Full night had settled over San Felípe by the time Price left the livery and started toward the nearest of the town's two small cantinas. Inside, the place was smoky from a combination of tobacco and the kitchen fires. He looked around for Schaefer, didn't spot him, and decided that he must be dining at the town's other café. Price had an impulse to go looking for him, but he throttled it.

Sweet solitude, after two long days on the trail.

It would've been ideal if he could lose the other fifty-odd patrons packing the place.

Price started with a beer, drank it while standing at the bar, and made a swift scan of the tavern for familiar faces. There was no reason to think that he'd know anybody in the crowd, and so it was. Strangers, a quarter of them Anglos like himself, two blacks positioned at the far end of the bar, the rest all Mexican. A few met Price's gaze as he surveyed the room, but none were in the mood for staring contests at the moment.

Price drained his beer and bought another, waiting for a table to be cleared. Two men left a small one near the bar some minutes later, and Price quickly claimed it for himself. He flagged the young barmaid next time she passed, ordered a third beer and a well-done steak, with rice and enchiladas on the side.

No beans.

Price sipped his second beer while waiting for his meal. Still no one paying any serious attention to him, at least that he could detect. A babel of conflicting voices filled the smoky air, frustrating his attempt to pick out any conversation dealing with the Schaefer ransom money. Any would-be eavesdroppers in the cantina had their work cut out for them.

And so he waited.

Price imagined Schaefer, finishing his grub across the street, a few doors farther down. Would he be drinking? Not too much, Price guessed, with the anticipation of a showdown later in the night. They had two hours before Price and Schaefer were supposed to spell Landry and Brooks at the hotel. They'd watch the money then, while their companions fed and drank a little something for their nerves.

Price didn't need the alcohol. He felt relaxed, at ease.

He simply liked the taste of beer.

The barmaid brought his plate, a charred steak hanging over one end, two fat enchiladas and a mound of rice three inches tall piled on the other side. Price thanked her, finished off his second beer, and dug in with a will.

It was delicious, cooked just right, which took him somewhat by surprise. The steak hadn't gone tough, though it was cooked clear through; the rice was almost fluffy, and the enchiladas were a dream of melted cheese and onions, topped with chili sauce. Price made a mental note to try the place for breakfast, if he was in any mood for eating after sunrise.

Price took his time, not bothering to check his pocket watch. It hadn't been an hour yet since he'd left the hotel. Too bad if Landry was impatient for his own turn at the trough.

Price didn't know his three companions well, but of the trio, he supposed he trusted Brooks the best. It was a stretch going that far, even when Brooks had shown a steady hand at killing for a rank beginner. On the trail today, there'd been no outward sign of qualms about the shooting, but Price knew they could sneak up on a man. The freeze might settle over Brooks next time he had to fight. But if he got through that one, possibly tonight, Price thought the worst of it would be behind him.

Price was nearly finished, mopping up some cheese and chili sauce with a tortilla, when a shadow fell across his plate. He straightened, raised his eyes to meet a red-rimmed pair set close together in the middle of a blotchy face. Their owner had a friend beside him, glowering at Price.

"You got our table, boy," the first man said.

"I didn't see your name on it," Price answered, setting down his fork.

"Look closer next time."

"Funny thing. I still don't see it."

"He don't see it," said the front man. "Wha's that tell ya, Ernie?"

"Tells me he's one blind sumbitch, Josiah."

"Tells me the exack same thing," Josiah said. And then to Price: "Is you a blind sumbitch?"

Price smiled. His hand had dropped below the table, found his Colt. "I've been called worse," he said.

"Tonight?"

"It's early yet."

"Might be a damn sight later'n you think."

"That so?"

"I'd say." The two heads bobbed in unison for emphasis.

"Well, then, I'd better clean my plate," Price said. "My

mama always told me it's a sin to waste good food, especially when there's trouble coming."

"Trouble's here," the front man told him.

"I can smell it."

"Wha's that s'pose ta mean?"

"You'll work it out," Price told him. "I have confidence."

"You got our table's what you got."

Price smiled, stalling for time. "They hold it for you, do they, in this fine establishment?"

"Tha's right."

"What's the procedure?"

"Huh?" No brains to speak of, which gave Price an edge.

"For reservations," he explained.

"I ain't no goddamn Injun, boy!"

"Reserving tables, that would be," Price said. "I'd hate to make the same mistake another time."

"Won't be no 'nother time."

"Did anybody ever tell you you're articulate?"

"Wha's that?" The rodent eyes had narrowed down to slits.

"Forget it. You want me to leave? Is that the deal?"

"Too late," Josiah said. "You done insulted me."

"How'd I do that?" Price asked. His right thumb freed the Colt Peacemaker's hammer thong.

"By sittin' in my chair, then sassin' back about it."

"Is that a serious offense in these parts?"

"Betcher ass. Somethin' like that kin putcha in the ground."

"My, my." Price heard chairs scraping on the floor around him, other patrons hastily retreating from the line of fire. He used the noise for cover, thumbing back the Colt's hammer.

"Ernie," Josiah said, "he still don't take us serious."

"I see that," Ernie answered.

"Oh, I do," Price interjected. "Are you sure you want to stand there, Ernie?"

"Huh?"

"Exactly where you are, I mean."

"Wha's wrong widat?"

"Nothing," Price said. "It's my mistake." Part of his mind was charting bullet paths and calculating for deflection.

"Last mistake you'll ever make," Josiah told him.

"I begin to get your drift. But still, I have to wonder."

"Wunner what?"

"How much it's worth to you," Price said. "This table."

"Worth your two-bit life, I'd say."

"See, that's my point."

"Whut is?"

"Some men will brace a stranger over small things, like you're doing now. They don't stop to consider, sometimes, that the stranger may be faster, stronger. And they don't think through the possibilities, because they never really mean to go that far. You with me, boys?"

Ernie leaned forward. "Bastid's sayin' you's too slow ta cap 'im."

"Did I *say* that, Ernie?"

"I jest heered ya."

"No. I said some men don't *think* about the possibility. The dumb ones, that would be. Two smart men like yourselves, I guess you've planned for all eventualities."

Josiah blinked at him, confused. "Shore did," he said.

"Which brings me back to my first question."

"Too much talk," Josiah warned him.

"Just a little more. I'm giving you a chance."

"You gimme nothin'. Whut I want, I'll take."

"And I don't think you care about this table, *any* table in the house, enough to die for it."

"Don't plan on dyin'."

"That's shortsighted of you, but you haven't answered me," Price said.

"About the goddamn table?"

"About why you want to die for it."

"You got a high opinion of yourself, mister."

"I've got a Colt Peacemaker pointed at your flabby gut, Josiah. Where your partner's standing, I expect to nail you both with one clean shot."

"Bullshit!"

"Try me."

They didn't try, but Ernie braced himself to change positions. Price rapped underneath the table with his Colt and shook his head.

"Stay put," he said.

"That ain't no Peacemaker," Josiah challenged him.

"Why would I lie?"

"To save yur ass. Could be a wooden leg down there, for all I know."

"So, make your move. You're not afraid of splinters, are you?"

"Ain't afeared a nothin'."

"Then you should definitely pull that Smith & Wesson."

"S'pose I don't?"

"Josiah—"

"Shet up, Ernie! S'pose I don't throw down," Josiah said.

"I still want answers."

"We'uns didn't come here ta palaver."

"No, you came to kill me. And I think we both know why."

"You's purty smart."

"It doesn't take a genius."

"Why *you* think we's here then?"

"For the money."

"Whut money's that?"

"Good question," Price replied. "You see it here?"

"See whut?"

"Try keeping up, Josiah. Do you see the money here?"

"I see ya sittin' at my table, boy."

"We're back to that?"

"Damn right!"

"You'd better move me then."

The room was quiet now, beyond a little whispering well back from where he sat. It let Price listen to the street. He kept his eyes on Ernie and Josiah, tuning out the nervous bystanders.

"You gonna move, or what?" Josiah asked.

"Too late for that, you said."

"Oh, yeah."

"You haven't really thought this through, have you. I hope the others do a better job, for your sake."

"Udders?"

Tempted as he was to spell it for them, Price abstained. "The *others*," he repeated. "Since you know the money isn't here with me, you must have someone going up to fetch it."

"Think so?"

"Sure. Unless they're all as dumb as you boys."

Angry color stained the faces looming over Price. "You gotta bad mouth, boy," Josiah said.

"I'm rude, no doubt about it. But you knew that when I took your special table."

"Right."

"That's right. So now, you're in the game. The only question is, do you intend to raise or fold?"

"I'm sick a waitin'," Landry muttered, shifting in his creaky chair.

"It hasn't been that long," Brooks said.

"Bullshit."

"We got the best part of an hour left."

"Two hours for a goddamn meal. Who ever hearda that?"

"You coulda argued when he set the time, I guess." It made him smile to think of Landry arguing with Jubal over anything.

"Wha's funny?"

"Nothin'."

They were in Schaefer's room, the one he meant to

share with Landry if and when they got to sleep. Two narrow beds, with Brooks perched on the foot of one, the suitcase filled with money resting on the other. Brooks kept both hands on the Henry rifle in his lap. Landry was fiddling with a double-barreled shotgun, breaking it again to check the load.

"Reckon the Messicans kin hear my belly growlin' in the street by now," he said.

"That what it was?" Brooks prodded him.

"Ho-ho. Ain't you the wit."

"Sometimes."

"One time too many, if ya ain't careful."

Brooks didn't take it as a threat. In fact, since last night's shooting, he'd discovered that he didn't hold Tom Landry in the same awe that he once had, as a seasoned hand. Landry had killed two men—or claimed he had at least—but neither of them recently. Brooks reckoned that if he was pushed to it, he might just hold his own against the older man. His own, and then some.

"They'll be back," he said. "It ain't like there's a shortage of tortillas."

"S'pose I wanted somethin' else, smart boy."

"Whatever. If they got it, we can find it."

"Ain't no 'we' in this," Landry replied. "First thing I want's a piece a poon."

Brooks frowned. "You heard what Jubal said about them whores."

"So what? You think he needed two hours for *supper*? How the hell long does it take to eat a couple a tamales?"

"I think he went off to have a look around the town with Mr. . . . Matt, just like he said."

"Mr. Matt," Landry snorted. "Tell me somethin, smart boy. How come *Mr. Matt* ain't sittin' here right now instead a you or me?"

"Because he's got an eye for things like this. Jubal wants him to have a look around."

"Uh-uh. I reckon Jubal don't trust your new friend ta watch the money."

"Jubal don't trust nobody," Brooks said.

"Oh, yeah? He leff us with it, didn't he?"

"That's 'cuz he don't think either one of us is smart enough to make off with it."

Landry thought about that for a moment, gnawing his mustache. "You sayin' I ain't got the brains ta *steal*?"

"I didn't say that, Tommy."

"And you goddamn better not!"

"Don't worry."

"'Cuz I'm damn shore smart enough ta steal."

"I always thought so. Still . . ."

"Careful."

"I was about to say that takin's one thing. Keepin's somethin' else."

"You wanna 'splain that?"

"Well, I mean, you steal a dollar offa Jubal an' he prob'ly wouldn't notice. Steal a hunnert dollars, an' he still might let it go, if he was in a easy mood. You steal a *million* dollars from him, though, you best believe he'd hunt you down."

"I'd slip him, don't you worry."

"With a million dollars?"

"Money makes it easy."

"Money that big leaves a trail," Brooks said. He hadn't been around so much, but everyone knew that, or ought to know it.

"Toss that suitcase on my horse and ride on out of here. Where would he look?" asked Landry.

"Anywhere he heard about a cowboy spendin' money like there's no tomorra."

"Let him find me then. I ain't afraid a Jubal."

He was flat-out lying now. Brooks had been working on the Schaefer spread with Landry for the better part of two years now, and never once had Landry talked back to the old man or his son. He'd bitch behind their backs like any other cowboy, but he wouldn't risk losing a paycheck.

"Damn him," Landry muttered, "thinkin' I ain't smart enough—"

"What's that?" Brooks asked, interrupting him.

"Wha's *whut*?"

"That noise." A creaking on the stairs perhaps.

"I don't hear nothin'."

"Hush and listen then."

"Now, boy—"

"Shut up!"

Landry was shocked into a momentary silence, groping for an answer as the stairs gave out another low-pitched groan.

"You hear *that*, dammit?"

"Yeah."

Brooks realized that both of them were whispering. He sat dead still, clutching the Henry tighter now to keep his hands from trembling.

"Someone's coming up," he said.

"It's a goddamn hotel. People *would* use the stairs."

"They're sneaking."

"You don't know that."

"Listen!" There was something furtive in the sound.

"It's Jubal comin' back," said Landry.

"I don't think so."

Landry stood and faced the door, his shotgun leveled from the hip. Brooks rose and joined him, was about to cock his rifle when he heard a scratching sound behind him.

They had left the bedroom's window open, letting air and noise in from the street. Most of the talk that drifted up to them was Spanish, punctuated by the sound of horses passing now and then. The scratching noise was different, though. Another furtive sound.

And it was close.

"You hear *that*?" Brooks demanded.

"Yeah. Whut is it?"

Brooks recalled the outward look of the hotel. Three stories tall, windows above the street with narrow balconies just large enough for tenants to step out and scan the street. The windows weren't that close together, but he guessed an agile and determined man might crawl between them.

"Someone's comin' over," he told Landry.

"Hell you say!"

"I hope I'm wrong."

"I'm ready, if you ain't." As Landry spoke, he cocked the shotgun's double hammers.

"Careful, in case I'm wrong."

"Make up your goddamn mind!"

"Just *wait*!"

Brooks left Landry to watch the door while he edged closer to the window. Barely breathing, he could hear the scratching noises better now. Louder. Closer?

Behind him, in the hallway leading to their door, Brooks heard footsteps. He thought it sounded like two men, but he was rattled now and couldn't really say. His hands were definitely trembling now.

Easy, Brooks told himself. *You've done this. You're a killer. You can handle it.*

Except he didn't have Matt Price to help him this time. He had fat Tom Landry quaking in his boots, despite the bluster from a moment earlier. The shotgun would be devastating at close range, but only if Landry had nerve enough to fire it.

Only if the prowlers didn't kill him first.

Passing the lamp, he paused on impulse, cupped one hand above the glass chimney, and blew out the flame. Landry moaned in the darkness, an animal sound.

The scratching stopped outside their window for a moment, then resumed with greater urgency. Brooks edged his way between the beds, knelt there, and cocked his rifle. Aiming at the open window frame.

"Come on," he whispered to the darkness. "Come and get it."

•   •   •

Schaefer was leaving the cantina, chewing on a toothpick, when a husky cowboy blundered into him and knocked his hat askew.

"'Scuse you," the clumsy stranger sneered.

Schaefer considered chastising the oaf, then reconsidered. He was due back at the room, to take his turn watching the money, and a few shots of tequila had done wonders for his mood. He showed the other man his back and never gave a thought to being followed.

Not until a rough hand gripped his shoulder, spinning him around.

"I didn't hear you 'pologize," the cowboy said.

Examining the sunburned, stubbled face, Schaefer initially supposed the man was drunk. That notion vanished when he smelled the cowboy's breath. The scent that made his nose wrinkle was rotten teeth, not alcohol.

"I guess your ears work better than your legs," Schaefer replied.

"You shove a man by accident," the cowboy said, "you oughta 'pologize."

"Do tell."

"Unless it weren't no accident."

"It was, on my part."

"Meanin' what?"

"Meaning I don't know if you're clumsy, or you're looking for a fight."

The stranger laughed, surprising Schaefer. "Hey, d'you hear that, Bob? Dude thinks I'm lookin' for a fight."

A second man appeared from nowhere, stepping out of darkness. Schaefer blinked and saw that he'd been hiding in the black mouth of an alleyway. "Dude could be right," Bob said.

"Yessir." The first one flashed a gap-toothed grin. "I guess he is."

Schaefer knew what they wanted now. "Are you with Reese?" he asked.

"Don't know 'im," Gap Tooth answered. "You know any Reese, Bob?"

"Nope."

"You don't know anything about my sister then."

"Ain't had the pleasure. Is she new in town?"

They snickered at him, gloating. Bob edged closer, while his friend stood fast. Schaefer counted three guns between them, two for Bob, all holstered at the moment. But their hands were flexing, itching for a draw.

"The money's in my room," he said.

"Don't worry none," said Bob. "We got it covered."

Schaefer almost turned to look at the hotel, behind him, but he knew the move would get him killed. Whatever might be happening with Brooks and Landry, or with Price, he had his plate full at the moment with these two.

It suddenly occurred to Jubal Schaefer that he might die here, in San Felípe. Any second now, he'd have to test himself against two strangers who were bent on killing him for money. If he couldn't stop them, it would all have been for nothing. Marcy would be gone, and—

"You look jumpy, boy," said Gap Tooth. "I think he's jumpy, Bob."

"I think you're right."

"You wanna take us to that money, boy? Is that wha's on your mind?"

"I don't think so."

"You'd rather jest have at it then?"

Schaefer considered the alternatives. They knew where he was staying, where the money was. They *had it covered,* Gap Tooth had said. That told him there were other shooters in the game, most likely sneaking into the hotel, trying to get the drop on Brooks and Landry. If he led these two across the street, Schaefer supposed they'd either shoot him when he turned his back or wait until they reached their destination, then cut loose to signal for the others to attack.

They clearly meant to kill him either way, and Schae-

fer didn't plan to make it easy for them. He would fight,
even if it was preordained for him to lose.

In truth, he'd never been much of a shooter. With the
money he was born to, fighting hadn't been a way of life
for Schaefer, growing up. His old man had encouraged
roughness to a point—boys'll be boys, all that—and
hunting had been part of it, but Jubal wasn't raised to be a
gunfighter. He'd fired at rustlers twice, and might've
winged one in the second incident, more than a year ago,
but that was the extent of his combat experience. He
hadn't even been at home the night Reese and his friends
came after Marcy.

When they killed his father.

"Boy, whut's wrong wi' you?"

He realized that Gap Tooth must've asked him something, but he hadn't heard the question. Covering, he answered, "Must be getting bored, I guess."

"Ya hear that, Bob? We's *borin'* him. Ain't that a cryin'
shame?"

"Shore is," Bob said. "He might get bored to death."

"You want the money," Schaefer told them, "all you
have to do is take it."

"Tha's whut I said." Gap Tooth graced him with another reeking smile. "Like candy from a baby."

"Like the five who tried last night," said Schaefer.

"Huh?"

He forced a smile. "Don't tell me. You boys thought
you had the game all to yourselves?"

"Don't see nobody else," Bob said.

"You wouldn't," Schaefer answered. "Not from here.
We left them for the worms, a day's ride north."

"Five men, you say?"

"Five dead men. Maybe you were watching when we
led their horses into town."

He saw a flicker of uncertainty in Gap Tooth's eyes and
felt the balance shift, albeit slightly. They would be calculating odds now, wondering how many of the five Schae-

fer had taken down. He wished it had been one of them at least.

Gap Tooth was thinking hard. Schaefer could almost see the rusty wheels turning behind the other man's dull eyes. At last he said, "How come I don't believe you, boy?"

"Maybe you really are as stupid as you look."

"Smart mouth'll get ya killed."

Schaefer stared back at them and answered, "Prove it."

He was waiting, frozen in the moment, when gunfire exploded on the far side of the street.

Price saw the move before Josiah made it, something in his eyes, the sharp twist of his mouth, a hunching of his shoulders. Ernie must've seen it too, because he faded to his right as Price fired through the tabletop into Josiah's chest.

He kicked back at the same time, sent the table crashing over with his plate and all dashed to the floor around Josiah's feet. The shooter wasn't thinking of his boots, though, with a spume of blood erupting from his shirt. He staggered backward, still apparently determined to complete the draw, while Price dropped out of sight behind the table, rolling to his right.

Two guns went off, almost at once, but only one shot struck the upturned table. Ernie's, Price supposed, as it blew past his face. Josiah's first shot drilled the floor as he lurched sideways, reeling toward the bar, his free hand clapped against his chest to stanch the flow of blood.

Price caught him turning as he cleared the far side of the table, fired again from floor level, and saw his bullet rip into Josiah's thigh. It was another gusher, and it dropped him, but he still had strength enough to fight while he was breathing.

Ernie got another shot off from the sidelines, peeling back a strip of floorboard ten or fifteen inches from the tip of Price's nose. Not close enough to worry him, but if he gave the second gunman time to steady up, he might do better next time.

Finish it.

Price vaulted to his feet, finding his target as he rose. Ernie was fanning now, putting his trust in speed when accuracy was required. He fired three times at Price and missed all three. Price felt an old familiar chill inside as he squeezed off a single round in answer, from a range of fifteen feet.

The slug hit Ernie in the hollow of his throat and punched him backward, lifting him a clear three inches off his feet. He went down hard, impacting with a force that raised a small dust cloud. His boot heels drummed the scarred floorboards, and he made liquid strangling noises as he died.

Josiah tried to rise, using his blood-slick left hand to support himself while ruby springs flowed from his chest and thigh, making the floor too slick to hold him. Giving up at last, he raised his Smith & Wesson, muzzle wavering, and tried to draw a bead. Hoping to take Price with him on his unexpected trip to Hell.

Price didn't want to fire a fourth shot, but he had no choice. His .45 slug made a wet sound when it slapped into Josiah's bloodstained shirt and nailed him to the floor.

At first, Price thought the gunshots from outside were echoes ringing in his ears. A heartbeat later he was racing toward the exit, no one in the place making a move to stop him. Trailing cordite fumes, he burst onto the sidewalk just in time to see the end of Jubal Schaefer's fight, across the street.

One man was down, a stranger, stretched out on his face in front of Schaefer. His companion had a six-gun in each hand, firing at Schaefer from a range that should've made it easy, but the trick in pistol fighting wasn't speed. Fast draws were useless if a shooter couldn't hit a man-sized target standing twenty feet in front of him.

And this one couldn't.

Price stood watching as he blazed three rounds in rapid fire. Schaefer was cringing from the muzzle-flashes, but he still found nerve enough to hold his right arm stiff and steady on the mark. His Colt spoke once and sent his adversary spinning off the sidewalk, to land facedown in the street.

"That's four," Price called across the street as he approached Schaefer. The nervous rancher spun to face him, leveling his gun, then lifted it as recognition hit him.

"You too?"

"In the cantina," Price confirmed as he reloaded his Peacemaker.

"That's what threw them off, I guess. The noise from over there."

"Whatever. Are you hit?"

Schaefer glanced down, as if expecting to see bullet holes. "Guess not."

"Okay. We're needed back at—"

"The hotel. I know," said Schaefer just as more shots echoed in the street.

Price raised his eyes and found the darkened window of the room where Brooks and Landry waited with the money. Muzzle-flashes winked like summer lightning in the shadows there, and he ran full tilt for the lodging house, with Schaefer cursing at his heels. Townspeople fled before them, anxious to avoid the crazy gringos in their midst.

When they were halfway there, Price saw a figure tumble through the window, jerking as a bullet caught him in midair. The man fell headfirst to the street and landed in a boneless heap.

Nearby, a woman screamed.

"Goddamn it!" Schaefer panted, overtaking Price, arms pumping as he ran.

They hit the door almost together, Schaefer leading by a stride or two. Across the lobby, toward the stairs they ran, and Price was suddenly aware of movement on his left. He swung around that way and saw a grizzled Anglo hunched behind the registration desk, where Price had left a slim young Mexican.

The substitute triggered a shot that missed Price by a hair. Price shot him in the face, spraying the wallpaper behind him, then almost ran into Schaefer as the rancher spun to face the action.

"Go on, dammit!"

Schaefer turned again and hit the stairs running. A shotgun blast rattled the ceiling overhead, and someone screamed—a man this time—as if he'd caught a terrifying glimpse of the hereafter. More shots sputtered as they climbed the staircase, pistols and a rifle's crack to put them in perspective.

On the second floor, they found one shooter lying on his back, trembling as if a powerful electric current surged through every muscle in his body. He was head-shot, and the tremors didn't last much longer.

Price stepped to his left and Schaefer took the other side, more cautious now as they approached the open doorway. Moaning sounds came from the room, another pistol shot, and then the flat crack of a rifle one more time. Price recognized the heavy impact of a body on the floor.

"Landry?" he called out from the hallway. "Brooks?"

Brooks answered him. "Is that you, Matt?"

"We're both here," Schaefer told him. "Are you clear?"

"I think so."

"All right, hold your fire," Price said. "We're coming in."

"Come on then."

Another corpse lay just inside the threshold, facedown with his arms spread, crucified in blood. The room was dark beyond him, someone having doused the lamp.

"Where are you, Early?" Schaefer asked.

"Here, Boss." A match flared, showing Brooks between the beds, just rising with the Henry clutched in his right hand. "I'll get the lamp."

"Jesus!"

Schaefer stooped over Landry, where the older man sat wedged into a corner with the shotgun at his side. Blood streaked his shirt and trousers, welling out between the fingers he held clamped against his stomach.

"Christ, it hurts!" he whimpered.

"Gut-shot," Schaefer said. "Does anybody know if there's a doctor in this town?"

8

There was.

Brooks said he'd seen a doctor's office near the livery when he took the horses down. He volunteered to fetch the medic, going armed with his reloaded Henry and the pistol on his hip. Price didn't wish him luck, but wondered if they'd ever see the kid again.

"Could take some time," he told Schaefer. "Figure the office must be closed by now. He'll have to track the sawbones down at home."

"Long as he finds him, brings him back," Schaefer replied.

Price didn't argue. They'd done what they could for Landry, short of digging for the bullet, and that needed expert hands. He occupied the floor in what had once, briefly, been Price's room, with folded hand towels pressed against his stomach wound to slow the bleeding. It was bad, Price realized, but Landry still might live if proper help arrived in time.

Schaefer held the sodden pad against his hired man's

belly, watching Landry fade. "I make it eight," he told Price, "with your two."

"I count the same."

"You think we missed somebody?"

Price had already considered it. "I think he would've come in with the others," he replied. "Or else hightailed it out of town by now."

"I hope you're right. We're getting whittled down."

Price played a long shot, almost certain it would fail. "No one you recognize among this lot, I guess?"

"Reese didn't send them." There was no doubt in his voice.

"Somebody else then. We're still waiting."

"Right. They didn't know about the ones last night either."

A dozen dead so far, and they still hadn't met the kidnappers. "We're drawing flies," Price said.

"They knew where we were headed."

"Same as last night. You've got leaks at home."

The rancher scowled. "There's no denying it. I find out who's been talking, and they'll wish they hadn't."

"Think about that later," Price suggested. "We've still got a job to do."

Schaefer lowered his voice, leaning away from Landry even as he kept the blood-soaked towel in place. "We'll be one short from here on, even if he lives."

"And do the best we can with what's left," Price replied.

"You reckon it's enough?"

"We won't know that until it's done. If we're still standing, it was ample. If we're not . . ." He finished with a shrug.

"Is that what you call optimism?" Schaefer asked.

"I never won a fight by looking on the rosy side," Price said. "Expect the worst—"

"I know. I heard you on the trail with Brooks. Truth is, I didn't think the worst would be this bad."

"You likely haven't seen it yet."

"Meaning?"

"There's still the payoff. We still have to get your sister back."

"If she's alive, you mean."

"Your mother didn't want to hear it, but she might not be."

"You'd have to know Reese, how he feels about her. I don't think he'd hurt her really."

"Killed her father, didn't he? That had to hurt."

"Reese wouldn't see it that way. He's like something from a fairy tale, wanting to rescue her and carry her away."

"Rescue?"

"In *his* mind," Schaefer said. "Because our father wouldn't let her marry young, first stud she ever looked at twice."

"You think he wants your sister? Why ask for the money then?"

"Why not? He knows we've got it. This way, he can have the girl *and* make a fortune. Run away, forget about the mess he left behind."

"Happily ever after," Price remarked.

"That's what *he* thinks. Smart bastard's in for a surprise."

"You still intend to pay the ransom?"

"Oh, I'll *pay* it, sure. But Reese won't live to spend it. That's your job. Ten thousand for the four of them."

Price meant to ask, *And then what?* but an urgent rapping on the door distracted him. He drew his Colt and cocked it. "What?"

"It's me," Brooks said. "I got the doctor with me."

Price crossed to the door, unlocked it, and stepped back, still ready with his Peacemaker. Brooks entered first, the Henry clamped beneath one arm, then stepped out of the doctor's way.

The doctor was a small man, no taller than Price's shoulder, with aristocratic features that revealed a hint of his Castilian ancestry. His outfit was immaculate, as if he had been summoned from a formal dinner or the opera. Only the black bag in his hand was out of place. Price wondered if there was a single manufacturer who serviced every doctor in the world, so their bags all looked the same.

The doctor looked around, saw gringos everywhere, and spoke to them in English. "I am Dr. Sanchez. Gentlemen, you have a grave emergency?"

"Right here," said Schaefer. "It's a grave we hope to keep him out of."

Sanchez had a look at Landry, peering underneath the towel Schaefer held pressed against his abdomen, and shook his head. "We must remove him to my surgery."

"Not we," Schaefer replied. "Call someone else to help you carry him."

"Jubal—"

"Forget it, Early. We stay with the money till it's finished."

"We can take it with us."

"No. That's final. Call somebody, Doc. I'll pay them for their time and sweat."

"If you insist, Señor. Excuse me while I speak to Hector at the desk downstairs."

"If you can find him, be my guest," said Price.

"Señor?"

"He wasn't there when we came back and found the shooters waiting," Price explained. "There's been no time to look for him. We don't know if they ran him off, or what."

"Such violence." Sanchez shook his head. "I'll get the undertaker and his son."

Landry heard that and bellowed, "Undertaker? I ain't dead, goddamnit!"

"Hush," said Schaefer. To the doctor: "How long will you be?"

"Ten minutes, possibly fifteen. Continue pressure on the wound to slow the bleeding."

"Early, it's your turn."

"All right then."

Sanchez left them and Price locked the door behind him. Schaefer cleaned his hands at the washbasin while Brooks took his place. The young man spoke to Landry softly, calming him. When Landry closed his eyes, Brooks asked, "What now?"

"We wait," said Schaefer. "See who shows up next."

It was the doctor, with the undertaker and his boy. They brought a stretcher, all three looking solemn, and the two new arrivals lifted Landry, groaning, from the bed to place him on it, while Sanchez took over keeping pressure on his belly wound. Schaefer stuffed money in the doctor's pocket as they left and promised more when he was done, then locked the door behind them and sat down.

"That's done at least," he said.

"You think Tom's gonna make it?" Brooks asked Schaefer.

"How'n hell would I know?"

"Being gut-shot doesn't mean he's finished," Price advised. "The doctor has a lot to do with it."

"He should've nailed 'em easy with the scattergun," said Brooks. "I guess the first one hit him, coming through the door."

"It helps to aim, even with shotguns."

"Someone oughta tell 'im that for next time. If there *is* a next time."

"He's been taken care of," Schaefer said. "Stay focused on the job at hand."

"We're still waiting for Reese?" asked Brooks.

"One of them anyway," Schaefer replied. "I know he didn't send the ones I met."

"We might've scared them off," Price said. "At least for now."

"You think so?" For the first time since they had arrived in San Felípe, Schaefer seemed concerned.

"If they were nervous," Price replied, "wanting an easy

swap, this kind of thing could put them off. They won't want lawmen following the money."

"Tom says there's no law in San Felípe," Brooks chimed in. "He reckoned tha's why Reese and them picked it."

"Well, if he's right—" Price froze. "Somebody on the stairs."

Price drew his Colt. Schaefer did likewise, while Brooks cocked his Henry rifle. All three tracked the sound of footsteps moving down the hallway, hesitating near the threshold of the bullet-riddled room next door, then drawing closer. Price was ready when a sharp knock sounded on the door.

"Who is it?"

"If you please, I am Luis Hector Ramirez, the *alcalde*—mayor, I believe you say—of San Felípe. I would speak to you."

"Who's with you?" Price demanded.

"Juan Lopez de Jesus Aguinaldo," said the mayor. "Our magistrate—or justice of the peace, if you prefer."

Price cracked the door and peered into the hall. Upon confirming only two men present, neither of them armed, he stood aside to let them enter, holstering his gun.

"Good evening, gentlemen," Ramirez said.

"It hasn't been that good so far," Schaefer replied. "Our friend was damn near killed by thieves."

"And you've killed several men yourselves, I understand. Outsiders, thankfully."

"We didn't get a proper introduction, so I don't know where they came from," Schaefer said. "But they'll be staying here."

"Indeed, you have brought trouble to our village."

"And business for the undertaker," Schaefer said.

"We found the trouble waiting for us here when we rode in," Price interjected.

"And what business brings you from El Norte?" asked the mayor.

"Our own," Schaefer replied curtly.

"Perhaps it was your own, before the killing started. Now, Señor, it is a personal concern of every resident."

Price waited, watching Schaefer. It was his call how much—if anything—to tell the locals.

"We're supposed to meet some fellas," Schaefer said at last. "They have a package for us. We have cash for them."

"A sale of merchandise."

"That's right."

"And why, if I may ask, did you choose San Felípe?"

"That was their call. We're just following the terms."

The visitors locked eyes, not speaking, then both drew themselves up to their full height, unimposing as it was. "We think it best," the mayor proclaimed, "that you transact your business somewhere else. We have no need of such commerce in San Felípe."

"Sorry, but we can't oblige you," Schaefer said. "Much as I'd like to leave this pissant town for good, we haven't seen the men we're waiting for. And wait is what we mean to do."

"Also, there's Tom," Brooks added from the sidelines.

"And our friend," Schaefer agreed reluctantly. "We'll need to wait on him."

"If he survives his wound," Ramirez replied.

"Whatever. We've got business left undone."

"You do not understand, Señor. We must *insist* that you leave San Felípe."

"No."

The dignitaries blinked at Schaefer, as if they could not translate his monosyllabic response.

"Señor—"

"This is the part where you start threatening to run us out," said Schaefer, interrupting. "But I have to wonder how you mean to do that. We already know you've got no lawman here in town. Maybe you want to call up some militia, shopkeepers and such. Of course, they may not be so anxious to oblige you, with the recent killings fresh in mind."

"I might prefer the *federales*," said Ramirez.

"You might," Schaefer replied. "But if they were in town, they would've beat you here. Send for them, if you want. We'll likely be done with our business by the time they get around to us."

"You seem to think this is a joke, Señor."

"I don't see anybody laughing here. But something tells me I know how to make you smile."

"Señor?"

"Suppose I volunteer to pay the funeral expenses on the scum that shot our friend and tried to rob us. Naturally, there'd be a fee for two important men like you coming around to see us after hours, sharing your concerns. How'd that be?"

"Well . . ."

"You've got a sum in mind. I know you do."

"Perhaps—"

"I'll make it easy on you. How about a hundred dollars for yourself, same for the magistrate, and fifty more to get those ugly bastards in the ground. We got a deal?"

"And you'll be leaving San Felípe *soon*?"

"As soon as we conclude our business. That's a promise."

"There's still Tom," Brooks said.

Schaefer was counting out the money as he spoke. "Just point our friend north when he's ready, will you, Mayor? His horse knows the way home."

The cash changed hands. Ramirez examined it, as if it might be stained with blood, then put it in his pocket. He ignored a sharp glance from the magistrate.

"Then, gentlemen," said the *alcalde,* "I wish you a peaceful evening and a safe trip home. A *speedy* trip."

"Just watch our dust," said Schaefer, moving in to close the door behind them. When it was locked, he said, "Cheap bastards. I'd have gone five hundred in a pinch."

"You got a bargain then," said Price.

"Not quite," Schaefer replied. "We've got a million left to spend, and you've got ten thousand to earn."

• • •

"Goddamn it, they've got too much company," Ed Timmons said.

"You wanna tell Reese you run outa nerve?" asked Frank Bodine.

They stood together on the sidewalk opposite the small hotel, watching the gawkers start to drift away. It had been almost forty minutes since the shooting ended, and the spectators were finally deciding that the show was over for the night. They'd seen the bodies carried out, one picked up from the dusty street outside, and watched the undertaker take a wounded man out on a stretcher.

"That live'un looked like Tommy Landry," Timmons said, for want of any other way to stall for time.

"I don't care who it was," Bodine replied. "You gonna do this thing or what?"

"I'm workin' up to it."

"Uh-huh."

"You seen what happened, same as me." Timmons was getting angry now, on top of his pervasive fear. "Them others musta been after the money too."

Bodine allowed himself a smile. "Looks like they didn't get it."

"So, you think we will?"

"Whole differ'nt thing. We got somethin' they want. They's gonna hand it over nice and quietlike."

"You hope."

"We all best hope it, Eddie. Now, if you can't pull your weight . . ."

"Jus' lemme breathe a goddamn minute, willya?"

Timmons hadn't volunteered to meet the Circle S riders. He never volunteered for anything—or never would again, at least, after he had agreed to help Reese Johnson snatch the Big Man's daughter out of Santa Rosa. It started out as idle talk, then grew into a plan while Timmons wasn't watching. Then, next thing he knew, it had been time to do the job and he could either go along or have his three best friends think he was yellow.

Hell, make that his *only* friends.

It hadn't hurt to know he'd get a portion of the money, though he wasn't great with numbers and the payoff had been hard for him to visualize. A hundred thousand, Reese had promised. More than Timmons stood to earn in two hundred years of cowboying.

So, here he was in San Felípe, but the simple plan wasn't so simple anymore. A gang of strangers already had tried to grab the ransom, shot to hell like they were nothing much at all, and wasn't that a wonderment? Timmons wouldn't have thought the Circle S riders could fight that well. He reckoned Reese would be surprised to hear it too.

"They're gonna be riled up when I get over there," he said.

"Unrile 'em then. You know 'em. They know you. Make sure they reco'nize you goin' in. You'll be all right."

"They kill me, then I guess the joke's on you," Timmons replied, forcing a smile he didn't feel.

"I gotcha covered," Bodine said.

"Yeah, right."

"Just *do* it! Jumpin' Jesus, you're like some old woman."

"Screw you!"

"Do your job first, 'fore they go ta sleep."

Timmons stepped off the sidewalk, concentrating on the simple act of walking as he crossed the street. No one around him paid the slightest notice to another gringo. They were tired of waiting for more action, turning back to the enticements of tequila, cards, or women, some of them tired out and bound for bed.

Jealous of those who didn't have to speak with killers in the middle of the night, Timmons advanced until he reached the spot where he had seen one of the would-be robbers lying crumpled in the dust. He glanced up at the darkened window that the man had fallen from. There was a light next door, Timmons's destination, but he didn't want to go there.

As if Reese had given him a choice.

Timmons looked back across the street and saw Bodine glaring at him, jerking his head in the direction of the hotel's entrance. Subtle. Timmons almost hoped a lawman would appear and stop him, but there was no law in San Felípe. Reese had picked it for that very reason, sounding wise as they discussed it over shots of whiskey, nothing but a little wasted time at stake.

Now it would be his life if he proceeded. Then again, Timmons supposed the price would be the same if he refused. Reese hadn't been himself of late, after he'd killed the Big Man. Where he'd been a hothead in the old days, now Timmons regarded him as *dangerous*.

He clomped across the sidewalk and went into the hotel. There was no clerk behind the desk, where rusty-colored blotches stained the wall. Three old men standing in the lobby studied him, but made no move to stop him as he headed for the stairs.

The fifth and eighth steps on the second flight were squeakers. Timmons reached the second floor and hesitated, staring at the door to Number 2A, where the battle had been fought. No one had bothered mopping up the bloodstains in the hallway, and he guessed they'd need a new door to replace the one shot through with pistol slugs and buckshot. He imagined lying on that floor, *his* blood pooled on the boards around him, and he thought again that it was madness being there.

Ten paces, more or less, to reach his destination. All he had to do was cross that gap, knock on the door, and wait for someone to respond. They'd recognize him, know his business, and if they were serious about the ransom, he supposed they wouldn't shoot him on the spot.

He was a messenger, that's all.

Of course, they'd blame him for the rest of it, and Timmons couldn't rightly argue with them. He'd been in on it from the beginning, nodding while Reese sketched the plan and then refined it, riding through the night to face the Big Man in his lair and make it happen.

Jesus, how'd we come to this?

He almost turned around then, felt the yellow creeping up on him. It was a shame to come this far and risk so much, though, without getting rewarded for his trouble.

All he had to do was knock, walk in, dictate the terms, and walk back out again. Simple. They would be fools to kill him, knowing what his death would mean for Miss Marcella.

Fools, or maybe just pissed off enough and fired up from the killing that they didn't give a damn.

Get out of here, a small voice urged him.

And another answered back, *I can't.*

Trembling, clutching his six-gun in its holster, Timmons started toward the door of Room 2C.

"Awright," Brooks said. "We bought some time. What happens now?"

"We wait," Schaefer replied. "What else?"

"How long?" the young hand asked.

"Long as it takes. We've got a job to do."

"Your new friend, the *alcalde,* may have second thoughts," Price said. "He's got your money now, but when he thinks about it for a while, he may decide to tip the *federales* anyway."

"D'you suppose I didn't think about that?" Schaefer asked defensively. "I wouldn't trust that prick as far as I can throw him. He'll send someone out tomorrow or the next day, if we're still in town. I bought tonight at least."

"That's fine," Price said, "unless those fireworks scared away the kidnappers."

"They'd come back for a million dollars, though," Brooks interjected. "Wouldn't they?"

Price shrugged. "Some would, for sure. I don't like second-guessing men I've never met."

"Reese wants his money," Schaefer told them confidently. "This isn't some game he dreamed up just to make us ride two days for nothing."

"Fair enough," said Price. "You want to sleep in shifts then, like before?"

"What sleep?" Brooks asked. "My nerves feel like I drunk ten pots a coffee."

"That's the action," Price told him. "Watch out. You could crash just as hard five minutes from now."

"Suit yourself," Schaefer said. "You go first then."

As they began to shift positions, Schaefer to the bed, Brooks to a chair beside the door, Price stopped them with his voice. "Two things we haven't talked about."

"What things are those?" asked Schaefer.

"We need to settle what we're doing if your sister's not around, and if she is, I need to know what happens after the exchange."

"You still think Marcy's dead?"

"I don't think anything. It's possible," Price said.

"I told you once before," Schaefer replied, "Reese loves her. *Thinks* he does at least. That's our ace in the hole."

"No chance the others might have different thoughts about the matter?" Price inquired.

"What are you askin' me?"

"Four men, one girl. Three of them might begin to think the fourth's a little greedy. They might want to share."

Schaefer immediately shook his head. "Reese wouldn't stand for that."

"Maybe you're right. But it's still three to one."

"You think they'd put him down?" Brooks asked, wide-eyed.

"It wouldn't be the first time thieves fell out," said Price.

"You're underestimating Reese," said Schaefer. "He's a two-bit piece of trash, I grant you, but he's still the smartest of the four."

"And three of 'em are blood kin," Brooks reminded him.

"I'm keeping that in mind."

"I won't release a penny of the cash till we've seen Marcy safe and sound," Schaefer declared. "Now, does that put your mind at ease?"

"As to the first part, it's a help," Price said. "That leaves the second."

"Meaning afterward."

"That's right."

"You're being paid ten thousand to make sure they don't enjoy the million," Schaefer said. "I thought those terms were clear."

"It's what you *don't* say that confuses me," Price answered.

"Meaning?"

"Think about it. We collect your sister and you pay the ransom. You and Brooks escort the lady home."

"With Tommy," Brooks chimed in.

"Whoever. Leaving me to settle up accounts with Johnson and his friends," Price said. "Is that about the size of it?"

"Sounds right to me," Schaefer replied.

"But you're forgetting something."

"Am I?"

"Think about it."

Schaefer took a moment, frowning to himself, then shook his head. "I don't see where you're going with it."

"What about the ransom?" Price inquired.

"You get it back," said Schaefer.

"And then what? Bring it back to Santa Rosa on my own?"

Schaefer blinked twice, then said, "Well, shit."

"You see it now, the hole in your umbrella. You'd be leaving me alone to watch the cash. Hoping I'd rather have ten thousand than a million. Somehow, Jubal, you don't impress me as the trusting sort."

"You're right. I never thought about it."

"But your mother did."

"Say what?"

"Unless I'm very much mistaken," Price replied, "that

lady doesn't miss a trick. One eye or not, she would've seen this problem coming from a mile away. And I believe she would've filled you in on what to say if someone raised the question."

"Maybe I—"

"Forgot? I'll buy that. You've had other matters on your mind. Maybe they shook you up a little. But you're thinking now. So what's the answer?"

Silence filled the room. Price was prepared to wait it out, watching while Schaefer racked his brain for a response, but Brooks was nervous. Finally, he blurted out, "Jubal, why don't you—"

"Shut up, Early!" Turning to Price, he said, "If you've got something on your mind, why don't you spit it out?"

Price was about to do that when the sound of squeaky floorboards brought him to his feet, six-gun in hand. Facing the door, he raised a finger to his lips. The others nodded, leveling their weapons.

Price supposed this would be Schaefer's chance to shoot him in the back, but that would spook the prowler in the corridor outside, and Price knew that their mission dominated Schaefer's every waking thought.

Even if he'd concealed its true purpose from the beginning.

There would be time to sort that out, Price thought, after they had discovered who was lurking in the hallway. Someone who was trying to be stealthy, though the hotel's architecture had defeated him. Someone who—

Price was ready for the rapping on their door, and still it almost made him jump. Brooks *did* jump, rifle wobbling dangerously as he brought it back on target.

Price opened the door and pushed his Colt into a startled face. The new arrival swallowed hard, then found his voice.

"Ya'll gonna shoot me now," he asked, "or do ya wanna see Marcy?"

9

"Ed Timmons," Schaefer said when they were all inside the room, door closed. "I might've known they'd send the runt."

"No call for insults, Jubal," said the messenger.

"'No call for *insults*'?" Schaefer snorted. "After you shits kill my father and Isaiah, blind my mother, steal my sister, and demand a million dollars for her? Do you feel *insulted*, Eddie?"

"I guess not."

Ed Timmons was a small man, five-foot-three or -four with boots and hat, reed-slender in his baggy clothes. He might've been nineteen. Price wasn't sure where he had found a gun belt small enough to cinch around his waist, but the LeMat revolver riding on his left hip in a cross-draw holster dragged his pants down on that side. Price couldn't tell if he was any good by looking at him, but his eyes were jumpy and his tongue flicked out incessantly to moisten peeling lips.

"Where's Reese and Marcy?" Schaefer asked point-blank.

"We'll git ta that."

"Uh-huh. You want to sit a spell before we talk? Maybe I'll have the desk clerk send us up a bottle and we'll all be sociable?"

"I wouldn't mind a drink right now," Timmons replied.

Schaefer glanced back and forth from Price to Brooks, smiling. "He wouldn't mind a drink. I have to give you credit, boy. I never thought you had the goddamn nerve."

"Guess you was wrong."

"Was I?"

"Damn right."

Price gauged the distance separating each man in the room. He stood nearest to Timmons, maybe six feet to the short man's right. Schaefer was twelve feet out in front of Timmons, with a bed between them and the suitcase filled with cash behind him, on the second bed. Brooks was beyond the messenger, some five or six feet to his left, across from Price.

It wasn't good if someone felt the urge to draw a gun. While Price and Brooks had Timmons boxed in for a cross fire, they would also be aiming directly at each other, nothing but the short man's slender torso in between their weapons. Schaefer had the only clear shot in the room, and Price wondered if he could pull it off before Timmons cut loose with his LeMat.

The hell of it was that their caller's weapon packed an extra kick. LeMats were awkward, chunky-looking pistols for the simple reason that they had two barrels. One fired .44-caliber rounds from a normal six-shot cylinder, while the second held a solitary shotgun cartridge. Although virtually useless beyond twenty feet, the scatter-shot was deadly at close range and spared the shooter any need to aim on his first shot. Within the confines of a small room like the one they occupied, Price calculated that Ed Timmons could wreak bloody havoc that was swift and steady.

Schaefer was moving, slowly circling the bed. "It wouldn't be my first mistake," he told Timmons. "I try to learn from each one as I go."

"Makes sense," Timmons replied, and licked his lips.

"I've changed my mind, Ed. I don't want to drink with you."

"Awright." Their caller didn't seem to mind. "Le's just talk bidness then."

"That's all my sister is to Reese? Business?"

"I wouldn't know 'bout that. He sent me here to give our terms."

"Your *terms*?" Schaefer had closed the gap between them by one third. Price couldn't tell if Timmons noticed, but the short man wasn't backing up. "I've got your money sitting in that suitcase, and you want to give me *terms*?"

"For the exchange," Timmons replied.

"Oh, that." Schafer nodded. "You didn't give my father any terms, though, did you?"

"He was after Reese and all. You know the way he use ta get."

"When he was still alive, you mean? When trash broke in his house at night to steal his child?"

"Jubal, you know as well as I do—"

Schaefer closed the gap between them with a snarling leap, driving a fist into the small man's face. His other hand clutched Timmons by the throat as Schaefer rode him down, the two of them all flailing arms and legs as they thrashed on the floorboards between Price and Brooks.

Price reached for Schaefer, but a boot swept past his face and drove him back. Brooks tried on his side, setting down the Henry first, but one fist or another caught him on the cheek and nearly toppled him. Recoiling with a curse, Brooks snatched up his rifle and raised it above the combatants, butt poised for a strike.

"Watch it there," Price commanded. "We don't want to crack any skulls."

"Serve him right if I did," Brooks replied, leaving Price to decide who he meant.

The grapplers held their clinch, slugging away to poor effect. Timmons was bleeding from the nose, while Schaefer had a thumbnail gouge along his jaw, but otherwise their contest had devolved to awkward body blows and breathless curses. At the first glimpse of an opening, Price darted in, grabbed one of Schaefer's legs, and hauled him backward from the fray.

"Goddammit, turn me loose!" the rancher ordered, lurching to his feet. Timmons was up on one knee, reaching for his pistol, when Brooks jammed the Henry's muzzle flush against his forehead.

"Let it go!" Price snapped at Schaefer. "If you want your sister back, save all this schoolyard nonsense for another time."

"Who do you think you are?" Schaefer demanded. "I don't take my orders from some saddle bum."

"Your mother isn't here," Price said. "So back off. Now."

Schaefer was clawing for his Colt when Price drove a hard right into his gut. He doubled over sharply, whooshing wind from startled lungs, and met a rising knee between the eyes. It dropped him like a sack of feed, and Price relieved him of the pistol as he turned to face Timmons.

"I won't apologize for him," Price said, "but that's an end to it. Before you pull that weapon, keep in mind that you came here for gold, not lead."

"Awright," said Timmons as he struggled to his feet unaided. "But you keep that piece a shit away from me."

Price glanced at Schaefer, huddled on the floor. "He won't be rushing anybody for a while. Let's talk about those terms."

"Okay."

"You're here about the money, yes?"

"What else?"

"You may have seen we had a little problem hanging on to it. Some other fellas thought they'd help themselves. We had to talk them out of it."

"I heard."

"No doubt you're grateful."

Timmons shrugged. "It ain't my problem. Reese won't give ya Marcy if ya don't deliver."

"He could've come himself, and brought the girl," Price told him.

Timmons shook his head. "We can't do business here," he said. "Too many folks around."

"Eight less than an hour ago," Price replied.

"Still too many. Reese has a new place."

"Does he now?"

Timmons nodded, then asked, "Was that Tommy they took on the stretcher?"

"You saw him?" Brooks asked.

"From the street."

"He might be dyin', Eddie, while we're talkin' here."

A shrug from Timmons. "Not my doin'."

"This is *all* your doin'," Brooks retorted. "You, Reese, and the rest. The men I killed to get here."

"Before you start another fight," Price said, "let's get to business. What's the great new plan?"

"Reese wants a differ'nt meetin' place," Townsend replied.

"And where would that be?"

"There's a place called Amorada, 'bout a day's ride south of here. Reese calculates you should be there by sundown if you leave by six o'clock or so tomorra mornin'. Won't be no one interferin' with us there."

"You've found a smaller town than this?" asked Price.

"We found a *ghost* town," Timmons said. He swabbed blood from his lips and nostrils with a sleeve. "No border trash or lawmen buttin' in. If *he* don't spoil it"—indicating Schaefer—"ever'thin' should be just fine."

"I hope so, Ed."

Timmons was focusing on Price now, studying his face. "I never seen you at the Circle S."

"I'm temporary," Price replied. "But you could say that for most everyone."

"Wha's that suppose ta mean?"

"Forget it. Tell us how to find your ghost town."

"Amorada," he repeated, "but you won't be seein' any signs. Ride south two hours, more or less, until the road forks. One way takes off southwest to Ojos Verdes, but you don't want that. Keep on due south until you pass through foothills and come out the other side. The road looks like it wants ta peter out, but don't give up. Sundown'll get ya there, or close enough."

"Foothills," Price said. "You wouldn't mean to bush-whack us by any chance?"

"Reese doesn't want no killin' if he can avoid it," Tim-mons said. "I don't expect ya to believe it, but that thing with Mr. Schaefer and the old'un weren't our fault. We only went in for the girl."

"You mean the money, right?" asked Price.

"Same thing." This time, when Timmons licked his lips, he must've tasted blood. "You really got a million dollars in that suitcase?"

"That's the rumor."

"Can I see it?"

"Absolutely. Just go fetch the girl."

"I reckon not."

"You'll have to wait then. Just like everybody else."

Timmons retreated slowly toward the door, seeming to gain nerve as the distance widened. "Don't go losin' it along the way," he said, smiling with bloody teeth. "Reese wouldn't like that."

"We'll hold up our end," Price told him, "against any-one who tries to take it short of Amorada. Make sure Reese knows that. This is the last time we accept a change of plans without a fight."

"No problem," said the small man, standing with one

hand on the doorknob. "Just be there when you're s'pose to be, and we'll all have a happy day."

"Some happier than others, I suppose."

"Sundown."

Price let him have the last word as he scurried out the door. Brooks rushed to lock it, then came back to stand above Schaefer.

"I don't like none a this," he said.

"That's two of us."

"Jubal is gonna want a piece a you when he wakes up."

Price eyed the crumpled form and said, "Unless his brains are scrambled, he can wait a while for satisfaction. While he's dozing, though, I've got an itch to scratch."

"Say what?"

Brooks followed Price around the prostrate form of their employer to the second bed. They stood over the suitcase, watching it as if they thought it might sprout legs and make a mad dash for the window.

"I've had something in my craw the past two days," said Price. "It won't go down."

"Guess I don't follow you," Brooks said.

"The money," Price replied. "We've all been guarding it and killing men to keep it safe, but now that we're about to part with it, your boss strikes me as just a bit too casual."

"I'm still not with you," Brooks admitted, frowning.

"Has anybody *seen* the money, Early?"

"Well, o' course. Hell's bells. They had ta *see* it."

"Who?"

"Jubal and Mrs. Schaefer. Who'dja think?" The frown had turned into a smile.

"Nobody else?"

Brooks shrugged. "I reckon someone coulda helped 'em pack it. There's a maid they got, a Messican, if they could trust her."

"But *you* haven't seen it?"

"Me? No, sir."

"Or Landry?"

"He'd a mentioned it."

"Before we ride off through the hills to some ghost town, I'd like to see it. Wouldn't you?"

"Well, I don't know. I mean . . ."

"A little peek while Jubal's snoozing. What's the harm?"

"You don't mean *take* none of it, do ya?" Early's knuckles whitened as he clutched the Henry in a tighter grip.

"A peek is what I said and what I meant," Price answered. "When's the next time either one of us will see a million dollars?"

"Likely never," Brooks agreed. "Le's do 'er then."

Price tried the suitcase latches, but they wouldn't yield. "It's locked," he said.

"That figgers. It was worth a go, I guess, but—"

"We're not beaten yet." Price doubled back to Schaefer, patting down the rancher's pockets. From his vest, Price took a small key on a metal ring. "Let's see if this'll do the trick."

It did. He opened one latch, then the other, and threw back the lid. Brooks stiffened at his side and moaned, "I'll be goddamned and go to Hell!"

"You may at that," Price said.

Before them in the suitcase, neatly stacked and banded, lay countless strips of newspaper cut to the size and shape of greenbacks. There was not a single dollar in the bag.

"What does this mean?" Brooks asked, sitting slump-shouldered on the bed beside the open suitcase. "Can you tell me that?"

Price thought he knew the answer, but he wanted to be sure. To hear it from the horse's mouth. He fetched a jug of water from the room's plain dressing table, came back to the middle of the room, and started dribbling the luke-warm water slowly onto Schaefer's face. It took a while to rouse him, nearly half the water gone before he sputtered back to consciousness and lurched onto all fours. He spent another moment there, head hanging low and dripping on the floor, then shook himself as if he were a dog fresh from the river.

"Price," he moaned, "goddamn you!"

Reaching for his empty holster almost cost Schaefer his balance, but he managed not to topple. Only leather filled his hand, bringing another curse to his tight lips.

"I've got your Colt," Price said. "You won't be needing it right now."

"Damn right," Schaefer replied. A bitter effort brought him to his feet, reeling before his legs remembered how to work. To Price he said, "You made your last mistake, you slick son of a—"

"Where's the money, Jubal?"

Schaefer blinked at Price, then at the suitcase, Brooks seated beside it with the Henry rifle in his lap. At first, the rancher didn't seem to understand what he was seeing; then his face resumed its typical expression of defiance.

"I don't owe you any explanations," Schaefer answered. "Neither one of you. You're being paid to do a job. It makes no difference if I fill that bag with gold or road apples. You want your money, do your work."

"Sounds reasonable," Price agreed, "but there's a couple problems with your pitch."

"Enlighten me," sneered Schaefer.

"First, we just found out that you're about to cheat the men who took your sister hostage, when they're bound to notice. If you'd stab her in the back that way, there's no good reason either one of us should trust you with a dime, much less the ten grand I was promised."

"Listen now—"

"And second," Price said, cutting through his answer, "you've been lying to us from day one. We've gunned down thirteen men to save a pile of newspaper. We're owed an explanation, and you won't be leaving here until we've got it."

"That sounds like a threat."

"At least we know your ears still work," Price said.

Schaefer turned angry eyes on Brooks. "Is this you talking, Early?"

Brooks considered it, then nodded stiffly. "Tommy still might die for what's inside this bag. I wanna know."

"All right then. Do you mind if I sit down?"

"It's your room," Price reminded him.

"You'd never know it." Schaefer winced as he lowered himself to the bed across from Brooks. "You should've let me finish Timmons, Price."

"You weren't that close to winning," Price replied, "but if you had, we wouldn't know where we're supposed to find your sister."

"What? They changed the drop? Where is it?"

"After you," Price said. He stood and waited, eyes on Schaefer's battered face.

"Okay, you want the truth? We couldn't raise a million dollars cash. The price of beef's been down the past two years, on top of which my old man wasn't what you'd call a mastermind of finance. We lost money on the ranch last year, barely broke even two years running prior to that. We're strapped."

"You couldn't borrow on the ranch?"

"For what? A bank won't loan you ransom money. Christ, they'd never get it back and they already know we couldn't make the payments."

"I guess you've got ten thousand, though?" Price prodded Schaefer.

"More or less. Ma reckoned she could talk you down some if . . ."

Price finished for him. "If I managed to live through it."

"Right."

"And maybe you were planning to make sure I didn't."

Schaefer squinted at him. "Hey, do I look stupid?"

"Pretty much. You're gambling with your sister's life, running a bluff the kidnappers are bound to call. What did you have in mind for when they cracked the bag?"

"I thought we'd take them."

"Just like that, your sister in the cross fire."

Schaefer shrugged, wincing with pain the effort cost him. Price felt nothing in the way of sympathy.

"Jubal," said Brooks, "you coulda got us kilt."

The comment earned another sneer. "You didn't seem to mind when you were guarding cash," Schaefer replied. "It was a big adventure then, the killing. I saw how you looked that first night, giddy with it. What's the difference whether it was scrap paper or greenbacks? You weren't getting any of it anyhow."

"I trusted you," Brooks said.

"Grow up, why don't you. Two years working on the Circle S, you think we've got money to burn?"

"This is your *sister*," Brooks protested.

"Don't remind me," Schaefer answered scornfully. "When did she ever lift a goddamn finger to do anything around the place? Whoring around with Reese and God knows who else, till we're all a laughingstock. If it was my choice, I'd a let her go and said good riddance."

"So, your plan was—what?" Price asked him. "Were you hoping that she'd catch a bullet when they saw the payoff, or did you even give that part of it a passing thought?"

"I figured we could pull it off with you along," said Schaefer. "And if not . . ." Another shrug.

"Was that your mother's plan as well?"

Schaefer retrieved his fallen hat and grimaced at another stab of pain inside his skull. "She still wants Marcy back, in spite of everything," he said. "Just couldn't raise the money."

"So you mean to go ahead with this?" asked Price.

"What else? Turn back and tell Ma I decided not to bother with it?"

"I'm just making sure," Price said. "With money in the suitcase, you had choices. This way, killing's guaranteed."

"So be it."

"And you won't be ducking it."

"I never meant to!" Schaefer challenged. "What was that you said about a change in plans?"

Price briefed him on the ghost town, still the best part of a day beyond their reach, while Schaefer cursed and shook his aching head. "Bastards!" he hissed. "I knew they'd try to pull a fast one."

"Look who's talking."

"You don't *trust* them, do you?"

"Right now, it's a toss-up which of you I trust the least," Price said. "Speaking of which, you won't mind if I hold on to your Colt a while."

"Damn right, I mind!"

"Too bad. You take first watch, and give a shout if we have any company."

"I'll keep an eye on him, if that's all right," Brooks said. He sat with Schaefer's Winchester beside him, his own rifle held across his knees.

"Suits me," Price answered, smiling to himself as he lay down to sleep. "Wake me at midnight."

Price had a plan in mind, but he wasn't prepared to share it yet. He didn't care for strangers dictating their group's departure time, but the group still needed rest before a day-long ride across the desert. If they split the difference, Price decided, it might work to their advantage in the end.

Or not.

He spent a moment listening to Schaefer, almost smiling as the ex-boss of the expedition muttered to himself. Brooks had him covered, wide awake, and midnight was only three hours away.

When Price woke up, they would be in for a surprise.

His plan was simple. They would pack their gear at midnight, fetch their horses from the livery, and leave town well ahead of time. There was a chance one of the kidnappers had stayed in San Felípe to observe them, but Price didn't think so. If Reese Johnson had his wits about him, he'd want all three of his shooters present at the rendezvous in Amorada, ready for whatever happened when the cash arrived.

The cash.

In retrospect, Price thought he should've asked to see the money back in Santa Rosa, but he'd let the moment pass. Now he could only fold or play the cards he held, and thinking of the girl he'd never met kept Price from throwing in his hand.

He didn't know what Marcy Schaefer looked like, whether she was sweet and virginal or the outrageous slut her brother made her out to be. In truth, Price didn't care. He had been hired to bring her safely home—albeit under false pretenses—and he meant to see the job done if it lay within his power.

As for getting paid, he had a few ideas on that score too.

He settled into sleep with one hand on his Peacemaker, the other hand on Schaefer's pistol, tucked into his belt. If Brooks should doze off unexpectedly, Schaefer might jump him, but the ruckus would wake Price in nothing flat. Together, they could overpower him—or shoot him, if it came to that.

In Price's mind, Schaefer was now expendable.

The job came first.

Helping a girl he'd never met for money he might never see. It made a change from bounty-hunting anyway, though so far at a higher cost of lives.

Almost asleep, he heard Schaefer whisper to Brooks, "You'd best remember where your paychecks come from, boy."

"For all I know," Brooks said, "the next one might be newspaper."

"There won't be any *next one* if you side against your betters."

" 'Betters,' is it? I weren't raised to make my sister out a whore and throw her life away."

"Damned fool. You don't know half of it."

"Reckon I know the half that counts," Brooks said. "When this is over, don't expect to see me on the Circle S."

"I'd better not."

"Meantime, there's four eyes watchin' ever' move you make, and don't forget it."

"Don't you worry, boy. I'm not forgetting anything."

They lapsed into tense silence then, yet Price felt more relaxed for what he'd heard. There'd been a chance that Schaefer might sway Brooks with threats or promises, the habit of their time together in the past, but Brooks was standing firm. He obviously felt let down, and that would carry through the last phase of their mission, with a little luck.

A little luck.

Dozing, Price thought he'd need a good deal more than that to see the sun come up the day after tomorrow. Anything could happen when they reached the ghost town, and he guessed all of it would be bad. The kidnappers were bound to be inflamed by Schaefer's trick, and it would be a toss-up whether they vented their anger first on Price's party or the girl.

Marcy.

Her disembodied name evoked no mental images for Price as he slipped closer to the realm of sleep. She had no face, and when he tried to picture her, his mind could only offer Mary's features, Mary's shape.

They're not the same.

Helping this girl wouldn't relieve the aching void he felt inside. Price knew that much, but still he felt compelled to try. For her sake.

And for his.

At last he slept, knowing that he would wake to yet another day of blood and pain.

10

"You look like hell," said Frank Bodine.

"Feel like it too."

Ed Timmons didn't think his nose was broken, but it hurt like hell and he was having trouble breathing through it, with the clotted blood inside his nostrils. That would be a bitch to clear, and every time he thought about it Timmons mouthed another curse at Jubal Schaefer, wishing that he'd put a bullet in the bastard's gut.

Later.

They had to get the money first, then see what happened. If he saw a chance for payback and he didn't have to cross Reese in the process, Timmons thought he just might take his shot.

Why not?

They'd stopped in San Felípe for a stiff shot of tequila after Timmons hobbled out of the hotel, but it had failed to dull the throbbing ache inside his skull. He hoped Schaefer was hurting just as bad after the stranger kneed him in the face, but Timmons got no satisfaction watching someone else do what *he* longed to do himself.

Just wait, you prick, he thought. *You'll have a damn headache yourself. Forty-four-caliber.*

The prospect made him smile, but that hurt too. He gave it up and tried to concentrate on the report Reese was expecting from him back at camp, but Bodine wouldn't let him focus. He wanted to talk, and Timmons didn't know a way to shut him up.

"Jubal just waded into you without a word?" Frank asked.

"We had some words," Timmons replied. "He didn't like 'em."

"I guess not. Who was the shooter pulled him offa you?"

"I didn't catch his name. Said he was temporary."

"Temporary. Huh."

"Somebody hired to help 'em bring the money down, I guess. A shooter."

"Pretty tough?" Bodine inquired.

Eight dead and Jubal laid out on the floor, he thought. *Pretty damn tough.*

"Seems like," he said.

Of course, the stranger hadn't shot all eight himself. Timmons had seen enough to know it was a group effort, and Early Brooks was going on about the men he'd killed.

"They didn't beef about the change in plans, though. That's the main thing," Bodine said.

"Not much. The stranger didn't like it, but he went along. Gave me a warning."

"Oh?"

"He made it clear they'd fight if anybody met 'em on the trail, and said they wouldn't go for any other changes in the plan."

"Jubal was out by then?"

"Out cold."

"Can't say for sure he'll buy it then. The change, I mean. He may be so pissed off about his own man drop-pin' him, he calls the whole thing off and goes back home."

"Without Marcy?"

"There's no love lost between them two," Bodine replied. "You know as well as me."

"Still, he come all this way and brought the money."

"'Cuz his mama made him do it. Mark my words on this. He don't do nothin' on his own."

"You think?"

"I'm gonna watch that bastid like a hawk at the exchange. Gun him if he so much as twitches."

"Get in line."

"You're mad he spoilt your purty face." Bodine unleashed a cackle.

"Sucker punched me's what he did. I woulda whupped him if the shooter hadn't got betwixt us."

"Maybe you'll get another chance."

"I want the money first."

"I heard that," Bodine said. "What're you gonna do with your share?"

They'd been over this before, the four of them, but Timmons couldn't seem to fix an answer in his mind. They shifted, slipped away from him like daydreams. One time, he imagined traveling back East, maybe around the world. But then, the next time he was asked, he'd thought about a nice big spread somewhere, with cattle, maybe horses on the side. Or gambling like a damned fool in New Orleans, till he'd thrown it all away and died a burned-out, happy loser.

"I been thinkin' I might go and see Tahiti."

"What the hell's Tahiti?" asked Bodine.

"It ain't a *what*," Timmons informed him. "It's a place — an island way off on the far side a the world."

"Bullshit."

"A lot you know. I read about it in a 'cyclopedia."

"Readin'. You must be tetched."

"Just 'cuz you never learned don't make it bad. Out in

Tahiti, they got skinny trees called palms, with big nuts full a milk."

"Sounds like *my* nuts," Bodine said, cackling.

Asshole. Timmons had saved the best for last. "Tahiti women run around naked, all day and night," he said.

"My ass."

"Last thing they'd wanna see, I reckon. Prob'ly think you was some kinda sea monster."

"There ain't no place like that. You made it up, or someone did."

"You're wrong," Timmons insisted. "People get there on a sailin' ship. Takes months and months without no sight a land; then up it pops, with naked women on the beach."

"Somethin' pops up, I'll bet."

"And you'd be right." It didn't hurt so much this time when Timmons smiled.

"Don't think I'd wanna be stuck on no boat for months. Storm comes along and drowns your ass, whatta you do?"

"Well, if it *drowns* your ass, you die."

"Damn right. I guess I'll spend my hunnerd thousand on dry land."

The number struck a chord with Timmons, made him frown. He shifted in his saddle, tried again to inhale through his nostrils, but it was no good.

"Tell me again," he said, "how come we're gettin' less than Reese and Abel."

"Jesus. We been over this time and again."

"You oughta know the answer then."

"All right. Reese planned the job from scratch, so he gets half. Abel's his brother. Kin always gets more."

"You're kin," Timmons reminded him.

"Third cousin on their mama's side. That ain't much blood between us really. Anyway, a hunnerd thousand bucks is more'n I ever thought I'd see."

"It's one tenth, Frank. There's only four of us."

"Don't start this now. You knew the deal when you signed on. We both did."

"Deals can change, just like Reese changed the plan."

"So ask him, if you wanna."

"I already took a beatin' that wasn't in nobody's plan. Don't tell me things can't change."

"Tell him yourself. We're almost there."

And so they were. Timmons saw firelight up ahead, and seconds later, someone called out of the night, "Who goes there?"

"Frank and Ed," Bodine called back. "We got the word."

"So bring it home, boys. Bring it home."

"You look like hell," Reese Johnson said.

"So I been told."

Firelight and shadow made the bruising more dramatic. Reese thought Timmons looked as if someone had kicked his face around the block.

"Must hurt."

"A bit." Timmons was sipping coffee, favoring a swollen lip.

"Who did it?"

"Jubal, like you'd figure."

"When he heard about the change of plan?"

"He didn't hear it."

"Say again?"

Timmons hunched forward, elbows on his knees. "He never lemme get that far. Just started goin' on about his old man bein' kilt, then sucker punched me."

"And you took it?" Abel asked him.

"*Hell,* no. I was on the way ta whuppin' him before this shooter got between us. Jubal took off on him, and then next thing ya know, the shooter knocked him out."

"Jubal's own man?"

"Ya wouldn't know it, seein' 'em together."

"What's this shooter's name?" asked Reese.

"I didn't get it."

"Jesus, Ed."

"I axed him, but he wouldn't say. Told me he's tempo-rary. Just for now."

"I know what 'temporary' means."

"Okay."

"So, Ed, what happened *after* Mr. Temporary knocked old Jubal out? You ever get around to tellin' them our terms?"

"Sure did. The stranger didn't like ridin' an extra day through hills and all, thinkin' we mean ta bushwhack him or somethin', but he got no choice."

"They bought it then?" Reese prodded.

"Right. The two of 'em."

"Which two?"

"The new man and Early. They'll have ta sell Jubal, I guess."

"There's just three of them?" Abel inquired.

"They had four, but Tom Landry got hit when them others tried takin' the money."

"Hit bad?"

"He was gut-shot."

"Fat bastard," Reese muttered. "His gut's where he lives."

"Maybe he's dead by now then," Timmons said.

"How did the money look?" asked Abel.

"Like a suitcase."

"*What?*"

Timmons recoiled. "Hey, now. Nobody said I had ta *see* the money. I axed did they have it, and they points me to a suitcase. Jesus, Reese, ya never said nothin' about—"

"Relax, Ed. It's all right. They got the money. That's what matters."

"Maybe not," said Abel. "You know Jubal's stingy ass. What if he only brought us half?"

"In that case, baby brother, you can take the rest out of his hide."

"Don't think I won't."

"I'm countin' on you," Reese replied. Turning to Timmons once again, he said, "Tell me some more about this temporary shooter."

"Well, he's on the tall side. Nothin' much to say about his face, excep' I never seen him at the Circle S before. Somebody they picked up 'cuz he can shoot, would be my guess."

"And can he?"

Timmons shrugged. "We didn't see him work first-hand, but they kilt eight betwixt 'em, tryin' for the money."

"Two men each," Reese said. "That's not so much."

"With Tommy shot," Bodine reminded him.

"Okay. We'll have to make allowances. What are they packin'?" he asked Timmons.

"Pistols. One apiece, from what I seen. Early was car-ryin' a Henry rifle. I suppose the others might have long guns too. Oh, and a shotgun on the bed, next to the suit-case."

"Nothin' special," Abel said. He spit into the fire.

"The men are what's important," Reese replied. "Jubal's a hothead, flyin' off the handle all the time. We'll need ta watch 'im. Early might've kilt some men today, but he was still a virgin when he left the Circle S. He may be shaky when the time comes, givin' us an edge."

"That leaves the new boy," said Bodine.

"The wild card," Abel echoed.

"If it starts to fall apart," Reese told them, "try'n drop him first. Don't give 'im any breathin' room, just put 'im down."

"I'll handle it," said Abel.

"*Ever'body* watch 'im. Watch 'em all."

"We only got so many eyes," said Timmons.

"Keep 'em open's all I'm sayin'. They're outnumbered as it is. Don't make no dumb mistakes."

They nodded all around the fire. Timmons was darting glances at him, small eyes flicking back and forth between his coffee cup and Reese's face.

"What's on your mind, Eddie?" Reese asked.

Timmons looked startled, gave a shifty look to Frank Bodine, then shook his head. "Nothin'."

"Frank? How 'bout you?"

"Not me. Un-uh."

"You boys got somethin' we should talk about, now's the best time to spit it out," Reese said. "I don't want any hitches when we get to Amorada, so let's hear it."

Timmons slumped lower on his rock, beside the fire. "I got a headache, Reese. Tha's all."

"Wish I could help ya out with that. There's nothin' else?"

"Naw, that's about the size of it."

"All right. I'm glad we had this little chat." Reese glanced behind him, at a small tent standing several paces from the fire. He rose, saying, "I'll go get Marcy ready for the trail. Oh, Eddie . . ."

"Huh?" Timmons peered out from underneath his hat.

"You told 'em when to leave for Amorada, yes?"

"Shore did. Six in the mornin', like you said."

"And they agreed?"

"They didn't *not* agree. Didn't say boo about it either way."

"Okay. We'll be ahead of 'em regardless."

Turning on his heel, he moved off toward the silent tent.

"When are we leaving?" Marcy asked him, sitting in the semidarkness.

"Soon," Reese said. "An hour, maybe less."

"There was trouble," she said. Not a question.

"A bit. It's all right."

"Did Jubal bring the money?"

"So I'm told."

Her face was veiled in shadow. Even sitting close, Reese had to imagine the features he'd fallen in love with. Green eyes. Bee-stung lips. Teeth so even and white they looked store-bought. Her body . . .

"This won't be the end of it," Marcy informed him.

"They're paying. I told you."

"And I'm telling you, they *will not* let it go."

They'd been through it before, with the threats. Reese was tired of it. Marcy kept pushing.

"They're *paying*," he told her again.

"You're not listening. Payment is one thing. They'll still want revenge for my father. For me."

"Then I'll deal with it."

"Jubal will hunt you wherever you go, or he'll pay men to do it."

Reese frowned in the darkness. "It's funny you say that."

"Why funny?"

"He's got a new man with him now. Eddie saw 'im."

"A gunman?"

He shrugged. "I don't know. They've got guns. There was killing."

She waited a moment, then prodded him. "Tell me."

"In town. San Felípe. Some shooters tried taking the money. They didn't get far."

"Jubal killed someone?"

"Maybe. I don't know exac'ly."

"Who else did he bring?"

"Early Brooks and Tom Landry. Tom's hit, Eddie says."

"So much blood."

"It'll be over soon."

"I hope so."

"We'll be leaving before long," he told her. "The payment's arranged."

"They'll surprise you."

"We might surprise them."

"Are we leaving now?"

"Soon." He relaxed, let his mind drift. "Remember the first time I saw you?"

"How could I? You spied on me out of the trees."

That was true. He'd been hunting on Circle S land,

tracking mule deer, and stopped by a small lake to water his pinto. A splashing noise urged him to caution and Reese had crept up through the trees, being careful, to see what was causing the sounds. He'd seen Marcy, refreshing herself with a swim in her birthday suit, glistening when she emerged from the water. The sight of her left him inflamed with an ache that still lingered inside. To possess such perfection was all he could hope for, a treasure beyond most men's reach.

"All right then. The first time we met face-to-face."

"I remember."

A barn dance. She'd come with her brother, the old folks abstaining. The young men avoided her, stunned by her beauty or terrified of her old man. Either way, Reese had felt their eyes on him as he crossed the floor, bowing low from the waist like a knight in some story, and asked her to dance. She'd been nervous but happy. She'd felt like a gift from the gods in his arms.

"Jubal hated me then," Reese recalled.

"He still does."

"But with reason." He reached out for Marcy, his fingertips grazing her cheek and the line of her jaw. "He'd go crazy to see us right now."

"Reese, he'd kill you."

"He'd try. Let's say that."

"You're no gunfighter."

"Neither is Jubal."

"But he'll hire the best," she said. "The worst."

"Forget about that now." His fingers trailed along the hollow of her throat, across her collarbone, and slipped inside the neckline of her shirt. "We got some time before we have ta ride."

"Reese, please."

"You just relax now."

Opening the first button one-handed took some effort, but the second one was easier, the third one quicker still. When he'd released the fourth, Reese eased the fabric open just enough to slip his hand inside.

"I don't feel right," she said.

"You will. Just wait." His fingers working, Stroking. Teasing. Pinching.

"No."

"You don't mean that."

He tugged the shirttail from her waistband, giving both hands room to work. Reese heard the hitch in Marcy's breathing. Felt her tremble at his touch.

"You like that."

"No," she stubbornly insisted.

"Liar."

Marcy tried to pluck his hands away, but Reese was eager now and wouldn't be denied. He leaned in closer, smelling her, and put his tongue to work.

"Damn you!"

Reese couldn't answer with his mouth full, didn't bother trying. When he heard her make that little sobbing sound, his hands dropped to the buttons of the men's pants she was wearing.

"No!"

He bit her, made her squeal. Her clawing hands retreated. She resisted, squirming, as he pulled the pants off, down her legs, and tossed them to the side. Reese wished it wasn't dark inside the tent. Next time, he'd bring a lantern.

Next time.

If there *was* a next time.

Thinking of the handoff and its dangers almost wilted him, until his fingers found her and she made a different kind of sound.

Damn Jubal and his shooter anyway.

Marcy had clamped her legs together on his hand, squirming, but Reese was stronger. Inch by inch he worked her thighs apart, then ducked between them.

"Oh! Stop that!"

She muffled his response, and that produced a tremor that ran the slim length of her body, emerging from her own throat as a gasp. She clutched his hair, twisting until the pain brought tears to Reese's eyes, but he was adamant, devouring her.

"Damn you!" she sobbed.

When Reese began to roll her over, moments later, Marcy offered no resistance. She was pliant in his hands, as if exhausted or defeated. He positioned her, moved up behind her, felt her welcome him.

"Try to be quiet now," he whispered. "We don't wanna make the others jealous."

"Christ, wouldja listen to 'em?" Bodine muttered. "It's enough to drive a man crazy."

"I don't hear nothin'," Timmons said. He washed the lie down with another sip of bitter coffee.

"Mebbe ya went deaf when Jubal slugged ya."

"Eddie's just a decent boy," said Abel, grinning from across the fire. "Don't wanna soil his virgin ears."

"Ears ain't the on'y thing about 'im tha's a virgin," said Bodine, cackling.

Timmons flushed crimson from his collar to his hairline, wishing he had nerve to throw his coffee in Frank's face and hammer him until he didn't know his own damned name. He was disgusted with himself for cringing, even with his friends. What would he do tomorrow, when the showdown came and lives depended on his nerve?

One thing for sure. He wouldn't hesitate if Jubal made a crooked move. He would remember the embarrassment and pain he felt right now, looking for an excuse to use his pistol at the handoff.

But he'd have to watch the others too. Especially the new man riding for the Circle S. They all would. That one had a look about him, as if one false move was all he needed.

That one was a killer.

Timmons felt it in his bones.

"This time tomorra, we'll be rich," said Abel. He retrieved the coffeepot and poured its dregs into his cup.

Timmons felt Bodine watching him, willing him to repeat what he'd said on the ride back from San Felípe. He bit his tongue, knowing that trouble was the last thing any of them needed at the moment. They could talk about the cut tomorrow night, after they had the money safely in their hands.

Until then, it was all just hopes and promises.

Pipe dreams.

They'd planned the operation and the payoff for the best part of a month. Now that the wait had dwindled to a day or less, Timmons had run into a private wall of disbelief. The kidnapping felt like a dream he couldn't wake from. The delivery and payoff loomed before him like a nightmare.

"Now he's poutin'," Bodine said with a chuckle.

"Go to hell, Frank."

"Boy, I been ta hell. It's where ya got no money and the women got no time."

"Someplace we'll never be again," Abel remarked.

"Amen!" Bodine emptied his coffee cup and shook it dry over the fire. He nodded toward the tent and asked, "Ya think they'll be much longer?"

"Reese is workin' off his nerves," Abel replied. "We got all night."

"We all got nerves too when ya think about it," Bodine said. "I don't s'pose he's inclined ta share."

"Feel free to ask him," Abel said with a blank expression.

"I reckon not."

"You ever seen this ghost town?" Timmons asked.

A nod from Abel. "Me'n Reese found it together 'bout a year ago. I'd guess it's gone downhill a bit since then."

"You 'fraid a ghosts, Eddie?"

Bodine reached out to poke him in the ribs, and Timmons slapped his hand away. "Fuck you!"

"No, thanks, darlin'." Another cackle.

"What's it like?" Timmons asked Abel. "The town, I mean."

"About what you'd expect. Old run-down buildin's. Snakes and lizards."

"How'd you know its name?"

"We asked around in San Felípe," Abel said. "Somebody said it use ta be a mining camp. There ain't much to it."

"Long as we got cover," Bodine interjected, "if there's trouble."

"Cover's not a problem."

"Were there any people?" Timmons asked.

"Eddie, I tole ya. It's a *ghost* town."

"Dead people, he means." Bodine raised clawed hands in the air and made a ghostly moaning sound.

"I don't remember any dead folks," Abel said. "I saw some rabbit bones. Looked like coyote leavin's."

"I just wondered if the Messicans go in there," Timmons said. "Or drifters. We don't want no interruptions."

"There'll be time to check it out," said Abel. "Ridin' steady, we should have a half day's jump on Jubal."

"If we ever saddle up," Bodine complained.

"Don't take it hard," Abel told him. "Marcy ain't your type, or you ain't hers."

"The hell you know about my *type*? You sayin' I ain't good enough to please some snooty bitch?"

"You got the charm. I'll give you that."

"Charm, hell. Young thing like that just needs a firm hand on the bridle, till she learns her lessons right."

"I never saw you as a teacher," Abel told him.

"All depends," Bodine replied. "With this'un now, I might use spurs. She looks all gentle, but I reckon she can buck. I just might have ta—"

"What?" Reese stood above them. He'd been quiet coming from the tent, but now his tone made Timmons smile into his coffee cup.

"Oh, nothin'," Bodine answered, shoulders hunched as if in expectation of a blow. "We just got talkin' about mustangs. Breakin' 'em and all."

"You turned into a bronco buster, Frank?"

"Mebbe."

Reese laughed. "Well, saddle up the horse you got right now. We're ridin' out as soon as we break camp." He turned to Timmons. "Eddie, would you take the tent down?"

"Sure, Reese."

Glancing that way, he saw Marcy Schaefer standing by the tent flap. She was dressed just as he'd seen her last, nothing to signal what she'd been through but some tangles in her hair, maybe a rosy glint that wasn't firelight on her cheeks.

"Appreciate it, son."

Reese moved off toward the horses. Timmons scrambled to his feet and left his coffee cup beside the fire, avoiding Marcy's eyes as he approached the tent. She stopped him with a soft hand on his sleeve.

"Eddie, you're hurt."

"It ain't bad."

"Jubal did that?"

He shrugged. "We mixed it up a little bit."

"I'm sorry."

Timmons blinked at her. "Not your fault."

"Can I help you with the tent?"

"It's easy."

"Well, then."

"Marcy!" Reese called her from the shadows, out beyond the fire. "We need to saddle up."

Reese snickered over that, and Abel punched him on the shoulder. Marcy moved away as Timmons started breaking down the tent, pulling its pegs and placing them inside the canvas, which he folded to the size and shape of a bedroll. Finally, he tied it off and hoisted it beneath one arm, going to fetch his things.

They had a long night ride ahead of them, but it would be daylight before they reached the ghost town. Timmons wasn't worried about spirits—not much anyway—but he preferred a clear view of the place before they settled in to wait for Jubal and the others.

If they came.

Why wouldn't they?

He thought about the trouble between Jubal and his shooter. Would the new man quit if Jubal pushed him, or haul off and put a bullet in the rancher's son? In either case, Timmons supposed the ransom payment would be jeopardized, and all their risk would be for nothing.

Reese had his horse and Marcy's saddled by the time Timmons retrieved his gear and joined them. Abel and Bodine were kicking dirt over the fire, checking the camp for anything they might've left behind. Ten minutes, give or take, and they'd be on their way.

Timmons drew comfort from his weapons, even as he prayed he wouldn't have to use them. All he wanted was the money and some room to breathe.

He hoped that wouldn't be too much to ask.

II

Price woke five minutes early, to a scene of silent tension that was gratifying. Brooks was hanging in there, stung by the deception that had prompted so much bloodletting. He didn't have the Henry aimed at Schaefer, but its muzzle hovered near enough that he could aim and fire without a heartbeat's hesitation.

Price wondered what Brooks would do for work when they were finished, then decided that the kid would likely get along all right.

It wasn't Price's problem anyway.

Brooks had been looking for adventure, and he'd found it. Now he had to reconcile the fantasy with stark reality.

And they weren't finished yet.

Price rose, both of them watching him. Brooks visibly relaxed, now that he didn't have to watch Schaefer alone.

"We're leaving soon," Price said. "We have a fair day's ride ahead of us, and likely killing at the end of it. The men who have your sister," he reminded Schaefer, "are expecting money and you brought them scrap paper. They'll want to take it out on anybody they can reach."

"So, let them try it," Schaefer answered.

"That's the problem. Normally, I'd say that three-to-four was decent odds, but we can't go in fighting one another and expect to walk out on the other side."

"Get to the point."

"It's this: I'm bound to try bringing your sister back, if she's alive, but neither one of us"—a nod toward Brooks—"can sheepdog you and fight at the same time. If I can't trust you till it's over, I'd prefer to leave you here."

"You can't believe I'd wait for—" Schaefer seemed to read the look on Price's face and understand Price didn't mean to leave him breathing. He swallowed hard, then told them, "Damn you both. I'm no backshooter, but I mean to finish this. I owe you, Price."

"You'll have a chance to pay me," Price replied. "Right now, or when the job's done."

"Now?" The strength had dribbled out of Schaefer's voice.

Price palmed the rancher's Colt and tossed it back to him. The catch was awkward, muzzle pointing up toward Schaefer's chin, but he made no move to secure a better grip. Instead, he made a show of easing it around, slipping the gun into his empty holster.

"When we're finished, like I said," he muttered.

"It's a date," Price answered, "if we're still alive."

He glanced at Brooks and saw the young man's subtle nod. Price knew that Brooks would watch his back, and would expect the same from him. It was an awkward way to travel, openly mistrusting one man out of three, but Price was strapped for nonviolent alternatives.

"All right," he said, "let's go."

They cleared the room, walked past its bullet-riddled neighbor, and descended to the lobby, Schaefer leading on the stairs. He couldn't pull a trick that way, and if a trap was waiting down below, he'd be the one to spring it.

There was nothing, not even a clerk behind the registration desk, where blood from Price's lucky shot had stained the wallpaper a rusty brown. The cantinas were still doing business, smoke and music wafting from their open doors, but Price's party had the main street to themselves.

It was a short walk to the livery. Price watched the darkened alleys, doors, and windows on their route, while Brooks watched Schaefer. No one challenged them along the way, and their arrival roused the stable boy from his small quarters near the entrance. Even tousle-haired and sleepy, he still knew enough to smile for gringo customers.

"You want to settle for the extra horses now or take them with us?" Price asked Schaefer.

"I don't care."

"We'll leave two then, and take the other three along in case we need fresh mounts."

"It ain't that far," Brooks said.

"Still makes a long walk back," Price told him, "if your animal gets shot from under you."

"Oh, right."

The boy agreed to Price's offer, putting on a brighter smile, and went to saddle their three horses. Price and Brooks picked out the other three to take along, Schaefer feigning indifference. Price chose a sorrel; Brooks picked out a pinto for himself and a bay mare for his ex-boss. The packhorse made it seven, with the suitcase on its back.

The stable boy was good. He had them saddled up and ready for the road in twenty minutes flat. Moonlight showed them the way, and San Felípe dwindled slowly on their backtrail as the riders traveled south.

They rode in silence, Brooks alert to any move from Schaefer, while Price ran the sequence of events in his head. The kidnappers had told them to leave town at six o'clock, predicting their arrival in the ghost town around dusk. Call it a thirteen-hour ride, with minor stops along the way. Leaving at midnight ought to put them on the scene by early afternoon.

And then what?

Price assumed their adversaries would arrive before them and be waiting, possibly expecting tricks on Schaefer's part. Daylight would make it harder, moving into Amorada unobserved, but Price imagined it could still be done. With care and discipline, some planning in advance, they had at least a chance to infiltrate and turn the tables on their enemies.

Were they his enemies?

Price didn't like kidnappers, but they'd stolen no one near or dear to him. Without a hard cash offer, he wouldn't have volunteered to join the party, much less guarantee rough justice for the other side. He could've ridden out and left the others over Schaefer's double-dealing with the ransom and the threat that Price himself would not get paid, yet something made him stick.

What was it?

Surely not a girl he'd never seen, whose body could be lying in a shallow desert grave. Price didn't think he'd gone that soft.

And yet . . .

Another thought of Mary came to him unbidden, piercing Price's heart. He wondered if the pain would ever go away, then caught himself and hoped it wouldn't. Some days, he believed that only hurting made him human.

But there'd be no room for weakness at the end, when they were facing Marcy Schaefer's kidnappers. It would be blood and thunder then, after the suitcase was opened and the badmen got their rude surprise.

As for her brother, Price would face that problem if and when he had to, without thinking twice. Maybe delivering a daughter balanced out taking a son.

But what then if the girl was dead already, and Price had to kill her brother to protect himself? What of Joan Schaefer, waiting for her children at the Circle S?

Price shook his head resignedly.

In that case, he supposed that he wouldn't be going back for his ten grand.

       •   •   •

Brooks broke the silence of their moonlight ride two hours south of San Felípe. "Have you thought about the ghost town? How we're gonna work it?" he asked Price.

"A bit," Price said. "We can't make any solid plans until we've seen the place."

"Oh, sure."

"Brilliant, that is," groused Schaefer.

Price ignored him, while Brooks settled for a dirty look. "You think they'll try ta jump us goin' in?" the young man asked.

"Depends on what they have in mind," Price answered. "If the girl's all right and they intend a straight exchange, there's no good reason for them shooting first. Of course, their errand boy may still be mad about his nose."

"Smart bastard had it coming," Schaefer said. "Lucky I didn't gun him down on sight."

Lucky for us, Price thought, *and lucky for your sister.* But they'd covered that already, and he kept it to himself.

"You plan on sneakin' into town?" Brooks asked. "Is that the way it's done?"

"There's no set way, but we could use an edge," Price said. "The odds aren't terrible, but they'll have cover and they'll know the ground. Better than we do anyway."

"But if there's no ambush—"

Price interrupted him. "I said there's no percentage in bushwhacking *if* the girl's healthy and *if* they want a straight exchange. We can't predict a thing right now."

"You still think Marcy might be dead?" The prospect seemed to sadden Brooks.

"Best we can do on that is keep our fingers crossed," Price answered.

"Sure. What did you mean by sayin' 'if they want a straight exchange'?"

Price shrugged. "Sometimes kidnappers get what they asked for, and they're not satisfied. They figure if the money's paid too easily, they should've asked for more."

"Well, *that* won't happen," Brooks said dourly.

"Others that I've heard of changed their minds for different reasons."

"Such as what?" The question came from Schaefer, sounding curious and angry all at once.

"You tell me this Reese Johnson loved your sister, or believed he did."

"You call it love?"

"I didn't pick the word," Price answered, "but it doesn't matter what you call it. If he feels the same today, he may decide that it would be a shame to let her go at any price."

"If that trash reckons he can keep her, after I've paid—"

"Nothing," Price interjected. "You brought newspaper, remember?"

"It's the principle," said Schaefer, drawing a derisive snort from Brooks.

"My point is," Price continued, "that they might not want to give her back, even if there was money in the bag."

"Just *keep* her?" Schaefer seemed to be caught somewhere between disbelief and outrage. "Why?"

"I'm no mind reader," Price assured him. "Because of Johnson's feelings, like I said, or some idea we won't know anything about until they spring it on us."

"I suppose we'll have ta kill 'em either way," Brooks said.

"Damn right!" said Schaefer from the sidelines. "We can't let them get away with this!"

Price frowned. "My guess would be they'll fight regardless, when they've seen inside the bag. Unless they want to hurt the girl first, as a lesson."

"Let 'em try it," Brooks replied. He sounded older, braver than his years. It made Price wonder if he had an eye for Schaefer's sister too.

It was a small world at the Circle S.

"There may not be much we can do to help her right away," Price said. "They've got a town of sorts to hide her in, and we should figure she'll be guarded if she's not at the exchange. One word from Johnson, or a wrong move on our part, and she could end up paying for it."

"How can we help her then?"

"It's part of why I want to scout the town before we meet them," Price replied. "If we can spot her first and drop whoever's watching her, the scrap paper won't matter."

"And we win," Brooks said.

Price yanked the rein on his enthusiasm. "That's just part of it. We'd have to deal with any who were left."

"But saving Marcy is the big thing, right?"

"She isn't saved until we've dealt with all the kidnappers," Price answered. "One way or another."

"Only one way's good for them," said Schaefer.

"And we'll likely have to do it, thanks to you." Price turned to Brooks once more. "Don't get your hopes up, Early. It's a rough game, and we're bluffing. We've got nothing in the hole except raw nerve."

"Then that'll have ta be enough," Brooks said.

Price sometimes marveled at the optimism of the young. Confronted with a situation where he knew he'd have to fight four men and bet a woman's life against his trigger finger, Brooks was busy looking on the bright side.

Even riding through the moonlight, Price could only see the dark.

I'm getting too damned old for this, he thought. Late thirties made him aged for a gunfighter. Time hadn't altered his reaction time or dimmed his eye yet, but he felt the weight of years and actions that no decent sort of man would brag about.

Price wasn't frightened, though perhaps he should've been. Incessant thoughts of personal mortality came with the territory he inhabited. Again, he didn't fear death as some people did, but neither would he welcome it.

Enough.

For now, he had a job to occupy his mind, finessing details that would be concealed from him until the last moment. With any luck, Price thought, he would succeed.

And if he failed, at least he wouldn't go alone.

They stopped at dawn to rest the animals and feed themselves. It was a strange experience, time falling out of joint as sunrise took the place of midday on the last leg of their journey. Brooks fried bacon, served on hardtack biscuits and washed down with water from a nearby spring that had a taste of rusty knife blades.

Price enjoyed watching the sun rise in the east. It meant he had survived another night, and if the day ahead posed challenges, at least he had a fighting chance. Whatever happened, there were always possibilities. It was the nearest thing to optimism that he dared allow himself.

"I guess we're halfway there," Brooks said to no one in particular.

"Should be," Price answered him. "Within an hour, give or take."

The fork Ed Timmons had predicted in their road was nearly four hours behind them. They'd continued south as he instructed, passing by the road to Ojos Verdes, holding true. He'd been correct about the southern track beyond that point. It "seemed to peter out" indeed, dwindling within a quarter mile to half its former width, its surface pitted and neglected, seldom used by all appearances.

"I guess nobody goes here anymore," Brooks had suggested when they marked the change.

No one but kidnappers and us, Price thought.

They hadn't asked about the ghost town back in San Felípe, leery as they were of putting other vultures on their trail. Price didn't know its story and he didn't care, except insofar as the knowledge might have helped him stay alive. A street plan would've been ideal, but he would have to plan the action as he went along and hope the others followed where he led.

Brooks wouldn't be a problem, he supposed. But Schaefer . . .

Never mind. If Schaefer caused a problem in the ghost town, Price would deal with him by any means required to settle it and keep the other two of them alive. He felt no debt of honor to the rancher. Oddly, that had shifted, when he wasn't looking, to the faceless person of a girl he'd never met.

"Daylight'll be against us," Brooks remarked around a mouthful of hardtack.

"It will," Price granted, "but the good news is, they're not expecting us till dusk. I'd bet on posted guards, but if there's only four of them and things work out the way I hope, we still might manage to surprise them."

"What things? Work out how?" Brooks asked.

"Jesus," growled Schaefer, "can't you just this once shut up?"

"I weren't talkin' to you," Brooks answered stiffly. "Matt?"

"The basics," Price replied, "are getting past the guards and looking for the hostage. I'd prefer not going through some kind of formal meeting in the street, since we've got nothing left to bargain with."

"All right!" Schaefer complained. "You've made your point about the money, damn it!"

Price ignored him, telling Brooks the obvious, in hopes that it would ease the young man's nerves. "If we can find the girl before they spot us, we've got half our problem solved. But failing that, we still might thin their numbers, maybe even turn the tables on the ransom."

"What's that mean?" asked Brooks, confused.

"Right now, they've got the hostage holed up, God knows where. They're counting on us to deliver payment sight unseen, and maybe wait while they go fetch the girl. Turn that around, we find a place to hide the bag their errand boy described to them, and we've got leverage."

Brooks didn't see it yet. "Because . . . ?"

"God help us," Schaefer said.

"Because they *think* we've got the money," answered Price. "They'll want to see it, but we'll say it's hidden somewhere. We won't tell them where it is until we've seen the girl alive and well."

"But there's no—"

"Money, right. That's where we bluff."

"They could start shootin' then."

"Not knowing where the ransom is? I don't think so. They'd never find it if we're dead."

"Okay. I get it now."

"Praise God and pass the chicken," Schaefer jeered, rolling his eyes.

Brooks flushed, trying to hide it with a scowl, but dawn's pink light accented the pink color of his cheeks.

It would be full daylight within another quarter hour, clearly marking them for anyone who watched the trail. Price didn't think the kidnappers would post a guard that far from Amorada, but they might not be the only threat remaining on his trek.

"We need to go," he said, rising.

Brooks scrambled after Price, while Schaefer stalled just long enough to make it feel like insubordination. Price ignored the petty gesture of defiance, mounted, and looped the sorrel's lead around his saddle horn. Soon they were on the move together, Price setting a pace that wouldn't risk laming their horses on the poor, untended road. They had five hours, maybe six to go, and it would soon be hot enough to fry eggs on the sandy desert's stones.

Price hoped they'd have a decent glimpse of Amorada from a distance, further hoping that its former occupants had built their habitation on the flats. If it was planted on a hill or squeezed into a canyon like some little towns he'd known, the plan for a covert approach would likely have to be discarded.

Give me room to work, he thought, not certain who he thought was listening.

If he could study Amorada from a distance, plot its layout, scout the town's perimeter unseen, Price reckoned he could find a way inside that wouldn't get them shot on the approach. From that point forward, it would be a cutthroat game of hide-and-seek until they found the prize or met their enemies.

The nagging thought that there might be no prize returned to trouble him. If Jubal's sister was already dead, their search.was doomed to failure and could only end in blood.

But if she was alive . . .

In that case, Marcy Schaefer was both prize and peril. Once committed to retrieving her at any cost, they'd have to pay the tab. Fifteen lives had been squandered from the night of the kidnapping—maybe sixteen now, with Landry—and Price saw no end to the killing. Today should pay all, but at what cost in bloodshed?

Whatever it takes, Price thought.

He focused on the bleak horizon, waiting for a glimpse of Amorada in the distance. They were headed for a ghost town, and smart money said there would be more ghosts in the village when they left.

Unless they stayed to join the haunted cast.

By noon, long hours in the saddle and relentless desert heat had sapped most of their energy. Price felt it, pitying the roan that carried him. They stopped briefly each hour and a half to dole out water for the horses from their spare canteens. Long treks through arid lands had taught Price to equip himself, but there was no escaping from the brutal sun.

"Damn crazy place to meet somebody," Brooks complained while watering the packhorse. "Snakes don't even like it."

"They're here," Price said. "But they come out at night, just like the men we're looking for."

"No wonder they got ghost towns," Brooks continued on his carping theme. "No good for crops or cattle.

Nothin' in the ground but weeds and cactus. Makes me wonder who'da built a town out here'n the first place."

"All we need to know is that they're gone. No witnesses, no townsfolk in the cross fire."

"And nobody helpin' us," Brooks said.

"You left help at the Circle S. We're on our own."

"Suppose we ain't enough."

Price shrugged. "We lose, and you move on from one adventure to the next."

"Jesus."

"Maybe. I wouldn't know."

"You ever think about what happens . . . after?"

"Not if I can help it," Price replied. He capped the half-empty canteen and wound its strap around his saddle horn. "Starting to think like that before a fight, you give too much away."

"I guess. It still preys on my mind sometimes."

Price checked to see that Schaefer wasn't eavesdropping. "Word of advice," he said. "You're three days on the killing road and worried that you might not see tomorrow. If it troubles you that much already, you should think about another line of work when you split from the Circle S."

"How'd *you* handle it?" asked Brooks.

"First thing, I didn't go out looking for a fighting job. It snuck up on me, more or less; then I was in the middle of it. Once you get a name for killing, there's no easy way to shake it off. As for the worry, some folks feel it more than others."

"So, you're never scared?"

"I didn't say that," Price replied. "But when you've lost enough, it doesn't seem to matter anymore."

"Like giving up," Brooks said.

Price shook his head. "When you give up, there's no fight left. The other fella walks over you and moves on to the next damned fool in line."

"You talk like it's some kinda game."

"It is," Price said. "Each time you ante up, you bet your life against the other fellow's."

"But for what?"

"Depends. In bounty work and such, it's for the cash. You spot a man with money on his head or pick a side that pays you for your skills. Range wars aren't what they used to be, of course. It's not a field with room for lots of growth, professionally speaking."

"And the rest?"

"You get a reputation; someone coming on behind you wants to top it. Try to hide, most times they'll find you anyway. They push it. Only one of you can walk away."

"You put it that way," Brooks observed, "it don't sound much like livin'."

"No," Price said. "But by the time most shooters work that out, they're too far down the road to turn around."

"I need ta chaw on this a while."

"Do that," Price said. "There's nothing here to hold you, now you've quit the Circle S."

"I didn't mean that." Brooks seemed anxious to correct him. "We gotta help Miss Marcy first. I just meant afterwards."

I hope you get the chance, Price thought. He mounted, waited while the others climbed into their saddles, then resumed the long ride south.

They were committed to the journey, each for different reasons. Schaefer had his family honor to uphold, although he didn't seem as worried for his sister's welfare as another might've been. Brooks likely harbored feelings for the hostage that he'd never share now that he'd burned his bridges to the Circle S.

And Price? Why was he sticking, when his promised fee looked more and more like smoke driven before a rising wind?

The simple answer would've been *for Mary*. Price had failed her when she needed him the most, and some folks might assume that he was working off the debt with

Marcy Schaefer, maybe even focused on their similarity of names.

Maybe.

But Price himself wasn't convinced.

He'd started for the money, but the job had turned to something else. It made a change from tracking misfits back and forth across the country, or enlisting with some rancher to keep greedy neighbors off his land.

Price didn't know about redemption, only what he'd heard from preachers as a child, and most of them weren't anything to brag about outside of church. They thrived on telling other people how to live, but when push came to shove, they were as soiled as anybody else. On rare occasions when he thought about it, Price believed in something greater than himself, but nothing much he'd seen on Earth so far gave evidence of any guiding hand.

Men did what they could get away with, for the most part. Women too. A few, in his experience, served others out of some compulsive need they couldn't shake, but saints were rare and commonly short-lived. It was a safe bet there'd be none in Amorada keeping score.

The cruel sun was an hour past its midday peak when Brooks called out, "I see it! Up ahead, there."

Squinting in the shade of his hat brim, Price followed Brooks's pointing finger toward a brown smudge squatting in the heat haze, still three quarters of a mile away.

"You think that's it?" asked Schaefer, momentarily forgetting that he hated them.

"We'll take for granted that it is," Price said. "Stay sharp now. Every step you take from this point on could get you killed."

12

Amorada hadn't been a large town when it was alive, and Price assumed the desert had reclaimed some portion of it in the years since it expired. The buildings that remained appeared through his spyglass as dusty, dried-out shells that might stand for another hundred years or flatten like a house of cards with the next breeze. From where he sat, a quarter mile due west, the place revealed no signs of life.

Which didn't mean that someone wasn't staring back at him, thinking one step ahead.

"Keep going," he instructed Brooks and Schaefer. "Slowly. We don't need a dust storm."

"We should leave the extra horses then," Schaefer replied.

"We'll find a place. Go on, now."

Schaefer went, albeit grudgingly. He seemed to have new energy about him, now that they had reached the ghost town, more or less. Price wondered whether that was eagerness to bring his sister out, or if the rancher had some other reason he was holding back.

They circled slowly southward, then turned east. When they'd completed half a circuit of the town, Price paused to use his glass again. He still saw nothing that suggested active human habitation, but he guessed the kidnappers were smart enough to take basic precautions. Hide their horses. Keep themselves tucked under cover during daylight hours. Whisper if they had to talk—or better yet, keep still.

As quiet as the dead.

They circled further still, back toward their starting point. Brooks seemed to know what Price was doing, whereas Schaefer didn't care. The rancher chafed at waiting, leading Price to think he'd never learned about postponing satisfaction as a child. Spoiled brats at any age were difficult to handle, but in killing situations they were fatal liabilities.

Price made his third stop east of town, wanting to know that he had checked all compass points before he chose their angle of attack. So far, the best approach was from the west. The town's one street was laid out on a north-south axis, with narrow east-west alleys serving in place of cross streets. Watchers would be expecting Schaefer's party from the north, and might direct a sharp eye southward, just in case some drifter came along to interrupt the party. On the eastern side, Price counted seven windows in assorted buildings, turning dusty eyes toward mountains at his back, and knew that any one of them could hide a spy.

The western side, however, boasted only two windows along its entire length. Price didn't understand that flaw, but rather simply recognized that it was so. He couldn't rule out watchers in those windows, but their odds were better coming from the west than from the other compass points.

If they were spotted, they would know it soon enough.

"We're going back," he told the others. "Come in from the west side."

Brooks made no complaint as they retraced their steps. Schaefer was muttering under his breath, but Price ignored him, hoping that they wouldn't have to shoot it out right there, when they were so close to the prize.

They spent another twenty minutes riding back, taking it slowly, kicking up as little dust as possible. The west side had one extra benefit that Price had noted on their first pass, namely a small stand of cottonwoods where they could leave their mounts with shade and forage for a day.

But what if none of them returned?

Price had a soft spot for the animals and didn't want them baking into buzzard pie if he and his companions never made it out of Amorada. When they reached the cottonwoods, he used slipknots to tie them, giving them the option of escape if they were spooked by something serious—or if the men didn't return and they began to starve.

Price unsaddled his roan as a final precaution, took his Winchester, and slipped an extra box of ammunition into a vest pocket. As he finished, Price saw Schaefer waiting with a rifle in his right hand, suitcase in his left.

"You're bringing that?" Price asked.

"Why not?"

"There's nothing in it worth the sweat."

"It's *my* sweat," Schaefer said. "Timmons will have them watching for the bag."

"We ain't suppose ta let 'em see us comin'," Brooks reminded him.

"I'm bringing it."

"Your call," Price said. "Keep up and don't make any noise."

They left the sparse shade of the cottonwoods and walked toward Amorada at a steady pace. Running the quarter mile to town was pointless. It would only leave them sick with heat stroke, raise more dust, and risk drawing attention to themselves. Better to walk the distance, watching out for snipers as they closed the gap and hoping that they wouldn't be observed.

An added benefit of coming from the west was that they had the sun on their side of the ghost town, blazing in a would-be watcher's eyes and raising shimmer-waves of heat haze to distort their images as they approached. It was the best that Price could do in terms of camouflage, hoping their enemies were spread so thin in Amorada that the western flank might go unguarded.

No one challenged them as they approached the old ramshackle buildings, standing slumped against each other in the afternoon heat. Long shadows stretched away beyond them, eastward, as the sun inched lower in the sky.

Price reached the nearest alleyway, slipped into shadow there, and started creeping toward the street.

Ed Timmons didn't have a headache anymore. He'd slept it off last night and awakened to find the pain had settled in his nose. It wasn't much of an improvement, but he'd take what he could get, waiting for Jubal and the rest to come along and make him filthy rich.

He'd taken Frank Bodine's advice to heart about the money. It was better to collect the ransom first and deal with any tricks Jubal might have in mind, before starting a quarrel about the split. For all he knew, one of the others might be dead by then, and he could argue for a bigger share on that basis, without offending anyone.

Reese had assigned him as a lookout on the eastern side of town, perched in the upstairs window of what looked to be a played-out brothel. Timmons judged it by the swaybacked beds left standing in the small rooms and the bar downstairs, which told him that it wasn't a hotel.

The thought of sweaty people rutting on those tangled, faded sheets did nothing to arouse him. Every place he'd been in Amorada smelled of rats and dry rot. Scorpions and spiders nested in the corners. Now and then, a tumbleweed distracted him from staring at the mountains, ten or fifteen miles away, but otherwise his watch was un-eventful.

Reese had begun to fret, now that the game was nearly over, all their cards thrown in. He worried about bandits and Apaches, about *federales*, about Jubal sneaking up on them somehow. He'd even talked about a flash flood once that morning, even though the sky revealed no clouds. Timmons could understand a certain nervousness—he felt a bit of it himself, in fact—but he'd begun to think Reese might've lost his grip.

Marcy.

She could do that to a man, just looking at him in that way she had, and Reese had done a damn sight more than looking since they'd snatched her from the Circle S. Timmons swallowed the sour bile of envy, concentrating on the threat Reese posed to their collection of the money if he lost his nerve.

Jubal might smell his fear and act accordingly, springing some kind of trap at the last minute. Sucker punches were his specialty, and Timmons meant to watch him closely, finger on the trigger, just in case. The first sign of a double cross would send him blazing into action, and to hell with Reese. Somebody had to watch out for the money, now that it was almost in their hands.

Almost.

A hundred different things could still go wrong, of course. Jubal and his new shooter could've fallen out and killed each other back in San Felípe. Early wouldn't try to pay the ransom by himself, Timmons was sure of that. Which meant that they could sit and wait forever without seeing one red cent.

That prospect troubled Timmons for a moment; then he put it out of mind. Jubal might be a sneaky, spiteful bastard, but he wasn't stupid. If he didn't mean to pay for Marcy, he'd have stayed home on the Circle S, instead of riding into Baja with a suitcase full of money.

Suitcase.

Abel had surprised him last night, in their camp, asking Timmons if he had seen *inside* the bag. Before that moment, there'd been no doubt in his mind that Jubal had the money, that he'd pay them every dime demanded for his sister.

But since then . . .

Timmons gnawed a ragged fingernail, trying to figure out what kind of rotten trick Jubal might have in mind to spring on them when they were least expecting it. He thought about a suitcase filled with dynamite, rigged to explode when it was opened, but that made no sense. He had to know they'd check the money first, at the exchange, when he was standing right in front of them.

Not dynamite.

But something . . .

He bit and twisted, spit a tiny sliver of himself onto the dusty floor. No matter how he riddled it, Timmons couldn't devise a trap that snared them all while letting Jubal and his shooters off the hook. Whatever happened at the trade-off, Mr. Jubal Schaefer would be standing close enough to feel the muzzle-blast when Timmons shot him if he tried the slightest little thing.

"Relax," he told the empty room. "It's gonna be all right."

He watched the desert, shadows lengthening across it, hiding features of the land that he'd already memorized. A cactus here, an orphan boulder there. Another tumbleweed came bouncing in the opposite direction from the last one he had seen, alerting Timmons to a shifting wind.

"Blow me some money," he beseeched the breeze. "I'm ready to be rich."

And he'd be ready too if Jubal tried to pull a fast one at the finish line. Ready and waiting to repay last night's assault with interest.

Looking forward to that prospect, Timmons didn't realize that he'd begun to smile.

•   •   •

The alley offered shade, but no real respite from the heat. Its dead air tasted stale to Price, as if no breeze had stirred it in the past five years. He smelled the nearby buildings rotting from within, a process slowed by baking in the desert sun for twelve to fifteen hours every day.

The others crowded in behind him, Schaefer with his suitcase dragging down one shoulder. Brooks was jumpy, but he tried to cover it. Price wondered whether it was worse for him this time, preparing to kill men he knew, but it wasn't the time or place for questions of that nature.

Leaning close to his companions so he barely had to whisper, Price reminded them, "We don't know where the others are, or if they're covering the street. They may shoot first, or call a parley. Watch your step. Remember why we're here." To Schaefer, he remarked, "You brought the bag. Now if you're smart, you'll leave it here."

"I need to hide it someplace," Schaefer said. "To bargain with."

Damn fool. "Be quick about it then," Price told him. "And be *quiet*."

At the alley's mouth, Price paused again. Only a small slice of the street was visible without emerging from concealment. Price examined it as best he could, noting the blank-eyed windows of a shop directly opposite. Its door was off the hinges, letting dust blow in and out, but Price saw nothing to suggest an enemy was hiding in the shadows there.

Of course, that didn't mean one *wasn't*.

Once he left the alley, Price would be exposed to fire from dozens of potential sniper's nests. Each doorway, window, rooftop, or the like could hide a gunman, waiting for the chance to take him down. Although they were expected for the handoff, their approach by stealth was not in keeping with a spirit of cooperation. Price, in the kidnappers' place, would take it as a hostile move and act accordingly.

Which meant they might be shot on sight.

But crouching in the alley, they would never find the girl.

Price turned to Brooks and raised two fingers as he mouthed the words, "Two minutes after me." Brooks nodded understanding, crouching with the Henry clutched against his chest.

Price risked a look around the corner, left and right, then eased from cover into daylight barely shaded by a narrow overhang of roof. He inched along the wooden sidewalk, felt it sag beneath him as he tried to cover every threat at once. It was impossible and wracked his nerves, until Price let it go and concentrated on the search.

There was no system to it, no advance plan, since they hadn't known the layout of the town when they arrived. Price meant to search the buildings in his path, while Brooks and Schaefer went the other way, along the same side of the street. It would take time, and when they finished—*if* they finished—they would have to cross the street and start again.

Somewhere along the way, they should meet members of the kidnap gang or find their hostage. Price couldn't predict if the abductors would be on alert or sleeping at their posts, but he anticipated mortal risk with every step he took.

The first place Price explored had been a dry goods store, according to the painted legend flaking from its window. The door stood half open and he shouldered it aside, mouthing a curse as rusty hinges squealed. To Price, the sound was like a woman's scream, cracking the ghost town's eerie silence.

Price edged out of sight, into the vacant shop. He scanned the drab interior in seconds flat, saw nothing that endangered him, then turned to watch the street. He waited, but no one emerged from hiding to investigate the noise.

Which didn't mean no one had *heard* it.

Price waited another moment, then admitted to himself that he couldn't spot enemies from where he stood unless they moved, did something to reveal themselves. A hidden sniper could lie waiting for him to emerge, and Price would have no inkling of the threat until he stepped across the threshold and a bullet cut him down.

All right then. Get to work.

He searched the store in less than sixty seconds. Two rooms were the full extent of it, both stripped of merchandise and furniture. In the back room, a sidewinder had turned an empty wooden crate into her nest. It seethed with little replicas of Mama, tiny forked tongues scenting Price as they recoiled in unison and shook their silent rattle-buds.

Price left them to their creeping lives and walked back to the open doorway. Stepping through could be his final act on Earth, but he would never know unless he tried it, and he couldn't stay forever in the dusty shop. Even the baby snakes would leave soon, wriggling out to face the world.

Price cocked his rifle, stepped out of the store—and felt no bullet ripping through his flesh. Embarrassed by the flush of sweet relief, he moved on to the next shop on his right. Glass from its shattered window crunched beneath his boot heels, telling Price the window had been broken from inside. No trace of explanation lingered in the dust before him, but a small sign on the door told Price the place had been a restaurant. He tried the door and found it locked, then doubled back and stepped in through the vacant window frame.

More dust, disturbed in little trails by shadow-dwellers who most likely did their hunting after sundown. Price didn't know what they were, and he didn't much care. He searched the dining room and kitchen, found no one to challenge him, and moved back to the street with greater confidence this time.

There was no sign of Brooks or Schaefer on the street as he emerged. Price left them to their work and went back to his own, searching for Marcy Schaefer and the men who'd stolen her from home.

* * *

"How do you know they'll come?" asked Marcy. Sitting by the window, face in shadow while the sunlight shone across her rumpled trousers, she could pass at first glance for a boy in his teens. It took a second, closer look to note the woman-curves beneath her baggy clothes.

"They'll come," Reese told her for the hundredth time, "because they want you back. Because your mama won't allow them *not* to come."

"But Jubal—"

"Never mind now."

Reese turned from the window, tired of staring at the desert while the sun went down, and went to sit beside her on the floor. He wished they'd picked a furnished room, but he'd been looking for a clear view of the road that entered Amorada from the north. He'd spent a long day watching and could only spare a moment from the task, but Marcy drew him as a magnet draws a rusty scrap of iron.

"Don't worry so much, girl. It puts lines in your face."

"I want this finished."

"Everybody does," he said.

"I want it finished *now*." That whine he hated, even though he'd never found the nerve to mention it.

"These things take time."

"What will you do after they pay you?"

"Just what we agreed."

"Promise?"

"You have my word."

She laughed at that.

"What's funny?" Reese demanded.

"You're a kidnapper and killer," she replied.

"And rapist. Don't forget that part."

"I won't."

"But have I ever lied to you?" He smiled.

"You might've. How would I know?"

"To your certain knowledge then."

She changed the subject. "Will you let them take me back?"

"I thought we'd settled that," he said.

"It doesn't hurt to ask."

"It hurts my feelin's. You should think of that some-time."

"Feelings?"

"I don't have time for this," he said. Rising, he walked back to the window and stood peering through the glass. He'd wiped a clear spot on the dusty pane to let him see the road.

Nothing.

All right. They weren't late yet. He'd calculated sundown, more or less, if they left San Felípe just at dawn. Of course, a smart man might decide to jump the gun and scout the town ahead of time, but they'd been watching since late morning without spotting any prowlers.

Waiting should've been an easy job, but it got on his nerves. Old women said a watched pot never boiled, but simple logic told him that it *had* to boil sometime.

Unless . . .

"I'll be back in a little while," Reese said.

"Where are you going?"

"I just wanna check the others. Make sure they're not slackin' off."

Reese picked up his rifle, going out the door, and clomped downstairs without giving the noise a second thought. He was already angry, thinking of the others leaving him to watch alone, although he hadn't caught them at it yet.

He felt that way a lot these days, angry at nothing, and it made Reese doubt himself. He should feel happy all the time, grateful that all his plans had fallen into place with minimal disruption and his life was rolling full-speed down the track he'd chosen.

Going where?

He didn't dwell on that so much. The future had seemed clear-cut once upon a time, but it was hazy now. He'd learned there was a difference between planning things, acting on plans, and knowing what would happen afterward.

It hadn't blown up in his face so far, but what did that prove? Even when they had the ransom money, when the rest of it was finished, they'd still have to find a hiding place. Watch out for bandits and for *federales,* not that there was any great difference between the two.

He'd heard it said that money couldn't purchase happiness, but what else was it for? Once rudimentary survival was accomplished, all the rest was gravy. Rich men had it better in the world, no matter how they tried to play their fortunes down. Only the rich made light of money, to forestall the poor from rising up and taking it away from them.

My money now, Reese thought. And he could almost feel it in his hands.

All it had cost him, so far, was a few small human lives. His own team hadn't suffered any losses, and there was no reason why they should.

Unless they let him down.

He reached the bottom of the stairs, moved through what used to be a doctor's office, vacant now. Only a dry husk of the town remained, devoid of life. And hiding somewhere in it, three men he would chastise if he didn't find them on alert, manning their posts.

"Ready or not," he muttered to them, "here I come."

The third place Price examined was an undertaker's parlor. Several coffins had been left behind when Amorada's people fled for parts unknown, as if they'd thought someone might come along one day and hold a funeral service for their dreams.

Price checked the boxes, just in case, and verified that all were empty. Prowling through the vacant rooms, he listened to the place—and to the town outside—in search of any clues that would direct him to another living human.

Nothing.

That was good, as far as Brooks and Schaefer went. At least they weren't running around, slamming doors and generally making noise enough to wake the dead. Given a choice of drawing fire or sneaking up on the kidnappers, Price preferred to sneak.

But first, he had to find out where they were.

So far, he'd covered three of six shops on the west side of Main Street, south of the alley that had served as his entry to town. Brooks and Schaefer had a roughly equal batch to search on their end, prior to checking out the other side. Their quarry had to be there, somewhere, if the ride to Amorada wasn't simply an elaborate ruse.

Price gave up on the undertaker's parlor and prepared to go next door. Again he hesitated at the threshold, scanning westward-facing windows bright with sun glare, peering into doorways dark with shadow. None yielded their secrets to his weary eyes.

The choice was simple. He could run, risk drawing their attention with his noise and sudden movement, or else take his time and watch the street for any sign that he was being watched.

Price finally decided it was too damned hot to run. He stepped outside and edged along toward the next door in line, keeping the wall at his back. Four paces brought him to another shop. He peered in through a window decorated with cobwebs and saw another empty room, with bare shelves on the walls. Price saw no sign, had no idea what they'd been selling in the town's heyday, but he could see the door to a back room standing ajar.

The shop's door, Price discovered, had been taken off its hinges at some point and leaned against an inside wall. Spiders had spun a tangled nest behind it over time, but nothing else was lurking there. Price concentrated on the doorway straight ahead of him, angling so that any snipers watching from the windows opposite would have no view of his retreating back.

His footsteps seemed unreasonably loud to Price as he moved cautiously across the dusty floorboards. Some of them were creaky, others loose, as if the whole floor had been rigged to sound alarms. It seemed to be for nothing, though, as Price reached the back room and found it empty, mottled sunlight falling through a small, dirty window that faced toward the afternoon sun.

He was alone.

Price searched in vain for any clues that might've told him what the shop had sold or serviced, then gave up the exercise as fruitless and a waste of time. He was about to leave when something caught his eye in the near corner to his left. A homemade wooden ladder, fastened to the wall, led to a trapdoor overhead.

It seemed to Price that no one had disturbed the dust beneath the ladder, but he'd come to search the place and meant to do it properly. Checking the front room of the shop again, and glancing through its window toward the street, he satisfied himself that no one from outside was creeping up behind him. Next, he leaned his rifle in the nearest corner of the room, where it would not fall and discharge by accident. He climbed the ladder slowly, testing every rung to make sure it would bear his weight. When he was five feet off the floor, Price used one hand to raise the trapdoor's lid and found it was a simple wooden panel without hinges, which he shoved aside.

Dust fell around him, Price ducking his head to catch most of it on his hat brim. Seeing only darkness in the attic when he looked again, he drew a match and struck it with his thumbnail, climbing higher with the tiny light extended overhead. A rush of tiny scuttling feet made Price's skin crawl as his head and shoulders cleared the trapdoor's frame.

Swift movement in the shadows drew his eye, its source eluding him. He turned and flinched at first sight of a horned toad staring at him, blinking bright eyes from a foot away. The lizard stuck its tongue out, as if mocking Price, then turned and fled into the darkness. When he raised the match above his head, spreading its light before it burned down to his fingertips, Price saw more of the thorny reptiles racing here and there, squat phantoms in the shadows.

"It's all yours," he informed them, shaking out the match as he descended to the floor. Price spent another moment grinding out the match head with his thumb and forefinger, eliminating any risk that any spark of his might set the tinder-dry ghost town ablaze.

Price retrieved his Winchester and left the storeroom, moving toward the exit and the street beyond. He'd almost made it when a gunshot echoed through the ghost town like the crack of Doom.

13

Despite his sense of urgency, Price didn't rush headlong into the street. He waited in the shadowed doorway, knowing he was fairly well concealed from prying eyes outside. The sun was well behind him now, sinking toward dusk from what had been late afternoon, but he could still see clearly every detail of the street outside. By shifting his position, Price could scan approximately one third of the town's full length.

But so far, there was nothing to be seen.

The pistol shot—for such it had been—must've come from *somewhere,* but he heard no further shooting, saw no bodies lying crumpled in the dust. The bullet hadn't broken any windows, for there'd been no sound of breaking glass. Price hadn't memorized each detail of the ghost town's street, but he saw nothing obvious to mark a bullet's impact on the walls within his range of vision. No fresh scars, no spill of dust from its time-honored resting place.

From what he'd heard, the pistol could've been a .44-

or .45-caliber. That narrowed the range of suspects to
Brooks, Schaefer, and several million other shooters in
the western half of North America. It galled Price, knowing one of his companions might be dead or injured
when he couldn't help, but rushing out to find them
would be worse than useless if he wound up lying facedown in the street.

And so he waited, listening. Ticked off a minute in his
head, counting the seconds one by one. No further shooting yet, but was that good news? The answer to that depended on who—if anyone—had been shot.

Only one round was triggered, but what did that tell
him? Price recognized the varied possibilities. Something
might've spooked Brooks or Schaefer, prompting one of
them to fire at a snake, Gila monster, a shadow—whatever. The same could be true for one of the kidnappers,
but Price deemed it less likely. They'd spent more time in
Amorada, he presumed, and thus should've been more acquainted with its creeping things.

More likely, he supposed, was that one of his companions had met the enemy. A single shot in that case meant
the target had been taken out of action, either killed or
physically disabled. Otherwise, there would've been return fire, shouting, running.

Something.

Amorada had relapsed into its age-old silence, and that
troubled Price more than the pistol shot a moment earlier.
He could press on without the others, but it would've
helped to know if they were still alive and on the move. If
nothing else, to stop him shooting one of them by accident.

Go on and have a look, the small voice in his head
urged Price. *Find out.*

He trusted that voice, more or less, though it was sometimes reckless. It had urged him into needless danger
more than once, asserting points of conscience or "moral-
ity" that damn near got him killed. Price had survived on

skill and ruthlessness in those cases, but he wasn't anxious to gamble with his life.

Why not? the voice prodded. *You do it every day.*

He shook it off, waiting, leaning a little farther from
the doorway. Still nothing. The street was empty, silent.

Price believed the shot had come from somewhere to
his left, though it was difficult to be precise. Sounds
would be batted back and forth between the storefronts,
maybe muffled if the shot was fired inside one of the
stores. There were still four or five shops to his right, an
equal number on the far side of the street. Price couldn't
positively rule out any of them as the source of the gunshot, but instinct told him it had come from somewhere
farther south.

Where he had last seen Brooks and Schaefer.

"Damn it."

Price knew he would have to go and look for them. He
couldn't simply act as if the shot hadn't been fired, ignore
it, and move on. It meant *something,* and if he found it
was a clumsy slip by one of his companions, he would—

"Hey, there!" someone shouted. "Anybody home?"

Price froze. He didn't recognize the voice, and didn't
plan to spring from hiding like a target in a shooting
gallery.

"I hope somebody's there," the shouter said. "'Cuz this
boy's bleedin' purty bad. He could be dyin'."

Price stayed where he was. Waiting.

The shouter dropped his voice a bit. "Say somethin',
boy," he ordered. "Make it good."

Silence was followed by a squeal of pain.

"It's me," cried Early Brooks. "I'm shot real bad!"

So what? thought Jubal Schaefer. *Serves you right.*

He overlooked the action from the second-story loft of
what had been a blacksmith's shop and livery. The place
still smelled of horse manure, with recent contributions

from the desert's rodent population, making Schaefer's nose twitch.

In the street below and fifty yards due north, he saw two men. Brooks was the whiner, wobbling on his feet and clutching at his side, held upright by a taller man whose hat shielded his face. His voice sounded familiar, but it wasn't Reese. The brother maybe.

What's the difference?

Schaefer only had four men to choose from, and he meant to kill them all.

He'd crossed the street when no one else was looking, leaving Brooks and Price to search the west-side shops. His sprint across that open space had been nerve-wracking, but no one had fired on him. Schaefer had found some ancient bales of hay, disintegrating from exposure and the ravages of mice, planting the suitcase in their midst and raking the shit-smelly straw across it with his hands until the bag was well concealed. From there, he'd climbed a ladder to the loft, to watch and wait.

It hadn't taken long.

He would've bet that Brooks would be the one to blow it. Young and eager to a fault, seeing himself in some damned fairy tale. Riding to save the damsel in distress. He must've stumbled onto someone in his searching, and he wasn't fast enough to drop his man. Now here he was, wounded and leaking, crying out for help like a dyspeptic child.

"You heard him," Early's captor called into the street after his prisoner's appeal. "He's hurtin', people. Are you gonna help 'im out, or not?"

Silence.

Schaefer lined up his rifle, found his target in its sights. It would be easy, firing through the crown of Abel's hat. If it *was* Abel. Either way, the .30-30 slug would put him down, leaving a shattered face his mother wouldn't recognize. He might hit Brooks as well, with lead or bone fragments, but Schaefer didn't care.

Smart bastard had it coming, siding with Price against

the Circle S. Schaefer had never liked him much, but he had no stomach for turncoats. Anything that happened to him, Brooks had brought upon himself.

One shot to drop the gunman, and if Brooks crawled off to die somewhere in Amorada, that was fine with Schaefer. All that stayed his hand now was a hope that more of the kidnappers would emerge from hiding, place themselves where he could cut them down conveniently, with little danger to himself. That done, he would be free to search the ghost town for his sister and find out where she was hidden.

Marcy.

He enjoyed the thought of their reunion.

It would be just like old times.

"Nobody home?" the gunman asked an empty street. "I can't patch up this boy myself. Don't wanna watch 'im suffer. Guess I'll have ta put 'im down."

Schaefer could hear the hammer draw back on the shooter's pistol. *Click-clack* in the silence of the street. Perhaps he ought to let the gunman finish Brooks, then shoot him. Make it look like angry payback, rather than a calculated move.

"He's not alone," another voice called out below.

Schaefer saw Matt Price step into the street, emerging from the third shop past the alley where they'd entered Amorada. Price held his Winchester left-handed, right hand hanging loose beside his holstered Peacemaker.

"You'd be the new man Eddie talked about," the faceless gunman said. "That still leaves Jubal. Where's he at?"

Schaefer considered firing then, simply to see what happened next. Would other gunmen in the shadows open up on Price? If so, their muzzle-flashes might betray them to a sniper poised above the street.

"I don't know where he is," Price said.

"Don't tell me Jubal lost his nerve." The shooter laughed, a mocking sound. "We always figgered he was yellow underneath. Still, I'da liked to seen his face once more, when—"

"Turn around then!" Schaefer bellowed from the loft. "My face'll be the last thing that you ever see!"

The shooter kept his eyes on Price, still smiling as he answered, "Are you gonna shoot me in the back, Jubal? Tha's about what I'd expect. O' course, you'll never see Marcy again. She'll be a dead'un 'fore I hit the ground."

Price used the moment to examine Brooks. He had been shot above the belt line, left of center. Blood was dribbling through the fingers of his two hands, clamped over the wound. He hadn't fallen yet, but Price guessed some of that was due to the support of the gunman who clutched him from behind.

Brooks was unarmed, as far as Price could tell, and seemed past putting up a fight. His face had paled alarmingly beneath the weathered tan, blood draining toward his wound. He would be slipping into shock soon, if he wasn't there already, and Price wasn't sure the shooter could support him when his legs gave way.

Price could draw then, give it a try, unless—

"I thought the girl meant somethin' to you, Jubal. Guess I had it wrong. Go on and shoot then. See what happens."

"Tell me where she is, damn you!"

Price had him spotted now. The loft down the street, above the livery.

"That ain't the way it goes, farm boy. You came to buy 'er, plain and simple. No more goddamn tricks!"

Price watched and waited, wondering when Brooks would slump enough to give him a clear shot. How many other guns were trained on Price himself, ready to fire when he did?

From the loft, Schaefer called out, "How do I know she's still alive?"

"You don't," the gunman answered. "And she won't be 'less you get your ass down here and bring the money with you in a hurry. Patience ain't my virtue, Jubal, and it's runnin' thin right now."

More hesitation. When he spoke again, the rancher's voice was filled with bitter resignation. "All right then. I'm coming down."

"Be quick about it. Y'all got lives to save."

Price watched for Schaefer in the stable's doorway, but another movement drew his eye off to the right. Midway between himself and Brooks, a man he'd never seen before stepped from the dead shell of a onetime barbershop. A week-old beard covered his lower face and he was carrying a shotgun, double barrels aimed at Price, the stock wedged tight between his elbow and his hip.

That left two unaccounted for. Price didn't feel like asking, and he didn't have to. Seconds later, still no sign of Schaefer on the street, he saw the first gunman glance to his left as footsteps crunched across the sandy street.

Price took a chance and glanced across his right shoulder. Two men stood waiting in the dusk, one taller than the other. He immediately recognized the messenger from San Felípe, hanging back behind a taller man who had to be the leader. Everything about his bearing said he was in charge, but Price also saw nerves at work beneath the tough veneer.

"We got 'em, Reese," the first man said.

"I see," Reese Johnson answered. Nothing in his voice to give his nerves away, but Price was sure of what he'd seen.

He'd bet his life on it, in fact.

"Goddamn it, Jubal," Early's captor shouted, "if you make me count to five, I swear I'll—"

"Save it, Abel," Schaefer answered. "I'm right here."

He came out of the stable, lugging the suitcase in one hand, holding his rifle in the other, index finger on the trigger. There was something odd about the suitcase, tufts of moldy straw adhering to the top and sides.

"Is that our money?" asked Reese Johnson.

"No," Schaefer replied. "I brought my dirty laundry by mistake."

Price frowned, thinking his clothes would've been worth more than the newspaper inside the bag, but the kidnappers weren't aware of the surprise that lay in store for them.

Not yet.

"I never knew you had a sense of humor, Jubal," Reese replied. "I'm glad to see there's no hard feelin's."

"Want there to be?" asked Schaefer.

"Come to think of it, Eddie's nursin' a grudge about his face," said Reese.

"Damn right," Ed Timmons echoed.

"I don't give a damn about his nose," Schaefer retorted. "Where's my sister, Reese?"

"I wanna see the money first."

"Forget it."

"S'pose ol' Abel kills your man."

"It's one less mouth to feed," said Schaefer.

"You're a hard one. All right then." Price heard him turn on one heel, calling toward the shadows on the east side of the street. "Marcy? Come out here for a second, will ya, girl?"

Early Brooks thought he was dying, and the notion made him scared and angry, all at once. He had the shakes so bad that he could hardly stand, beside which there was precious little strength remaining in his legs. He clenched his teeth against the pain and blinked his eyes to stop the black motes swimming in his field of vision.

It had gone to hell with startling speed. One minute, he was starting up the staircase to the second floor of an abandoned shop, smelling the mouse turds everywhere, and then a shadow loomed across the landing just above him. He'd been startled, swinging up the Henry for a hip shot, but the shadow-shape had spoken to him. Called him by his name, in fact.

"Early?"

And then it shot him.

Only afterward, as he was tumbling down the stairs, then huddled in a sobbing clutch of pain, did Brooks have time to analyze his terminal mistake. He should've fired instinctively, without a conscious thought. It might not have prevented Abel shooting him, but chances were they'd both be hurting now, and Brooks wouldn't have drawn his two companions into Reese's trap.

Brooks hadn't know that it was Abel Johnson on the stairs, until the man leaned over him and took his Colt, hiding the gun somewhere behind his back. His face swam in and out of focus. Abel only spoke again when he was satisfied that Brooks had been disarmed.

"Sorry about the gut, Early," he said. "At least you're breathin'."

For a little while, Brooks thought, but kept it to himself. A second later, Abel hauled him to his feet, ignoring gasps of pain along the way. He'd seen the blood that spilled from Early's wound more rapidly when he was upright, and supplied a well-used handkerchief to press against the hole. Before they reached the old shop's threshold it was saturated, and Brooks felt life leaking through his fingers.

It was nearly black, a sure sign that his liver had been damaged by the bullet. Brooks knew he couldn't last long, even if a doctor tried to patch him. As they'd moved into the street, he was already thinking of his next move, last move, hoping he'd have one more chance to get it right.

So far, it wasn't working. He'd had no choice but to call out for the others, hoping that they wouldn't take the bait. Unfortunately, Price had stepped out right away, showing the kind of man he was beneath the rough exterior. Price had to know it was a fool's play, but he took the chance for Brooks.

And Marcy. Don't forget Marcy.

It had been harder, talking Jubal down, but now Reese had them both and nearly everyone was in the street.

Brooks felt his strength fading, knees weakening. He pledged himself to stand as long as possible, but couldn't promise how much longer that would be. His belly ached, then burned, then ached some more, as if he'd eaten something that was fighting to escape.

Price met his eyes. Brooks thought a message passed between them, but it could've been his feverish imagination. There was something he could do, he realized, and Price might take advantage of it, even if he wasn't counting on assistance.

Just as Reese turned toward the buildings on the east side of the street and called for Marcy, Brooks let go. He folded at the waist, stooped over as if bowing to a queen, and let his knees buckle. Behind him, Abel tried to hold him upright with a tight grip on his belt in back, but Brooks was slipping.

Gunshots rang out just as his knees touched dirt, and he was suddenly released. The sudden freedom was too much for Brooks, and he slumped forward, facedown in the street. A jolt of pain shot through him on impact; then he rolled sideways, desperate to see what happened next, if he'd done anything at all to help the others.

Scuttling boots and trouser legs were all he saw, before a bullet hit the ground in front of him and spit sand in his eyes.

Reese Johnson had his back turned when the shooting started, calling out to Marcy, but the gunshots changed his mind and message. Shouting, "No! Go back!" before he even saw her, Johnson spun and drew his pistol, ready to defend himself.

His first glimpse of the street-turned-battleground was chaos. Early Brooks was lying on the ground, just rolling over on his side, bleeding to beat the band. Abel was down on one knee, squeezing off a shot at Early's head, missing and raising dust to make his target grimace. The rest were moving, scattering for cover, and it seemed to Reese like one damned fine idea.

He didn't want to leave his brother in the street, but what else could he do? Abel was rising now, his movements jerky, awkward. When his left hand reached around behind him for a moment, the returning fingertips were crimson-stained. Jubal, the backshooter, was levering another round into his Winchester, clumsy because he wouldn't drop the suitcase long enough to do it right.

Reese fired at Schaefer, cursing when his bullet hit the heavy bag. At least it spoiled the bastard's aim, gave Abel time to fire at him and miss from fifteen feet. Schaefer was ducking, weaving, firing blindly as he ran back toward the nearest vacant shop. Reese had his six-gun raised to try again, when suddenly a bullet plucked his sleeve and drew a line of fire along the underside of his right arm.

It was his turn to duck and dodge now, as he spun to face the shooter he'd forgotten when he first saw Abel down. The stranger was retreating, but he fired again as Reese tried lining up his sights for a quick parting shot. This time, the bullet nicked his hat brim, and it was enough to make him say *To hell with this,* running for cover with the speed of one who feels Death breathing down his neck.

He wasn't sure where Marcy was exactly, but she wasn't in the street and that was ample reason to be thankful. Just a few more seconds, and she would've been revealed. God only knows what Jubal might've done in that case. Now, at least, Reese had a chance to finish him.

But first, he had to save himself and deal with Jubal's shooter.

Reese still didn't know the gunman's name. It was irrelevant perhaps, but if the shooter had a reputation, maybe there'd be something in the word of mouth that Reese could use to get an edge.

Too late.

He stumbled on the rough edge of the sidewalk, nearly

falling, then lurched forward through the open doorway of the former barroom that he'd come from moments earlier. Upstairs was the room he'd shared with Marcy through that waiting day.

Where was she now?

"Reese?" Calling to him from the stairs.

"Go back up to the room," he ordered. "Get out through that hatch we found."

"The roof? I don't—"

"Just do it! I'll be right behind you, girl."

I hope.

She turned and fled, conditioned to obey him. Huddled by the door frame, peering out into the dusk with one eye, Johnson scanned the street for targets.

Early Brooks lay in the middle of the street, unmoving, whether dead or passed out from the pain of being gut-shot, Johnson couldn't say. The only other person visible was Abel, lurching toward the west-side shops and firing into one of them with his six-gun. A bloodstain six inches across and growing marked his back.

Go, brother, Johnson urged him silently, but all in vain. Another step, and Abel staggered from the impact of a second bullet. Dropping to his knees again, Abel prepared to fire at someone in the shadows, braced his six-gun with both hands.

Two shots rang out, almost together, bullets slapping into Abel's chest and side. Reese bit his lip and tasted blood, watching his brother topple slowly forward now, his last shot wasted on the dust before he fell across the pistol.

Abel. *Jesus.*

Reese craved vengeance, but he had no targets. Cursing bitterly, he rose and backtracked toward the stairs. Chasing Marcy toward the roof.

It startled Price when Early Brooks began to crawl across the street. He'd written Brooks off as a goner, but now the kid was moving, dragging himself through the dust toward the spot where Abel Johnson lay facedown.

Abel was dead, Price guessed, or damn close to it. Schaefer had hit him twice with rifle slugs, coming and going, and Price had put a .45 slug in his side before Abel fell. If he was still alive, there couldn't be much fight left in him now.

Price scanned the street from his doorway, reloading his Peacemaker while his eyes sought movement in the shadows. Nothing stirred except Brooks, inching through the dust, but Price knew there were still at least four living gunmen in the ghost town.

Jubal Schaefer might be wounded, but Price didn't think so. He'd seen one shot strike the rancher's suitcase full of newspaper before all hell broke loose, but Schaefer had been running at full speed and firing from the hip when Price last saw him.

Price had blown his shot at Reese Johnson, maybe winged him on the fly, but it wasn't enough to slow him down. He'd vanished in the scrambling rush for cover, shouting for the girl to run before Price ever glimpsed her.

Had she even made it to the street? Could the one-sided conversation be a cover for the fact that she was dead and buried somewhere?

Price dismissed that theory, based on Reese's own behavior. He'd been running for his life when Price last saw him. If he had the mental wherewithal to play a scripted part while bullets whistled past his head, he could've been a first-rate actor on the stage.

Aside from Reese and Jubal, there were two more shooters lurking somewhere close at hand. The messenger from San Felípe, Timmons, had escaped the first exchange of fire without a scratch, as far as Price could tell, and the fourth man—unknown to Price—had also fled after firing a blast high and wide from his shotgun.

Four gunmen, and three of them were definitely hostile. As for Jubal, he'd started the fight in the street when he shot Abel Johnson in the back. It was a risky move, all things considered, and it hadn't tipped the balance in their favor. Price resolved to treat Jubal with utmost caution if they met again.

His first job, though, was to pursue Reese and the girl, wherever she might be. That meant crossing the street, which was almost guaranteed to draw more fire. The shotgun was his greatest danger, though its owner had already proved himself a shaky hand. He might do better next time, but the threat wasn't enough to make Price fold and drop out of the game.

Not yet.

He put the Colt back in its holster, clutched and cocked his Winchester. Price knew where he was going—where he *hoped* to go at least. His target was a shop across the street and one door farther south, where Reese had first emerged from hiding. If Price made it that far, he hoped he would find his quarry waiting, or else pick up Reese's trail.

In any case, he couldn't linger where he was.

Price counted down from five and hit the sidewalk running, shoulders hunched against the impact of a bullet he might never hear. In front of him and to his left, a shadow moved behind a broad, dark window and he fired in that direction without making any real attempt to aim. The glass imploded with a crash, but Price's faceless adversary turned and fled, presumably unharmed.

Off to his right, the shotgun roared. Price ducked his head, a reflex action that would do no good at all against buckshot. A swarm of angry hornets hurtled past him, almost on his heels, but the shooter had failed to lead his target. Even with his weapon's sawed-off barrels, he had missed again.

Price fired back toward the sound, knowing he wasn't even close, and gained the sidewalk two strides later, diving headlong through the open doorway of the shop that was his destination. Gunfire followed him, another shotgun blast that brought the shop's front window raining down in jagged shards, and then a rifle shot that slapped the vacant room's back wall.

Jubal?

Price rolled clear of the doorway, out of sight from shooters on the street. His main risk now was Reese, if the kidnapper had delayed his flight to ambush any followers. Price swept the room with his Winchester, sighting first on stairs, then on the open doorway to a room in back, behind a bar, but no one challenged him.

He checked the bar and back room first, careful of snipers from outside, and found it empty. There was no rear window, no back door, no obvious escape hatch. Satisfied that no one had eluded him in that direction, Price retraced his steps and started up the stairs.

14

Brooks reckoned he was dying, but he didn't want to finish in the dusty street, without a fight. He hadn't fired a shot so far in Amorada, and it didn't seem the proper way for any man to go, gut-shot from ambush without taking down at least one enemy.

His main problem, after the deep soul-searing pain and weakness caused by loss of blood, was that he had no weapon. Abel had relieved him of his guns, back in the store where he was shot, and Brooks had no idea what had become of them. He saw a pistol, though, once he had blinked and wept the road grit from his burning eyes. And slowly, inch by agonizing inch, he went to claim it.

Abel Johnson lay facedown, with blood soaking the earth beneath him. Badly wounded, all unmoving. Maybe dead. Brooks dragged himself toward the six-gun that Abel had dropped when he fell. It lay just beyond the fingertips of Abel's outflung hand. A little stretch, and he could reach it.

The image prodded Brooks with greater urgency. He

clenched his teeth, clawed with his fingers, pushed off
with his feet. His body seemed to weigh a ton; the simple
act of dragging it exhausted him. Only determination kept
him going when his weary muscles cried for rest.

Another heave, and the six-gun would be within his
reach. Behind him, Brooks heard someone running, right
to left across the street. A rifle cracked in front of him, followed immediately by a shotgun blast from somewhere at
his back. Another rifle shot, runner trading fire, and then
it stopped. Brooks wasn't strong enough to turn and see
what it was all about, but he imagined that it must be
Price.

"You give 'em hell," he whispered to the dirt and
corpse in front of him. His trembling, outstretched fingers
clasped the pistol's butt and drew the weapon to him.

Pained and weakened as he was, Brooks still remembered Abel firing several times. He thumbed open the pistol's loading gate, half-cocked the hammer, and began to
turn the cylinder, counting spent rounds by their indented
primers.

Four rounds out of six were gone.

And one of them's in me, he thought. Another was
likely the shot that had kicked dirt into his face after he
fell, that bastard Abel going for his head and missing by a
fraction. The others had presumably been fired at Price or
Jubal.

Two rounds left to fight a war.

It wasn't good enough.

Slowly, laboriously, Brooks ejected the spent car-
tridges, replacing them with live ones that he took from
Abel's gun belt. Every moment that he spent out in the
open made his skin crawl—surely someone must be lining up another shot to finish him—but then he finished
and they hadn't shot him yet.

Maybe they didn't care.

Brooks thanked his lucky stars for that, then nearly
laughed aloud at the idea of being grateful for anything as
he lay with his blood leaking into the dust. He would be

dead soon; Brooks was nearly certain of it. But he had one final opportunity to fight.

If he could stand. And find a target.

With the revolver clutched in his right hand, Brooks crawled another twenty feet to reach the sidewalk. There, digging with knees and elbows, weeping from the pain, he struggled to a kneeling posture, then got one foot underneath him. Gravity almost undid him as he surged upright, but a hitching post came to his rescue, supporting him while he found his balance.

They'll drop me now, he thought. But no one did.

He reeled across the sidewalk, tottering, until he found a wall to keep him upright. Slither-striding to the north, keeping one shoulder constantly against the wall, Brooks passed one shop, peered through its window, and moved on when he saw nothing.

Silence behind him as he reached the next, squinted, and saw a ghostly hint of movement on the far side of the glass. Gasping from pain and the exertion, Brooks picked up his pace and staggered through the open doorway.

Eddie Timmons stood before him, well back in the shadows, barely visible. The sight of Brooks made him recoil.

"Jesus, you're bleedin', Early."

"Tha's what happens when you're shot."

"I didn't reckon it'd come to this."

"It has, though."

"I just wanna get the hell away from here."

"Too late," Brooks told him, firing even as he spoke.

Incredibly, he saw the first shot strike his target, low and to the left, but still a hit. Timmons fired back and missed, cracking the window. Advancing, Brooks squeezed off another shot and saw a crimson boutonniere sprout from his adversary's chest.

He felt like crowing, but a lucky bullet found him then and dropped Brooks to his knees. Roaring, he raised the six-gun in both hands and locked his sights onto the sagging target.

Both men fired again, this time together, gunshots merging in a smoky thunderclap. No witnesses beheld them as they crumpled into darkness on the dusty floor.

Price took his time climbing the stairs. He wanted to be sure they'd hold his weight, and that an ambush wasn't waiting for him at the top. Poised with the rifle butt against his shoulder, finger on the trigger, Price hugged the wall and cautiously planted his feet near the edge of each step, where a squeak was less likely.

Halfway up, he heard a rapid scuttling sound and froze, then let himself relax a little as a rat peered down at him, blinked beady eyes, and then retreated.

Cursing silently, he took another slow step, and another, kept it up until he reached the second floor. Darkness obscured the hallway there, but it served Price as well as any lurking enemies. He couldn't risk a light, knowing the first flare of a match would mark him, while illuminating little of the hunting ground.

Price waited, listened, even tried to *smell* another human being in the dark, but nothing registered. The building wore that same pervasive smell of rot and rodents that he'd found in every shop he'd searched so far.

Go on, damn it!

Hugging the wall again, he cautiously advanced. Price held the rifle at his hip now, leading with its muzzle. He was doubly careful now, knowing that Marcy Schaefer was—or recently had been—inside that very building. It wouldn't do for Price to shoot her by mistake, when he had come so far to save her life.

Small rooms lined both sides of the second-story hallway, putting Price in mind of a hotel or brothel. With the bar downstairs, he guessed the latter was more likely. Either way, the rooms made handy hiding places, and he'd have to check each one, until he found Reese Johnson or the girl.

A muffled burst of gunshots froze Price in his tracks.

Distance and instinct told him they'd come from the far side of the street, maybe inside one of the other buildings. He guessed it must be Jubal, dueling with the other kidnappers, but there was nothing he could do to help.

Not yet.

It frayed his nerves, checking the pitch-black rooms in order as he came to them, but there was no alternative. There was no third floor to the building, so his quarry must be somewhere in that musty warren, waiting for him. Reese to kill him, and the girl to . . . what?

Price followed the same pattern in each room along the left side of the corridor. The doors all stood ajar or open, saving him from awkward fumbling with the knobs. Each time, he went in low and fast, finding a wall to guard his back and crouching silently, his rifle probing empty air. After a moment passed with no attack or muzzle-flash, he'd begin to whisper names—Reese Johnson, Marcy Schaefer—hoping the distortion of his voice would keep the first gunshot from finding him.

But no shots came. No answers reached his straining ears. Price groped around each room in bitter darkness, braced to meet a knife blade or a flying fist, but each was empty in its turn.

He found out why in number four, the last room on the left side of the hall. It wasn't quite as dark as the last three he'd searched, dimly illuminated by starlight that glimmered through a ceiling hatch. Beneath it, wooden ladder rungs were mounted on the wall.

The roof.

Before he climbed the ladder, Price had to be sure it wasn't just a ruse. Running on nerve alone, he moved into the hallway, picking up his pace and fairly shouting now, as he invaded other rooms.

"Reese Johnson! Marcy Schaefer."

Only silence answered him.

Price ran back to the last room on the left and stood below the open hatch. Once he ascended, anything might happen. There would be no turning back.

One-handed, with the rifle slowing him, Price scrambled toward the stars.

Jubal was sitting on his bullet-punctured suitcase, well back from the street and covering the small shop's open doorway with his rifle, when he heard the sound of muffled voices through the wall immediately to his right. He pressed an ear against it, trying to make out the words, then instantly recoiled as gunshots echoed from the place next door.

He counted six in all, but guessed he might've made an error since they came so close together, rattling off in rapid fire. He waited two full minutes, counting off the seconds, *one-one-thousand, two-one-thousand,* then moved to the door and took a long look at the street.

Nothing.

Jubal left the suitcase where it was and crept next door and peered in through the window, where a bullet hole had drilled the glass but somehow failed to shatter it. He dimly glimpsed two bodies on the floor and ducked inside to take a closer look.

It startled him to find that Early Brooks had made his way in from the street, where Jubal had believed him to be dead. More startling yet was Eddie Timmons, sprawled against the back wall in a spreading pool of blood, where Brooks had gunned him down. They'd finished one another, taking two more players from the game.

Jubal appreciated that kind of arithmetic.

Encouraged, thinking there were only three men left to kill, he walked back to the door and stepped outside. Night had descended on the ghost town, still an hour short of moonrise. Feeling safer than he had all day, Jubal stared off to the south, where he had last seen Reese, Bodine, and Price.

Searching the town by night didn't appeal to him. It was a good way to get shot from ambush, when he'd rather be the one who lay in hiding, peering over gunsights at his enemies. A sudden thought occurred to Jubal, and he went back to retrieve the suitcase from its resting place.

Lugging its weight for the last time, Jubal retraced his steps southward, past the silent corpse of Abel Johnson, to the point where Price had run across the street a short time earlier. Jubal had missed his shot that time, a gamble that had failed to pay him any dividends, but he was confident he'd get another chance.

The whole mess would be settled soon, and wouldn't cost the family a dime.

Arriving at his preselected point, Jubal veered off the sidewalk, jogged into the middle of the street, and dropped the suitcase there, then ran back to the nearest open doorway. Hastily he checked the shop, then hunkered down in shadow, cleared his throat, and called out to the night.

"Hey, Reese! You want your money now? It's waiting for you. Come and get it!"

Only silence answered him. He counted sixty seconds in his head, then tried again.

"Last chance! It's one time only, now or never."

Maybe Reese was smarter than he thought. Not dumb enough to show himself at least. The trick had been too obvious, a waste of time. Disgusted, Jubal stood—and froze as he glimpsed movement on the far side of the street.

A moment later, starlight showed him that it wasn't Reese, but rather Frank Bodine who ventured out to claim the bag. Bodine still had the shotgun, covering the west side of the street as if he wasn't sure where Jubal had concealed himself.

So much the better.

"Here I come," the shooter said. "No tricks now, if you wanna see your sis again."

"I'll see her, don't you worry," Jubal muttered, framing Bodine in his gunsights.

"Just go easy, now, and I'll—"

The gunshot cut off any promise Bodine might've made. The bullet drilled his chest dead center, and its impact pitched him backward to the ground. As he fell, his finger clenched around the shotgun's double triggers and discharged a swarm of buckshot toward the sky.

Two left, thought Jubal with a smile.

Rising from cover, he glanced left and right, then dashed across the street.

Price lingered at the trapdoor's rim, aware that Reese or one of his companions could be waiting on the roof, mere inches distant, with a weapon pointed at the open hatch. Unseemly haste could get Price killed, but nothing would be gained from hanging on the ladder paralyzed.

A muffled voice called something from the street, but Price couldn't make out the words. The call was soon repeated, followed by a rifle shot and shotgun blast, then more oppressive silence.

Tired of waiting, Price decided on an awkward compromise. Right hand already filled by his Winchester, he leaned forward, braced his toes against the ladder, and released the topmost rung with his left hand. Slowly, afraid of plummeting to sprained ankles or worse, Price doffed his hat and placed it on the muzzle of his rifle. Anchored to the ladder once again, he raised the hat and weapon slowly, as a cautious man might lift his head, into the darkness just above.

No shots rang out; no bludgeon hammered down upon his Stetson. Did that mean the way was clear, or were his enemies too clever to be taken in by such a simple ruse?

Price raised the hat a few more inches, then decided he was wasting precious time. He shook the rifle, let his hat fall to the roof above, then scrambled after it as fast as he could climb.

And found himself alone.

He had expected something more, if not a glimpse of kidnapper or hostage, then at least some footprints on the dusty rooftop, but the desert wind was an efficient house-keeper. Crouching, Price glanced in both directions without finding any clue to which he should select.

He peered into the street below and found that Early Brooks was gone. A few yards farther south of where he'd been last time Price saw him, a new body lay near Jubal's suitcase. Price immediately recognized the shotgunner and reckoned Jubal must've finished him.

Where was the trigger-happy rancher now?

Hunting, no doubt. But hunting *whom*?

Price had another choice to make: He could descend to search along the street, or else pursue the instinct that had brought him to the roof. On one side, only two more buildings stood between Price and open desert, at the southern end of Amorada. To the north, a dozen rooftops beckoned, some separated by alleys that an agile man— or girl—could leap across at need.

Which way?

He chose south on a whim, because it was the shorter distance and it wouldn't take as long for him to search a pair of rooftops as it would to check a dozen. Furthermore, if Reese had no more attic hatches to assist him, he'd be forced to drop and run when he ran out of buildings. Price might see him on the flats below, perhaps still close enough to risk a rifle shot if Marcy wasn't in the way.

His mind made up, Price hastened to the next rooftop in line, found it unoccupied, then cautiously descended to its flat, tarred surface. Every step reminded him that dry rot might conspire against him, send him crashing down through weak spots in the roof, but he negotiated it without mishap.

The third and final building was approximately ten feet taller than the one on which Price stood. He took a chance, leapt up, and caught the parapet with one hand, while his other placed the rifle gently on its narrow edge. Price dropped, moved down a pace, then jumped again and

caught the roof with both hands, digging with his boots to
power up and over the crumbling adobe obstacle.

It was another moment when they could've had him,
but he met no adversaries on the other side. Instead, he
found another service hatch. This one was closed, and
while he briefly feared it might be locked from the inside,
it opened freely to his touch. Dry hinges rasped a warning
of his progress, but if anyone was listening below, they
made no sound.

This time, Price risked a light. He struck a match and
dropped it, following its firefly progress to the floor. The
small light showed an empty room, with no threats lurking in the corners. Price descended swiftly, grinding out
the match beneath his boot before it set the ancient place
on fire.

Jubal thought it would be a needless risk to follow Price
directly, so he veered off course in his mad rush across the
street, angling to reach the final shop in line. Beyond it,
starlit desert waited to reclaim the ghost town in due time.
It mattered not to Jubal whether Amorada stood for one
more day or for a thousand years, as long as he found
those he sought concealed within its shadows.

Reese and Marcy. Then Matt Price.

Or turn it all around. What difference did it make?

He hesitated on the sidewalk, sniffed the open doorway
as if he possessed a bloodhound's power to track by scent,
then edged across the threshold. Driven by a brother's instinct, Jubal half-imagined he could *feel* his sister, hiding
somewhere in the space that he now occupied. Upstairs?
In a back room?

Where to begin?

The second floor produced a furtive scraping sound. It
might be nothing but a rodent, or the breeze intruding
through a broken window, but ignoring it could place his
life at risk. More to the point, it might be Reese and

Marcy, cowering in darkness, the kidnapper hoping he'd be overlooked.

Not this time, Jubal thought. *This time we finish it.*

He started toward the stairs, then stopped dead in his tracks as a new sound reached his ears. A different sound, it was, more like a startled gasp of fear—and this one definitely came from the ground floor, a room mere paces from the spot where Jubal stood.

What should he do?

Climbing the stairs with enemies behind him could be fatal, just as chasing ground-floor targets while another lurked above might cost his life. He finally decided that the nearer threat should be his first priority. He'd check the back room first, while keeping eyes and ears alert to any traffic on the stairs.

He started forward, planting each step carefully, testing the boards before he trusted them to hold his weight without a squeal. The shop was small, no more than fifteen feet across, perhaps twelve deep. Four paces from the entrance to the back room for a large man in a hurry.

Jubal didn't hurry.

Nerves on edge, teeth clenched, hands trembling as they clutched his rifle in a death-grip, he advanced by inches, focused on the three-inch slice of darkness visible between the back room's door and doorjamb, where it stood ajar.

Slow steps on the approach, he reasoned, followed by a rush across the last three feet or so, burst through the door, and drop immediately to a prone firing position on the floor. Blast anything that moved.

If that included Marcy . . .

He had nearly reached the mental jumping-off point when the darkness blossomed into flame before him, echoing the throaty sound of pistol fire. Jubal recoiled, falling before he had a chance to tell if he'd been hit, and triggered a reflexive shot that slapped the wall without effect.

A second shot sent hot lead hissing past him. Jubal

didn't know if he was visible to anyone inside the back
room, or if they were simply firing at the sounds he made.
In either case, fear prompted him to lie rock-still and hold
his breath, praying for total silence in the night.

His ears still rang with gunfire, but Jubal imagined he
could hear two voices whispering, somewhere beyond the
doorway just in front of him. Wishes aside, he couldn't
track a target by the ghostly sounds, and if he tried, his
muzzle-flash would show the phantom shooters where he
was.

Shooters? Or was it only Reese, huddled with Marcy in
the shadows? If he made a lucky shot and took Reese
down, would that conclude his hunt?

Not quite.

Jubal heard footsteps overhead now, drawing closer to
the stairs. He couldn't turn and face in that direction without making sounds that would betray him to the back-
room shooter, but he wondered if Ed Timmons had circled
around to join them somehow, or if the prowler upstairs
was Matt Price.

If it *was* Price, how had he reached the second floor?

More to the point, would he help Jubal against Reese,
or had he recognized the rifle shot Jubal had fired while
Price was in the street?

A wave of nauseating fear washed over Jubal, driving
him to act before his strength and will deserted him completely. Snarling through clenched teeth, he rapid-fired
three rounds into the darkness of the store's back room,
then rose and chased the bullets in a howling charge.

All hell broke loose below while Price had one foot on the
stairs. Rifle and pistol fire exploded, punctuated by a
woman's high-pitched screaming and a man's harsh, inco-
herent shouts of rage. The man sounded like Jubal Schaefer, but Price couldn't swear to it.

Caution and haste competed in his mind as Price descended, smelling gun smoke, crouching on the stairs

when he saw muzzle-flashes in the room below. A dark
shape charged the door of a back room behind gunfire,
while more shots blasted at the runner from within. Price
thought he saw the rifleman stagger, but it could just as
easily have been a feint, ducking the hostile fire. The
whole shop rattled with impact as the attacker smashed
the door aside and breached the smaller room in back.

Price hurried then, as battle noises echoed from the
storeroom. He took time to scan the street, saw only the
familiar corpses there, then turned to join the fight in
progress.

Marcy Schaefer—who else could it be?—screamed
once again as gunfire battered Price's ears. He counted
three more shots, one from a rifle and two from a six-gun,
before ringing silence descended. He stopped, uncertain
whether anyone still living in the back room would be
deafened, or if they might hear his footsteps and send
slugs to greet him in the darkness.

Price cautiously edged to his left, away from the stairs,
to get a better angle on the open doorway. All was dark
within, but he could estimate the room's dimensions and
project a bullet's flight path from the threshold to the
nearest wall. It might not help him score, but it was an improvement over firing blind.

Price found the spot he wanted, crouched, and waited
for a moment, listening. A man's voice muttered something unintelligible, followed by Marcy replying, "I can't
see."

Beyond the doorway, someone struck a match. Price
saw Reese Johnson's face illuminated from below, almost
a tribal mask, and sighted just below it with his Winchester. It would've been an easy shot, before the gunman saw
him, but Price felt compelled to try another way.

"Don't move!" he ordered, holding steady on his mark.

Reese snarled a curse and dropped the match, raising
his pistol as he sidestepped to his right. They fired together, bullets crossing in midair, but Reese's panic shot
went high and wide. Although he'd only had a fraction of

a heartbeat to correct his aim, Price heard his target stumble, cursing once more as he fell.

Then it was Marcy cursing, sobbing out profanity young ladies weren't supposed to know in proper families. Price held his ground through fumbling noises, then rolled to his left as yet another gunshot blasted through the open doorway, this one coming close enough to peel a strip of pale wood from the floorboards.

He recognized the sharp metallic sound as someone cocked and tried to fire an empty six-gun. Quick to move before the shooter could correct his dangerous mistake, Price rushed the doorway, shouldered through, and aimed a kick at the figure crouching before him with pistol upraised. He heard a grunt on impact, followed by the clatter of gunmetal on the boards.

It was his turn to strike a match, holding the small light well out from his body as he scanned the room. In front of him, Reese Johnson huddled on the floor, clutching a wounded arm. Jubal Schaefer slumped against the wall to Price's left, slack-jawed but breathing shallowly while blood soaked through his shirt. Two yards away, his sister rose on hands and knees, shaking her head to clear out the effects of Price's kick. The empty pistol she had grabbed from Reese lay in between them, useless.

"Are you happy now?" she asked Price. "Do you want to finish it?"

15

"I don't know what you mean," Price said.

"Don't lie to me, damn you!" Her rage was incandescent. "She sent you to kill us. Admit it!"

Price didn't have to ask who *she* was, but the *us* surprised him.

"I was hired to fetch you home," he said, shading the truth a bit. "There was no talk of hurting you."

"Oh, no?" She aimed a pale, accusatory finger at her brother's slack-jawed form. "Explain *him* then!"

The match burned down to Price's fingers at that moment, causing him to curse and drop it, stepping on its still-red tip before the ancient floor could catch. "Nobody move!" he ordered.

"God." The girl's voice dripped contempt. "I have a candle. Wait a minute."

Price heard rustling cloth, and shifted silently away from where she'd seen him last. One long step and a crouch, to spoil the first shot if she brought out anything except a candle.

He felt silly seconds later when the match flared and she lit the dark wick of a candle stub, but Price preferred silly to dead.

"Are you afraid of me?" she asked.

"Let's say you don't exactly fit the mold of someone being rescued," Price replied.

"Rescued?" Her laugh was bitter, harsh. "Of course, you *would* think that. Why not? I need to help him now."

Without another glance at Price, she crossed the space that separated her from Reese and knelt beside him. He was sitting upright now, clutching his wounded arm. She gently pried his fingers free, to view the wound by candlelight.

"It's not too bad," she said. "We need to stop the bleeding, though."

Price glanced at Jubal, slumped against the wall, and couldn't tell if he was breathing, much less conscious. Turning back to Marcy as she worked on Reese's arm, Price said, "I take it you weren't kidnapped?"

"I was *rescued*, Mr. . . . What's your name?"

He saw no harm in sharing it. "Matt Price."

"I've never heard of you."

He let that go and asked, "How does a girl your age get 'rescued' from her home?"

"By friends," she said. "And it was more like Hell than home."

The way she looked at Reese, the way she touched him, told Price they were more than friends. Price saw how it could happen, a young girl in love or thinking that she was. The man a little older, though not much, craving her body or caught up in the bizarre adventure.

"What about the ransom?" Price inquired.

Reese spoke for the first time, telling him, "That was my idea."

"He's lying to protect me," Marcy said. "The money's frosting on the cake. We have to live on something, don't we?"

"You won't live long on cut-up newspaper," Price told them.

Reese and Marcy gaped at him, then stared at one another for a while. When Marcy spoke again, Price had to strain his ears to catch her words.

"She didn't pay. I should've known."

"I understand your family's a little short of cash right now," Price said.

"Who told you that?"

He nodded toward the slumped form of her brother. "Jubal here."

"It's bullshit," Marcy answered bluntly. "You can tell that bastard's lying if his lips are moving."

"So, your mother isn't broke?"

"My father used to pinch a penny till it screamed. I'll be surprised if Mama doesn't have the first dollar he ever made."

"What was the plan?" Reese asked. "You s'pose ta shoot us while we're lookin' at the funny money all surprised?"

"That sounds like Mama," Marcy said.

"You weren't supposed to get away with anything," he told Reese. "That's a fact." Turning to Marcy, he repeated, "But I say again, there wasn't any talk of harming you."

"She wouldn't spell it out," the girl replied. "That isn't Mama's style." Another scalding look at Jubal as she said, "She'd let her precious firstborn do the dirty work."

"I don't know why you'd think—"

She interrupted him. "Where's Early? He was with you, wasn't he?"

"Last time I saw him, he was in the street. Hit bad," Price answered.

"Hit. But was he dead?" The girl almost seemed frightened now.

"He crawled away somewhere," Price said. "But hurt the way he was—"

"We need to find out if he's dead," Marcy insisted. "He could sneak in here and finish it while we sit talking."

"I can promise that he means no harm to you," Price said.

"*You* say."

"I guess you haven't heard the way he talks about you, how he looks when someone drops your name."

Reese wheezed a laugh. "I told you, Marcy. Puppy love."

"He still works for my mother."

"No, he doesn't," Price corrected her. "He quit the Circle S last night, when he found out there was no ransom."

Marcy shook her head, hair swirling loose around her face. "I don't believe it. Mama could've paid him to pretend. We have to find him and make sure he's dead."

"You're wrong about him," Price insisted.

"You don't know her, how she *uses* people," Marcy answered, angry almost to the point of hissing. "She'll do *anything*. Sometimes I think she's worse than the old man."

"Your father's dead."

"Don't try to cheer me up," she said, still working on Reese Johnson's wounded arm. "Why can't I stop the bleeding?"

"We may have to cauterize it," Price suggested.

"Hurt him worse, you mean? I don't think so."

"I'd rather hurt a bit," Reese said, "than bleed to death. They'll want me healthy for the hangin'."

"No one's hanging anybody," she assured him. Then to Price: "How would you do it?"

"One thing at a time," he said. "I need to know why you believe your mother wants to kill you."

Marcy sneered. "So I can't talk, all right? That's why. She'll want me dead so I can't tell the world about her precious, rotten family."

"Shut up, you lying bitch!"

The curse from Jubal was his first clear sign of life since Price had barged into the storeroom. As he spoke, the wounded rancher tried to lunge across the space that separated him from Reese and Marcy, but his pain and weakness stopped him cold and put him back against the wall.

"You're dying, Jubal," Marcy said, smiling. "I hope it hurts like hell."

"Hell's where you're going, little girl," Jubal replied, gasping.

"Save me a seat, brother. I want to watch you burn."

Jubal slumped further to his right, facing toward Price. "Don't listen to a goddamn thing she says. Been lying all her life. Nothing but trash."

"I'm what you made me, *brother*. You and precious *Daddy*."

"Liar . . . not one . . . truth . . . filthy . . ."

Jubal had the look and sound of someone who was fading rapidly. His face was pale by candlelight, from losing so much blood. His clothes were dark and heavy with it, sopping wet. Price couldn't cauterize *that* wound. He guessed that Jubal would be dead within the hour, probably much sooner.

"Look at him," said Marcy. "Lying on the way to meet his Maker. That's my *family*, Mr. Price. Secrets and lies they'll kill to cover up."

"I still don't see—"

"Because they *raped* me, damn you! Daddy started in on me six years ago. I told Mama the first time, and she whipped me with a belt. Beating the devil out of me, she called it. Wouldn't give me anything to eat until I finally 'confessed' that it was all a lie. Made me apologize to *him* in front of her, to 'purge my sin.' "

"Lies," Jubal moaned. "Cheap bitch."

Price felt a hard knot in his stomach, wishing she would say no more, but once the gate was opened, Marcy couldn't stop the flow of angry words.

"About a year after it started, Jubal caught him at it, in the barn. You think Daddy felt any shame?" She laughed again, a hateful sound. "Hell, no. He saw a chance to teach his firstborn what it means to be a man."

A ragged, gasping noise escaped from Jubal's throat. Price turned in time to see a ruby bubble blossom on his lips, then burst and dribble down his chin. When Price leaned closer, Jubal's eyes were glazed, already dusty-looking.

"Is he dead?" asked Marcy.

"Yes."

"Too bad he didn't suffer more. You want to hear the rest of it? About the baby Dr. Janklow took from me the week before I turned fifteen? Or how about—"

"I've heard enough," Price said.

"A hard man like yourself?"

"There's no way I can change what you've been through," he told her.

"No. But you don't have to do my mother's bidding either."

"Never mind that now. She's got no claim on me."

"She may feel otherwise."

"Then she can take it up with me herself, next time we meet."

"You're going back?"

"She owes me money."

"You ain't done the job yet," Reese reminded him.

Price glanced at Jubal and replied, "Her side's a little short of witnesses."

"There's Early," said the girl.

"I'll find him when we're done here," Price replied. "If he's alive, we'll have a talk."

In fact, Price would've bet that Brooks was dead. The wound he'd seen before the shooting started in the street would likely claim his life. Crawling away to find another fight would only make it worse, and from the shooting that had followed, Price assumed that Brooks had found more trouble in the shops. There was no realistic likelihood of finding him alive.

"Go find him, please." The anger had deserted Marcy's voice, supplanted by a weary tone.

"We need to stop that bleeding first."

She couldn't cover her surprise. "You'll help?"

"Why not?"

"Because you shot him."

"Yes, I did. While he was trying to shoot me, as I recall. Are we past that?" he asked the wounded man.

"I'm done," Reese said. "You didn't see my brother on the street by any chance?"

"You've got two dead men there," Price told him. "One was carrying a shotgun—"

"Frank Bodine," Reese interjected.

"—and the other had a gun on Brooks, when you came out."

"That's Abel. Damn. I figgered he was kilt."

"I haven't seen the man you sent to San Felípe since the shooting started."

"Eddie Timmons." Reese shrugged. "If he's smart, he'll ride the hell out and keep going."

"We should hurry on this arm," said Marcy urgently.

Price drew his knife, moved closer to the pair of them. "You have another candle somewhere? This one's burned down to a stub."

"One more," she said, and rummaged in a pocket for it. It was hardly larger than the one already burning, but she lit the second one and set them both on the floor in small wax puddles, side by side.

"You want to roll that sleeve or lose it?" Price inquired.

"It's ruined anyhow," Reese said. "I got a clean shirt in my saddlebag, in case I ever need it."

"Fair enough."

Price leaned in close and ran the sharp edge of his blade along the shoulder seam of Reese's shirt. When he was done, Marcy peeled back the bloody cloth from Reese's arm, weeping at sight of where the slug had torn his flesh.

"I reckon this'll hurt," Price said.

"Hurts now," Reese said, "and I'm still bleedin' out."

"Just warning you."

Price held his knife blade just above the candle flames, letting their bright tongues lick the steel. He turned it slowly, back and forth, heating the two sides evenly. The flames weren't hot enough to make the blade glow cherry-red, but it would hold the heat he needed for a few short moments anyway.

"We may not get it all at once," he said.

"You always such an optimist?" asked Reese.

"Just—"

"Warning me. I know. Let's do it, huh?"

"You want something to bite on?" Price inquired.

Marcy leaned closer, stroking Reese's brow, and kissed him softly on one stubbled cheek. "I'm all he needs," she said. And then, a whisper in his ear: "You won't feel anything."

"I felt that," Reese informed her after Price was finished. Smoky whiffs of burnt flesh lingered in the air.

"I must've lost my touch," she said, and kissed him on the lips.

"I wouldn't go that far," Reese answered when they broke for air.

Price wiped his blade and sheathed it, telling them, "I'd better go and look for Early. Just in case."

"Be careful with him," Marcy said. "You really don't know Mama."

"I'm beginning to," Price said. He left the candles, but retrieved pistols from Reese and Jubal, tucking both inside his belt. Leaving the room, he scooped up Jubal's Winchester to carry with his own.

"You're leaving us defenseless," Reese called after him.

"I won't be far," Price answered. "Give a shout if you need help."

He was inclined to trust the girl's grim story, after seeing the emotion on her face, hearing the raw pain in her voice, but that still left Price far removed from trusting Marcy or her lover. They'd conspired to cheat her family, such as it was, out of a million dollars, and they'd killed her father in the process. Maybe he'd deserved a bullet, but Price also thought about the servant killed during the phony kidnapping.

Did they feel bad about his death? If Price had raised the subject, would the other dead man have been branded as a rapist too?

He passed the suitcase with its bullet scar on one side, left it sitting in the middle of the street, and walked back to the spot where Reese's brother lay unmoving in the dust. A trail like something a great lizard might've left led past his body, from the point where Brooks had fallen wounded, to a wooden sidewalk splotched with rusty bloodstains. Price followed that trail to the open doorway of a long-abandoned shop and peered inside.

The smell of recent death came out to greet him, like an old acquaintance who was never far from conscious thought. Price stepped inside, new moonlight helping him pick out the bodies. One of them was Brooks, a pistol clutched in rigid fingers. Back against the far wall, Eddie Timmons lay with eyes locked open, staring at a mystery no living man would ever solve.

Price had no words to say over the dead. Both young men had been volunteers for an adventure and had chased it to the bitter end. If they were disappointed in the outcome, it was too late to repair the damage done. Wherever they had gone—if there was anywhere at all to go—they would have ample company.

He counted twenty dead, with Marcy's father and her manservant. It was a grim toll for the pain and degradation she'd endured, and Price wondered whether it would ever be enough. Some things, he guessed, could never be put right.

Returning to the young survivors, Price paused long enough to heft the worthless suitcase, carrying the two

Winchesters underneath his arm. He had begun to feel like someone's beast of burden, with the extra weight, but he would soon be finished with the job at hand and safely on his way.

Knock wood.

It had been Mary's voice inside his head, the thing she used to say whenever Price said things were going well around the home they'd briefly shared. She wasn't superstitious really, but she'd always liked to hedge her bets.

Price thought about the seven horses waiting for him, west of town. He'd take them with him when he left, maybe retain a spare and sell the others when he got to San Felípe. Thinking of the town drew Price's thoughts to Landry, but he didn't plan on visiting the wounded cowboy. If and when Landry was fit to travel, he could make his own way home.

Price took it easy, coming back to the deserted building where he'd left Marcy and Reese. They could've plotted something in his absence, maybe ripping up a piece of lumber for a bludgeon, waiting for him as he came back through the door. Price used his normal caution, easing into the approach and walking softly on the wooden sidewalk for the last few yards.

A quick glance through the shop's front window showed him Reese and Marcy sitting where he'd left them, bathed in candlelight. Reese had his good arm around Marcy's slender shoulders, speaking softly to her, maybe telling her that everything would be all right, no matter how it looked.

Price wondered whether that was true.

Relieved to find no traps waiting, he let them hear him coming in. They both looked up, Marcy's expression bent toward fright until she recognized him. Price set down the suitcase, near enough for them to reach it.

"There's your ransom," he informed them.

"Brooks and Eddie?" Reese inquired.

"Both dead."

"Damn it."

Marcy unlatched the suitcase, raised its lid. Although its contents were no longer a surprise, her eyes still brimmed with tears.

"I should've known," she said again. "I'm sorry, Reese."

"It's not your fault, sugar."

"Your brother, all your friends . . ."

"Hush, now."

She sobbed against his shoulder as Reese gathered her into his arms, hiding a grimace from the pain it cost him. Price gave them a moment, then asked bluntly, "What comes next? Where will you go?"

Marcy drew back from Reese. When she faced Price, suspicion lingered in her red-rimmed eyes. "Why are you asking?" she demanded.

"Simple curiosity," he said. "I figure you've got horses stashed somewhere I haven't looked yet, but you must be short of money."

"We'll get by," Reese told him. "I'll be fit to work soon. Can we trust you not to tell Miz Joan we're still alive?"

"She'll send more men to hunt us if you do," Marcy explained.

"Don't worry," Price replied. "I'll think of something that should satisfy her." Facing Reese, he said, "I don't know what you want to do about your friends. So far, I haven't seen a spade or any other kinds of tools in town."

Reese nodded. "Folks that use ta live here picked it clean for sure. I'll have ta leave 'em as they are, I guess."

Price had a sudden thought. "About the horses—"

"We're all right," Reese interrupted warily. "I got 'em put aside."

"Okay," Price said. "But I've got half-a-dozen spares stashed outside town. I had in mind to sell them, but I'd say you need the pocket money more than I do. They won't fetch a million dollars, but you could do worse. It's better than nothing."

"What's the catch?" asked Marcy.

Reese reached out to stroke her hair. "She means to ask you where they come from."

"Three of them came with us from the Circle S," Price said. "We took the others from a bunch of sad *bandidos* on our first night out."

"And you don't want them?"

"I'll be keeping mine, of course. Maybe one spare. The rest are just deadweight to me."

"Awright," Reese said. "We'll take you up on that, with thanks."

"None needed," Price assured him. "I can fetch them in and put them in the livery. Maybe they'll have some feed left. When you're ready—"

Price swung toward the doorway at his back and froze there, listening. Marcy and Reese waited a moment, then the girl asked, "What? What *is* it?"

"Horses," Price replied. "Best douse the candles now. We've got company."

Price left the back room first, with Reese and Marcy close behind. He hung back from the door and window, letting darkness cloak him while he scanned the street outside.

Price couldn't see the riders yet. Their noise told him they were approaching from the north, still some distance away from where he stood, and slowing as they reached the heart of town.

They'd seen the bodies, he supposed. Whatever brought the riders into Amorada, fresh corpses in the street would likely make them stick around to find out what had happened there.

"*She* sent them," Marcy hissed.

"You don't know that," Reese answered.

"Why else are they here right now?" she challenged him. "This is a *ghost town*, Reese. Nobody's been here in a hundred years, and now it's like a market day in Santa Rosa. You think that's *coincidence*?"

"Quiet, the two of you," Price said. "They're getting closer."

The first rider was mounted on an Appaloosa that reminded Price of a good horse he used to own. It had been shot from under him some months ago, but he still thought about it now and then, the way it had responded to his needs almost before he issued a command.

More horsemen followed, four of them that Price could see from where he stood, and several others hanging back beyond his range of vision, by the sound of it. He made it ten at least, for safety's sake. Their leader sat and studied the façades of dark and silent shops.

"You reckon they's still here?" one of the others asked.

"Some of them are," the leader said.

"I mean *alive*."

"I took your meaning, Hank, but I can't see through walls."

Hank cast a nervous glance along the street. His bay mare felt the rider's sudden fear and shied. "Don't matter none," said Hank. "Me'n the boys can search this place in nothin' flat."

"You reckon *those* boys had the same idea?" the leader asked him, nodding toward the nearest body.

"I dunno."

"Maybe you oughta think about it."

"Jesus, Kirby. We come all this way—"

"Shut up a minute, willya?"

"Well, excuse me all to—"

Kirby swiveled sharply in his saddle, glared at Hank, and was rewarded with an instant silence. Price watched other riders shifting nervously, exchanging glances, but they didn't speak. There was no further doubt in Price's mind about who called the shots.

Behind him, Marcy whispered breathlessly, "They're after us. I know they—"

Price was turning, meant to shush her, when Reese clapped a hand across her mouth. She froze, and Price

turned back to find the horseman, Kirby, staring toward
the shop where they were hidden.

Could his sharp eyes penetrate the shadows? Had he
picked up Marcy's whisper in the night? Price clamped
his hand around the curved butt of his Peacemaker, ready
to draw, but Kirby turned away at last, addressing his
companions.

"We could search this place from one end to the other,"
he declared, "and maybe root 'em out by sunrise. On the
other hand, if they're dug in and watchin' us right now,
they just might gun us down before we know what hit us."

That made Kirby's riders nervous. Those who Price
could see reached for their weapons, scanning dark windows and doorways in a fruitless search for enemies.

"So, what we gonna do?" asked Hank.

"Same thing you'd do with rats in a corncrib," Kirby
replied.

"You wanna go and find a cat?"

"Hank, I believe the better part of you ran down your
daddy's leg."

That brought a laugh from several of the riders, while
Hank grumbled in his beard. "Just axed a simple goddamn
question, didn't I?"

"And here's your simple goddamn answer," Kirby said.
"We burn 'em out. Go back the way we come and start a
couple fires at the north end of town. This place'll go up
like a tinderbox, and we can pick 'em off when they come
out."

"S'posin' they don't," another rider said.

"Dead's dead," Kirby replied. "I don't care if they're
roast or buzzard bait, as long as we get paid."

"Just burn the town?" asked someone else.

Exasperated, Kirby turned on him. "You wanna move
in when we're done? Make this your home away from
home?"

"I reckon not."

"Then what the *hell* do you care if it burns or not? Just
turn around and do like you been told."

Sullen and smarting from their leader's acid tongue, the others reined about and started back along the street northbound. Price watched them go, noting that Kirby lingered for a moment where he was, sparing another glance in Price's general direction.

Price could take him now, but what would it accomplish? Some gangs fell apart without their leader, but he didn't get the sense that this crew was attached to Kirby in that way. A shot would only tell the others where he was and bring them whooping down the street with guns ablaze. At least, the other way, they had some time.

When Kirby finally withdrew from view, Price turned to find Marcy and Reese already huddled in the back room once again. Reese held the girl, but she was squirming, anxious to be gone.

"They mean to burn us," she protested. "If we run right now, while they're down at the other end—"

"We wouldn't get a hunnert yards," Reese said.

"He's right," Price told her. "They're expecting us to bolt. We have to turn the game around and make it costly for them. Use the fear against them, if we can."

"And how are we supposed to do that?" Marcy asked.

"By getting tough," Price said. "You planned a kidnapping and murder, didn't you? This ought to be a piece of cake."

16

It took a while for Kirby's riders to prepare a decent fire. They hadn't brought supplies of kerosene or coal oil with them, and were thus reduced to seeking fuel within the shops and on the open desert that surrounded Amorada. Dried-out lumber was in plentiful supply, but their collective genius wasted fifteen minutes on the kindling problem, after which the flames caught hold and started to consume the town.

Price used the time he had to find a sniper's roost. It was a matter of retracing his approach to the shop where he'd found Reese and Marcy—up the stairs and out the hatch, across two roofs, and back to where he'd started. By the time he got there, smoke was rising white and acrid from the northern end of town.

The riders couldn't see Price from the street, if he stayed well back from the edges of the roof, and even when he ventured closer they had handicaps. The blazing firelight ruined their night vision and made those who stood behind it, flames rising between themselves and town, as good as blind. Kirby was smart enough to have most of his men positioned with the fire behind them, but the light still made it difficult to see more than a few yards past their noses.

Price used his advantage, spotting where the shooters were positioned, some afoot, some still on horseback. It was his first real chance to count them, twelve in all, which made the odds against him that much longer.

Reese could fight, but he was injured, which would slow his movements and reflexes. As for Marcy, if her rage could be directed through a weapon she'd be deadly, but sheer malice wouldn't send a bullet straight and true to find its target.

Price cocked his Winchester and moved up toward the street. He sat and braced one elbow on the flat roof's parapet, marking his targets at the far end of the street. He couldn't drop them all before they saw his muzzle-flashes and began returning fire, but with some luck Price calculated that he could reduce their numbers for the final rush.

And what would happen then?

They'd force him to retreat, first thing. Once he was spotted on his perch, gunfire and torches would combine to drive him back to Reese and Marcy. His opponents wouldn't know immediately where he'd gone, but they would either search the shop or burn it down in an attempt to smoke him out. If they discovered the trapdoor, it wouldn't take them long to find out where he'd gone. And if they didn't, burning out the shop would bring flames that much closer to his final hiding place.

It was a devil's choice, but the alternative was scarcely better. They could buy a little time with frightened silence, waiting in the dark while fire devoured Amorada from the other end, but Kirby's men would follow the advancing flames, and Price would ultimately have to lead the others in a break, regardless of the odds.

He didn't plan on being burned alive. Beyond that, everything about the night was up for grabs.

Price knew the mounted gunmen were more danger-

ous, in terms of swift response. He didn't have a decent
shot at Kirby, hidden now behind a rising wall of flame to
Price's left, but several other riders were exposed. Price
chose the nearest of them, as the one most likely to react,
and framed the gunman's torso in his rifle sights.

He took a deep breath, then released half of it through
his nose and held the rest. Price closed his left eye, waited
for the space between heartbeats to squeeze the trigger,
and absorbed the sharp kick of the Winchester into himself.

Downrange, the rider somersaulted backward from his
saddle, rolling off the horse's rump before it shied and
bolted from the rifle shot. By that time, Price had pumped
the lever-action to eject his empty cartridge, while a fresh
one filled the chamber. Tracking, he acquired a second
target while the echo of his first shot still resounded in the
smoky street below.

His next mark was an older man whose unkempt beard
couldn't describe the shocked expression on his face.
Kirby's gunmen had been expecting action of a different
kind, where targets ran in panic from the flames to be cut
down, their dying screams accompanied by laughter from
the killers.

Price meant to change that view and let them taste the
panic for themselves.

His target was about to bolt when Price squeezed off
his second shot and spilled the rider from his mount into
a boneless heap of flesh and fabric, crumpled in the dust.
The horse couldn't decide whether to rush the flames or
brave the crack of gunfire from its other side, but finally
it chose the darkness, galloping full tilt through Amorada
toward the south.

Price heard the first sputter of pistol fire below him,
shots squeezed off on instinct, but he knew they'd have
his range in seconds. He had time for one more shot at
least, but if he wanted it to count he'd have to hurry.

Mounted target number three was facing toward him,
squinting in the firelight, holding reins in one hand and a

six-gun in the other. Price went for a body shot, no fancy marksmanship, and slammed the dying rider into space before his piebald gelding could react.

A couple of the others saw his muzzle-flash that time, shouting and pointing as they triggered quick shots toward the rooftop. Price retreated, knowing he was out of time. The battle was about to overtake him, and he didn't want to be there when it happened.

Racing through the night, hearing a swarm of bullets sweep the space where he'd been standing seconds earlier, Price scrambled to the next rooftop in line. The hunters couldn't see him there, would only know they'd missed him when they scaled the roof or brought it tumbling down in flames. And by that time, with any luck, a few more of them would be dead.

Waiting in the musty dark, Marcy asked Reese, "You reckon he'll come back?"

The question startled Reese. "Why wouldn't he?"

"Why *would* he, Reese? You're hurt, I can't fight worth a damn. Without us, he could likely slip off to his horses and ride out before the others noticed him."

The thought hadn't occurred to Reese, but now it troubled him. Why *should* Price stay and help them after all? They'd tried to kill him just a short time earlier, and even if he sympathized with Marcy's suffering, releasing them took money from his pocket. Or it would've, anyway, before the other shooters had arrived.

Marcy was right, though. Even if Price lost his payment from her mother—which seemed certain now—he still could slip out with his skin intact and leave them to their fate. Price owed them nothing, wasn't friend or kin, and had no stake in keeping them alive.

Why would he fight against long odds to help them, when the easy thing—the *smart* thing—was to run away?

Reese didn't give his trust away for free, and yet . . .

If Price was leaving them, he could've done it earlier,

before he cauterized the wound in Reese's arm. He didn't
have to help with that, or bring the suitcase back to prove
his tale about the phony ransom. He could've just as easily walked out, taken their guns if he was so inclined, and
left them to the desert.

But he hadn't. And—

The first sharp sounds of gunfire drove Marcy into his
arms. Reese liked feeling her there, but this wasn't the
time. After a quick hug, he stepped back and told her, "We
need to be ready when they come."

"So, tell me how," she said.

"Take Jubal's Winchester. Make sure it's loaded, with
a live round in the spout."

"All right."

Marcy had told him countless times about her fantasies
of killing Jubal and their father. She had practiced with a
rifle, dry-firing to keep it quiet and save ammunition, but
Reese had volunteered to do it for her when he heard
about the home life she endured with her so-called family.
Marcy had thanked him for the gift in ways he'd never
have imagined, sealed the bargain with her flesh, and
promised her undying love if Reese would set her free.

They weren't there yet, and the "undying" part was
looking shakier with every passing moment. Reese had
smelled wood smoke before the shooting started, knew
the gunmen Marcy's mother had employed were making
good their threat to burn the town, but there was nothing
Reese could do until he found out whether Price was
really on their side, or if he'd ditched them in a hasty ploy
to save himself.

The shots had settled it. A Winchester, then pistols an-
swering. Reese hoped he'd taken down a couple of the
shooters anyway. Whatever Price could do to shave the
odds, it had to help.

"I'm ready," Marcy told him, standing over Jubal's
body with his lever-action rifle in her hands. "What
now?"

"We watch the street," Reese said. "They'll be here

soon, whatever happens down the block. That's when we fight."

And die, he almost added, but he couldn't say the words. They didn't have much chance, but Reese still clung to hope, no matter how faint it appeared.

"What if they set the place on fire?" she asked.

"Don't worry. We'll be fine."

I'm not about to let you burn, Reese thought. *Not while I have a bullet left.*

If seeing Marcy safe and happy was beyond his capability, at least he wouldn't let her die in agony, screaming away the final moments of her life. That much was still within his power, and the bastards sent to hunt them couldn't steal it from him.

Not unless they killed Reese first.

He heard a sudden thump and rush of footsteps overhead. With Marcy at his side, Reese moved from the back room to watch the stairs, raising his Colt and thumbing back the hammer. If he needed more than six shots, he had Jubal's pistol tucked inside his belt.

"It's me," Price warned them, rapidly descending from the second floor.

Reese shuddered with relief, lowering the weapon to his side. "I thought they mighta picked you off."

"Not yet. All ready here?"

"As ready as we'll be."

Price frowned and said, "Let's hope that's good enough."

Kirby McGowan watched his riders firing up at shadows on the left side of the street. He was convinced their shots were wasted, but he let them vent their fear and anger for another moment while he counted bodies in the street.

Three down, which left eight shooters and himself out of the twelve who'd started south from Santa Rosa two days earlier. The lady who had hired them had made it sound like easy pickings, but it wasn't turning out that way. He'd have to have a word with their employer when the job was done. Make sure she understood the risks involved and how a bonus might not be amiss.

Their orders had been simple: Find the woman's son in San Felípe and make sure he settled all their family problems. She didn't care about the hired hands, one way or another, but she was concerned about her son and his ability to carry out the mission. Namely, she'd paid extra to make sure that Kirby didn't let a certain girl and her boyfriend return alive.

They'd tracked their quarry on from San Felípe to the ghost town, where a quick glance seemed to indicate that someone had already done part of the dirty work. So much the better, but McGowan didn't feel like waiting overnight to search a bunch of broken-down old shops and houses, when more shooters might be waiting in the nooks and crannies there to bushwhack him.

Better to set the place afire and watch them run—until one of the trapped rats started shooting back with deadly accuracy, dropping riders left and right.

"Goddammit, *stop*!" he bellowed at his small group of survivors. "Stop it now!"

The message took a while to penetrate their fright and fury, but it finally hit home. The eight still standing held their smoking weapons ready, scanning roofs and windows while they waited for their marching orders.

"Now you see what happens," he informed them, "when you stop paying attention. Look around you, damn it! Three men dead, and you've wasted a hundred rounds on God's thin air. You wanna shoot, for Christ's sake pick a *target*. I'm surprised they didn't drop the rest of you while you were playing games."

"I seen his flashes," answered Zeke, a scruffy rider who spent more time growing hair than tending it. "Right up there!"

McGowan scanned the rooftop where a couple of his men were pointing, but he saw no movement there. He would've made an easy shot himself, sitting astride his stallion in the middle of the street, backlit by flames. That told him that the sniper must've run, maybe decided to play games.

"Who's sure about that target?" he inquired.

Two hands shot up, followed reluctantly by one more on the sidelines.

"Right," McGowan said. "So why'n hell are you just standing here? *Do something,* damn it! Do I have ta lead you by the nose?"

Embarrassed by his rage, they rushed off to pursue the gunman who had dropped their comrades. Several paused long enough to wrench crude torches from the nearest burning shop and carry them along for comfort. McGowan spurred his mount ahead and to the left, ducking his head to clear the awning as the horse clopped onto the wooden sidewalk.

He was covered there, protected from a sniper on the west side of the street, and from at least a few roofs on the east. The fire was coming on behind him, but he'd have no trouble staying well ahead of it. McGowan's horse would do that for him, if it somehow slipped his mind. Meanwhile, he had a clear view of his troops, advancing with their guns and torches down the ghost town's only street.

McGowan hoped they'd trap the shooter, either blast or burn him out—it hardly mattered which—and thereby make an end of it. He worried, though, about their grim employer's son, who hadn't showed himself and wouldn't stand a chance if he stayed hidden in the clapboard buildings while they burned.

McGowan worried. But not much.

He had a story ready for the woman, if they couldn't find her baby boy. Killed by their adversaries, wasn't he? And after some dumb bastard struck a match, setting the town afire. McGowan would've saved the body for her, but the flames were too intense. Of course, if she was paying, he'd be glad to make another trip and bring back Sonny's blackened bones.

Or someone's anyway.

McGowan shouted rude encouragement to his gunmen. "Get in there, damn it! Root him out! What are you waiting for?"

They fired a ragged volley through the windows, blowing out whatever glass remained but likely missing anyone inside. One of them scuttled to the door and peered inside, then ran back to the street and huddled with a pair of torch-bearers. McGowan saw the two rush forward, pitch their torches through a ground-floor window, and retreat.

The place went up in seconds flat. McGowan's horse shied from the sudden heat and light, urging him toward safety in the middle of the street. But *was* there any safety there? Where was the sniper who had killed three of his men?

Burning? Or waiting at another vantage point to choose his next target?

McGowan wouldn't let the fear control him. Scowling, he deliberately turned and spurred his mount into the open street.

"They're coming," Price told Reese and Marcy. "Hold your fire until I give the word."

"How did they find us?" Marcy asked, tearful.

"They haven't yet. They torched the shop I fired from last. Now they'll be moving on, until they've finished off the town."

"And us," Reese said.

"Not necessarily. I trimmed a dozen down to nine. They bleed like anybody else."

"Okay." Reese nodded, putting on a smile that clearly didn't suit his mood. "Let's make 'em bleed."

"Can you two hold the door a while?" Price asked.

They blinked at him in unison. "Us two?" asked Marcy. "Where will you be?"

"On the roof. I need an angle for my Winchester."

The lovers hesitated, traded glances. Marcy answered

for them both. "All right then. Go ahead. And give them hell."

Price started toward the stairs, halting as Reese caught up to him and gripped his arm. "You wouldn't plan on ditching us by any chance?" the wounded kidnapper inquired.

"It never crossed my mind," Price lied.

"Jesus." Still torn, Reese stepped back and released his grip. "Go on. We'll try'n hold 'em here. But just remember, bullets won't stop fire."

"They'll stop the men with torches, if you're quick enough," Price said.

He climbed the stairs as rapidly as possible, afraid of crashing through them if he sprinted. On the second floor, he found the now-familiar ladder, mounting nimbly to the rooftop.

Two roofs farther north, Price saw smoke belching from the hatch where he had crouched and fired at Kirby's riders moments earlier. Flames shortly followed, leaping toward the sky. It wouldn't take long for the roof to buckle and the walls to follow. In the meantime, flames he couldn't see were gnawing through the walls, preparing to engulf the shop's neighbors.

Price had no time to lose. He was embarking on a strategy both bold and perilous. Firing on Kirby's gunmen from his new post would invite them to attack in force, but he saw no alternative. The fire might reach them first, if they sat waiting passively, and Price preferred a bullet to a blazing preview of eternity in Hell. His way, if nothing else, he'd take more of the shooters with him, giving Reese and Marcy some faint opportunity to flee.

And if they all died there, in Amorada, who would really care?

Who'd even know that Price was gone, in fact?

Dismissing further idle thought, he stepped up to the parapet and found five gunmen visible below. Price guessed the other four were somewhere on the sidewalk, hidden by the awning roofs on his side of the street.

Do what you can with what you've got.

He raised the Winchester and sighted down its barrel toward a runner brandishing a torch and pistol. Price followed the shooter as he made a beeline for the next shop in between the blazing pyre and Price's hideaway. A light touch on the trigger sent a bullet hurtling out to drop the target in his tracks.

At first, Price thought the others might've missed the gunshot's echo, shouting as they were and partly deafened by the roar of hungry flames. Another second, though, and he saw Kirby pointing at him, leveling a pistol while he shouted orders to the rest.

Price fired at Kirby without aiming, knew he'd missed the mark as bullets sizzled past him in the night. He stood his ground, pumping the rifle's lever-action, letting Kirby gallop free as other targets clamored for attention.

There! The only other mounted gunman Price could see was charging toward him, squeezing off a shotgun blast one-handed as he came. It wasn't even close. His buckshot pocked the wall six feet below where Price stood on the parapet, drawing his bead.

He didn't miss that time. The charger, suddenly divested of its rider, veered off course and fled the smoky battlefield. Price wished it well and focused on the strangers who were bent on killing him.

He had a third mark lined up in his sights when suddenly the shooter crumpled, clutching at his chest. Marcy and Reese had joined the battle, taking down the nearest threat with close-range gunfire. Price immediately shifted to another target, caught another torch-bearer with arm drawn back to make his pitch, and dropped him with a quick shot on the fly.

The wounded gunman fell, but quickly wobbled to his feet again. He'd lost his torch but clung tenaciously to his six-gun, turning to fire a shot through the front window of the shop. His pistol and the Winchester went off together, Price's bullet striking with sufficient force to spin the shooter in his tracks and plant him facedown in the street.

Kirby was shouting orders down below, cursing the four survivors of his posse when they started to retreat. His anger or the threat of his reprisal rallied them and got them moving forward in a ragged skirmish line, unloading whatever they had as they charged.

It could've been a good move, with enough determined troops, but four disoriented, frightened men would never make it work. Price shot the nearest of them through the chest, and by the time he pumped his rifle's lever-action for another shot, Marcy and Reese had dropped two more.

Price winged the last one, saw him stagger, falling to one knee. Before he had a chance to finish it, another rifle shot rang out below and slapped the gunman over on his back.

Marcy.

That left the leader, Kirby, and he wasn't wasting any time evacuating Amorada. Riding hell for leather with salvation on his mind, he'd covered half the distance to the night and open desert when Price shot him in the back and spilled him to the earth. His horse ran on without him, possibly relieved.

The place next door was burning fiercely as Price scrambled down the ladder, then descended smoky stairs to reach the shop below. Marcy and Reese were standing on the sidewalk, ready to resume the fight if any of the dead stood up and asked for more.

"I hope you didn't stash your horses in the livery," Price said to Reese.

"They're right next door," Reese answered, nodding to the last shop on his left. "Turns out it was a feed store and the townsfolk left some stock behind."

"We'd better get them out of there," suggested Price. "The way this fire is closing in, it won't last long."

Five horses, saddled for the trail, stood waiting in the last shop on the west side of the street. Price saw that they'd been sharing gutted bags of feed with mice that skittered off from his approach. It seemed that neither species minded sharing, but sounds of battle and the smoke that stung their nostrils now made all and sundry anxious to be gone.

They led the horses out and well away from the advancing fire. The west side of the street was burning faster than the east, since Kirby's men had jumped the fire line chasing Price and torched the extra shop halfway along. That side would be consumed before the other, but Price saw that all of Amorada would be burned down to scorched earth before sunrise.

"What about your animals?" asked Reese.

"A quarter mile that way," Price told him, pointing farther west. The firelight didn't reach that far, but he had memorized the spot.

"We might as well ride over," Reese suggested, "since we've got the spares."

Price chose a roan gelding, hoisted himself aboard, and met no opposition from the animal. Ten minutes later, riding at an easy pace and watching out for pitfalls in the dark, they reached the stand of trees and found the other horses waiting.

"I'm on the roan," Price said as he dismounted. "You can take the rest, if you've a mind to."

"We appreciate it, mister. All of it, I mean." Reese wasn't used to thank-yous or apologies. The words stuck in his throat, but he was working on it.

"We talked about it," Marcy told Price, "and we're heading south. If Mama wants to send more gunmen looking for us, she can try." After a moment's hesitation, Marcy added, "If you wanted to ride with us for a while . . ."

"No, thanks," Price said. "I've spent a lot of time in Mexico already recently. I'd like to see if I can break the habit."

"Are you going back to Santa Rosa then?"

He thought about it. Marcy's mother had already paid the Dermott Jackson bounty, and while Price could claim the ten grand he'd been promised, it would likely take a bloody fight to get the money.

If he ever did.

And truth be told, he hadn't done the job.

"I reckon not," he said at last, resigned to let it go.

Both Reese and Marcy seemed relieved. "Where will you go then?" asked the girl.

Price shrugged. "Back to the States, first thing," he answered. "Find a marshal's office. See who's posted on the board."

"Seems like a hard way to get by," Reese said.

"I grant you," Price replied, "it doesn't have the charm of kidnapping."

"I see your point."

The roan was pleased to see him, nuzzling Price's hand. He loosed its reins and mounted, moving off to one side while the youngsters climbed down from their saddles and began collecting their new horses. Reese was hampered somewhat by his wound, but it should heal with tending, and he had a caring nurse along to help him.

Price had no idea how long they'd last, and he resolved right there to put it out of mind. Their story wasn't his, and in a short time they'd be parting ways forever. If they thought of him at all, after that night, he'd be a part of ugly, bloody memories best left behind.

Across the flats, he saw the skeletal remains of Amorada burning, shadows dancing with a kind of frenzied, disembodied life. It wasn't every day Price got to watch a ghost town die.

He watched and wondered where the ghosts would go to rest.

An epic Western from the author of
The Gun

REBEL GUN

by Lyle Brandt

When Matt Price rides into a dusty
Mexican town, he knows all he
should do is get in and get out
without any trouble. But the posters
announcing an upcoming public
execution steer him away from that
plan, as the man scheduled for the
hanging is an old comrade, an
Apache named Gray Wolf who
once saved Price's hide.

0-425-20298-4

AN EPIC WESTERN FROM THE AUTHOR OF
THE GUN

VENGEANCE GUN

BY LYLE BRANDT

JUSTICE HAS A NEW PRICE. MATT PRICE.

RETIRED GUNMAN MATT PRICE'S IDYLLIC WORLD HAS
SHATTERED WHEN A DANGEROUS GANG OF ROBBERS
TAKE THE ONE LIFE HE HOLDS DEAR—HIS WIFE'S.

NOW HE'S ON THE TRAIL AGAIN, HUNTING THE
MURDEROUS THIEVES WHO CRUELLY STOLE HIS PEACE.
HE'S THROUGH LIVING BY THE LETTER OF THE LAW—IT'S
TIME TO FOLLOW HIS OWN RULES, AND GIVE THIS GANG
THE TYPE OF PUNISHMENT THEY REALLY DESERVE.

0-425-19383-7

AN EPIC WESTERN FROM THE AUTHOR OF
THE GUN

JUSTICE GUN

LIVE BY IT. DIE BY IT.

BY LYLE BRANDT

GUNMAN MATTHEW PRICE DID NOT THINK
HE WAS GOING TO MAKE IT OUT OF
REDEMPTION, TEXAS, ALIVE.
BUT AS HE STUMBLES OUT OF TOWN
GUT-SHOT AND DYING, HE IS RESCUED BY A
BLACK FAMILY PIONEERING THEIR WAY TO
FREEDOM. NOW, MATT MUST RETURN THE
FAVOR AND HELP THEM WHEN
TROUBLEMAKERS IN THEIR NEW SETTLEMENT
OFFER UP A NOT-SO-WARM WELCOME.

0-425-19094-3

B678